MW00848547

AND THEN THERE WAS SILENCE

CANDACE ROBINSON

Copyright ©2023 by Candace Robinson
Edited by Jackie Turner
Cover Design by JV Arts
Hardcase Cover Art Design by Aude Ziegelmeyer

This is a work of fiction. Names, characters, places, and incidents either are the product of the author's imagination or are used fictitiously, and any resemblance to any actual persons, living or dead, events, or locales is entirely coincidental. This book may not be used or reproduced in any manner without written permission from the author.

For those who have ever lost someone they love

1

"I would give you everything."

*H*onk!

"Jesus, slow down, River," Sadie hissed, gripping her chest.

"The fucker literally just cut me off." River motioned out the window at the red pickup truck in front of them, speeding ahead.

"Yes, but did you have to turn the window washer fluid on first?"

"Sadie, he was riding my ass."

She rolled her eyes and relaxed back into her seat. "One day we're going to get in a car wreck, and I suppose then I'd find out if ghosts do exist."

"You'd make a pretty ghost." A charming, sly smile played across River's lips. His hand fell to her knee, squeezing gently. "But seriously, do you think I'd ever let anything happen to you?"

Sadie studied her husband's face, his chiseled features, his light gray irises, the locks of dark hair swept behind his right ear. Even now, after a year of marriage and five years of being together, moths still swarmed within her at the sight of him. However, when she'd first met River Hawkins at the adult novelty store where they'd worked together, she'd been uncertain of him. But she'd fallen for his charm, the way he would quarrel with her over films, his caring and sweet side, the dark side of him that came out through his art. The art he'd started selling at an early age that she hadn't known he'd become wealthy from.

"What if a ravenous monster from another dimension was crawling around our world and caught us both but only had an appetite to eat one of us…" A devious smile lifted at the corners of her lips as she spoke. "Who would you choose to be ground to death between its razor-sharp teeth?"

"Ah, that's an easy question. I would choose me, my sweet nightmare." River grinned, his hand squeezing her thigh once more before resting it against the steering wheel. "And who would you choose?"

"Why you, of course, my vicious dream." Sadie laughed, recollecting when they'd first started using the nicknames for one another—it had been after a disagreement over what the top ten horror films of all time should be. A cliché tale to pass down to any future offspring they might have.

"You're wrong. Vampires don't do it for me," Sadie argued, dusting the top of a shelf when her foot slipped on the step of a ladder and sent her careening backward.

Two arms caught her just as she was about to collide with the floor and break her neck. "Then what would, my sweet nightmare?"

River's fingers drifted to her knee again, slowly skimming up to her thigh, her pulse speeding from his touch. "You'll get a spanking later for that answer."

"I hope you'll be dressed in your finest monster attire." Sadie waggled her eyebrows at him, then returned his hand to the steering wheel. "Now, keep quiet and watch the road, Victor. Your parents need you alive for their party."

River groaned, fidgeting with the gray tie at his chest. "We leave as soon as boredom levels reach critical mass." He was dressed as Victor from *Corpse Bride*, and she his dead counterpart, Emily. To this day, even though the character Emily had been dead, Sadie still wished they would've ended up together. Victoria was a sweet choice in the end for Victor, but Sadie believed the flame would've burned brighter if Emily had been his wife.

She peered out the window to the night sky, blanketing the city in ebony, only a few stars decorating its inky darkness. The sliver of a crescent moon smiled down at her through the trees lining the streets.

River steered the car down a lamplit street leading to a neighborhood full of mansions, each distinct in its own style. Bricked or stucco exteriors, some holding large balconies, others showing off massive windows. All having perfectly trimmed landscaping. His parents' mansion looked like a modern-day castle, with the front portion curved and a cylinder of beige brick at its top. Vines wove through the iron bars of the balcony, and several stone angels stood in the garden, their hands folded in prayer.

While River drew the car to a stop in the long

driveway, Sadie checked her makeup in the mirror. The blue body paint she'd meticulously applied wasn't as smooth as she would've liked, and the dark eyebrows and decaying piece of flesh on her cheek weren't perfect, but they would do. She would never be a special effects makeup artist, yet one day, possibly, her screenwriting dream—or beautiful nightmare—would come to fruition. It was something she'd focused on for the last five years since she'd turned eighteen. And thus far, there hadn't even been a teensy piranha nibble.

Adjusting her wedding gown, Sadie ran her fingers through her blue wig, her brown hair hidden beneath. A real autumn never came to this part of Texas, and she knew her makeup and costume would be heavy against her the instant she stepped outside into the blasted humidity.

River helped her from the car, breathtaking in his suit of grays, his pinstriped pants, the costume perfectly fitting his lithe and muscular form. "You should've worn this on our wedding day," he purred into her ear, his hand brushing across the curve of her hip, his light gray eyes meeting hers a moment later.

Warmth coursed through her at his touch, as it always did. "I should've." Instead, she'd settled on a red gown with lace and tulle that mirrored the dress from one of her favorite classic horror comedies.

River circled his arm around Sadie's waist, pulling her close, his honey and sandalwood scent enveloping her. He guided her along the curved sidewalk, beside the pristine shrub garden, toward the wide porch. Sadie rang the doorbell, and a few moments later, the maid, Valentina, answered, dressed in loose navy pants, a black blouse, and a silver bird mask hiding the top half of her face, only her deep brown eyes peering out.

"It's good to see you, River," Valentina said, her words coming out with a hint of a Spanish accent as she smiled. "And you as well, Sadie." She was in her mid-fifties with gray streaks peppering her black braid and only a few fine lines near the edges of her mouth.

Valentina motioned them inside, then led them through the living room decorated with leather furniture, a grand piano, and large replicas of famous paintings hanging across the walls. They turned down the marble-floored hallway, enhanced with portraits of fashion gowns, that opened to the dining room where eight of the ten chairs were occupied around the rectangular ivory table set with glittering crystal and red roses.

River's mother, Coral, sat at one end of the table, an ivory silk gown hugging her thin frame, and an alabaster mask, speckled with silver glitter, concealed half her face. Her hair, dark like River's, hung in loose curls to her waist. Gabe, River's father, was at the opposite head of the table, wearing a golden wolf mask, his gray hair swept back. The six guests—four women, two men—seated around the table all wore gowns and suits, along with ornate animal masks.

"I thought I said this was a masquerade party," Coral said, the hint of a smile playing across her red lips as she studied her son.

Sadie side-eyed River. He'd never once mentioned a masquerade party, but she preferred what they were wearing over the matching styles of the others.

"You said *Halloween* party," River drawled.

"It's fine." Coral waved a hand and gestured at the

empty chairs to her right. "Have a seat." She then introduced the other guests at the table who worked at her fashion design studio.

They each nodded and said hello, to which Sadie gave a polite wave, already forgetting most of their names. River drew back a chair for Sadie to sit, and her gaze drifted around the table to find that the guests' eyes were pinned on her. She frowned and looked down at the empty crystal glass diagonal from her. When she glanced up a few seconds later after River lowered himself beside her, everyone's stares still lingered on her.

Strange… She fidgeted with her dress, casting her attention on River's mom.

Coral and Gabe didn't seem to notice as Valentina carried in tray after tray, delivering bowls of steaming soup. Valentina set the last two in front of Sadie and River. Sadie peered down at the bowl and arched a brow—dark chunks of meat swirled within a thick ruby-red substance. Valentina then filled their glasses with another red liquid.

"Have you never seen blood before?" Coral asked, her voice cool. Sadie blinked, unable to tell if she was serious. But then Coral laughed a high-pitched laugh that sounded nothing like her as she continued, "It's just food coloring and red wine. So, how is everything going for you, Sadie?" Coral drank a sip of her wine. "Did you find a steady job yet?"

"I'm still writing short stories and articles on the side while working on screenplays." The money wasn't much, but she wanted to bring in something so she didn't feel like a leech, even though River said he didn't mind if she focused on her screenplays since he made more than enough for the both of them.

Coral ran a red-painted fingernail across her matching crimson lips. "Maybe you should try harder, dear."

"Mother," River hissed in a low voice. Sadie's stomach dropped as everyone at the table fixed their gazes back on her. It was a conversation she would rather not have with an audience.

"I'm only being honest." Coral shrugged. "She could work for me at the studio and write fashion design articles instead."

Sadie had finished college with a degree in English and could get certified to become a teacher, but she'd been procrastinating, not really wanting to go down that career path. Yet now she was second-guessing what she was doing—what she'd been doing. How even her sister had nudged her to try something else. The only ones who hadn't were River and her good friend, Skyler. "I don't even know the first thing about fashion."

River frowned. "She helps me at events and conventions, which makes it so I don't have to hire an assistant."

Gabe lifted his glass of wine. "How about we show the guests some of your art, son?"

"We don't need to do that tonight." River ran a hand across his jaw, peering at Sadie. She'd never once been envious of him having the center of attention—his dark art always pulled at her in an alluring way that was hard to describe.

"Let them see what you can do," Sadie said, clasping his hand. "Your art is beautiful."

Valentina left the room and returned a few moments later, carrying two small sculptures. She set them in the center of the table. For the first one, an alabaster form leaned to the side as if melting, and two obsidian horns curled from the head, its face without features. Beside it, the other statue was black and white checkered, resting in a crouched position, fangs protruding from its wide mouth, its wholly dark eyes taking up most of its face.

They were perfect as always, and Sadie glanced up, noticing everyone was not only watching her but wore broad smiles spread across their faces.

As her pulse raced, drumming inside of her, she couldn't keep silent and pretend she was imagining it. "What's going on?"

River followed her stare, looking around the table. "Mother?" he asked, his hand folding over Sadie's.

A wicked smile spread across Coral's red lips as she drew out a jeweled dagger from beneath the table. "I think Sadie will make a lovely sacrifice, won't she? Now we can fill our glasses and toast with her blood."

River's expression changed from worried to mirroring his mother's eerie smile. A villainous look she'd never once seen on him. "Shh," he whispered, his eyes crazed as he took out a dagger from under the table. "You always did love a good horror film, my love. How about I bestow on you the gift of a real one?"

Sadie's heart slammed against her ribs as she took a deep swallow. This couldn't be happening. But everyone around the table was now standing, blades in their hands. She stumbled back from the chair, turning to run for the front door, when she caught River fighting a smile.

"You ass!" Sadie shouted, glaring as she slapped him on the arm.

"Dammit, River, couldn't you play along for once?"

Coral huffed.

"What?" River chuckled, setting the dagger on the table, his body shaking with laughter. "I told you I'm a terrible actor."

"This was your idea?" Sadie's brows shot up as she faced Coral.

"I figured maybe we could give you a bit of a creative nudge." The corners of Coral's lips drooped. "I'm sorry for what I said earlier. I just wanted to make this appear real. You know Gabe and I both believe in you."

Sadie's shoulders relaxed and her lips formed a smile, her fingers begging to write words that would take her to dark, imaginative worlds. "This was perfect. A game that could have gone deadly, nonetheless. But perfect!"

"Sorry I couldn't play my fucked-up part well enough." River smirked as he started the car.

"It was positively glorious until you smiled." Sadie bit her lip. "For a moment, I really thought you wanted me to be a sacrifice."

"Never." River grasped her hand and laced their fingers together. "Maybe I shouldn't have agreed for us to do that."

"Are you kidding me?" Sadie laughed. "It was the most amazing thing ever. I mean, now that I know I'm not going to be slit open with a dagger."

"And this is one of the reasons I love you." River chuckled, turning up the music to an older song they both liked.

Sadie stared out the window, humming softly to the melody as he drove them home. The rest of the party had gone well, and she'd awkwardly chatted with Coral's fashion team. One designer had pitched a horror fashion line, but Coral denied it with a flick of the wrist, saying she would possibly consider something on the gothic side though.

Once they arrived home, Sadie tossed her purse on the counter. "You can take a shower first. I'm going to work on my screenplay for a bit since, you know, I now have good inspiration." She rubbed her hands together and grinned.

"I want to read what bloody goodness you come up with after I finish." He waggled his brows.

"Tut, tut." She laughed, ticking her finger in the air. "Only after I complete it."

"So secretive." River tickled her beneath the ribs, making her laugh harder before he headed into the bathroom. Sadie relaxed in a chair at the dinner table and opened her notebook. She wrote down *bloody soup* but debated on whether to make the liquid real body fluids. Later she would revisit that scenario. She jotted more things down about betrayal and surprise, then added a few lines of dialogue.

Sadie was about halfway into the scene when the bathroom door opened, and River swaggered into the living room littered with his art supplies, wearing only a towel around his narrow hips. "I'm going to continue where I left off at the party before the sacrifice," he purred, his voice deep, seductive, as he approached her.

With a grin, she set her notes aside and folded her

arms across her chest. "Go on then. Do your best, my vicious dream."

A few beads of water ran down River's taut chest as he swept a wet lock of dark hair behind his ear. "I've come to take your soul," he cooed.

"Oh really?" She laughed, then leaned forward, giving him a daring look as she whispered, "Where are you taking it?"

"I suppose you'll find out." He scooped her up from the chair and cradled her close, his nose nudging hers. "You deserve a break."

"I just started, but..." She tilted her head to the side as if mulling it over. "Only if you confess how you would reap my soul."

"All in due time, my sweet nightmare." River couldn't hold his serious expression, a smile breaking free while carrying her into their room and laying her on the bed. His expression turned serious once more as he trailed his finger between her breasts, directly to her heart. "Straight through here is how you would die. Even in my wicked state, I want your heart to be mine."

"My choice mirrors yours." Sadie pretended to hold a dagger and pierced the invisible blade into his heart. She then skimmed her hands up his bare chest to cup his face. "I love you," she murmured.

"I could hear you say those words for all eternity." He crawled on top of her, caging her in, and she bit her lip in anticipation. "After the fright I caused earlier, tell me how you want to be ravished tonight."

Sadie's eyes fell to the blue smudge marks she'd left behind on his chest and cheeks. "You'll be covered in blue makeup, and so will the bed."

"Fuck the bed being clean." He smirked, his eyes hooded. "And I *want* to get dirty with you."

"Are you—"

River cut off her words with his mouth, tasting of honey, and she easily gave in to his delicious touch. His tongue flicked the seam of her lips, prying them open, then tangled with hers as his skilled hands hiked up the skirt of her costume. He slowly drew her panties down her legs, teasing them both, before he left her mouth to trail kisses up her inner thigh.

"I love you. Don't ever forget that." He lifted her legs over his shoulders and pulled her closer to his mouth. She moaned in pleasure as he stroked that delectable tongue of his up her center.

2

"Write the tale, my sweet nightmare."

The trees' limbs whispered as they rustled and sang, their low hum spilling through the air like a gentle lullaby.

Sadie squeezed her eyes shut, imagining the trees were filled with blood, traveling through their veins. A heart beat at their center as their lungs pumped beneath their barked flesh. A swarm of colorful insects cloaked the entirety of the woods, guiding her along a path to where giant monstrous forms, with obsidian flesh that glittered like diamonds, reigned. Bloody crowns rested atop their heads, their smiles holding razor-sharp crimson teeth.

She flicked open her lids and jotted down a few sentences inside her notebook—the inspiration still flowed through her, courtesy of the party from the evening before. For most of the night afterward, she'd been awake with River, his mouth on hers, her tongue tasting his salty skin, the paint from her costume smearing *everything.*

A gust of wind blew, rattling the trees. It was fall, but by the green color of the leaves, and the lack of coolness, it didn't seem much different than summer. Not like when she and River had gone to Salem the year before, catching glimpses of the beautiful autumn foliage. She wanted to visit the area again—it was the perfect time of year for them both to gather eerie inspiration there.

Sadie brushed a tendril of chestnut-colored hair from her face and peered around the woods, watching the branches dance with the warm breeze. "And the skin of the trees turned into human flesh, the insects drifting to their branches and becoming their leaves. The monsters crouched at their trunks, waiting." Sadie grinned, adding another sentence to a possible scene, hoping it wouldn't become erased words. For the past few weeks, her focus had been on the short stories for anthologies and magazine articles to bring in a pitiful amount of money, but finally, the itch was there—the *drive*—aching to spill out a screenplay. The trick last night at the party was the very kick she'd needed to get her act into gear.

A craving thrummed inside Sadie's rib cage, thirsting for at least one screenplay to be turned into a film, to be watched, loved, hated, *anything.* Just as long as her characters could be given the breath of life.

Maybe I should try writing a novel instead… But she wouldn't be good at writing a full-length book—she was lucky to manage short stories. The process would be much more tedious, less character-driven than a screenplay, and she relished the dialogue the most. She'd been dabbling in stories ever since she was ten years old—some awful, some satisfying. With her screenplays over the past five years, it had been continuous failures. Failed submissions. Failed attempts to get an agent. Failed words. Maybe she just wasn't good enough…

Sadie's phone dinged, startling her. She grabbed it from beside her bag, finding a text from Skyler.

River looks like a poor version of Victor, but you look all right.

She rolled her eyes and messaged him back. *At least we dress up still. You're never too old to have fun.*

Hey, I wear a police uniform for nearly the whole year.

Sadie had been friends with Skyler ever since they'd met in elementary school. He'd had a crush on her older sister—Charlie—for years, then they finally started dating in high school. That was until Skyler broke off the wedding a few months ago. Not because he didn't love Charlie—he was worried he wasn't good enough for her, that she could do better. He just needed time to find himself, but Sadie's sister refused to talk to him. Charlie was hurt—she loved him too much and wanted to protect her heart.

Sadie looked around the woods again, the setting's mood now lost on her. She needed to find inspiration somewhere else.

Packing her things into her bag, Sadie glanced toward the cabin where a murder-suicide had occurred—the main reason she liked to come to these woods was to get the juices flowing. Twenty-something years ago, a young man had decapitated his girlfriend outside the cabin with an axe, then slit his own throat. Years before that, deeper in the woods, a man had shot his fiancée, then himself while camping.

As many times as Sadie had been out here, she had

never once experienced the slightest bit of supernatural anywhere in these woods. Brushing the dirt from her jeans, she headed toward the cabin, its paint faded and chipped. However, the structure had been kept up, the slate roof still in good shape. The place had been abandoned for several years, but a sold sign now rested near the road. She peered through a window, and there were no longer missing wooden floorboards or warped walls. Instead, new glossy boards covered the floor, their color a dark cherry stain, along with vintage-style wood paneling across the walls. It was perfect, her dream home. Envy crawled through her.

The garden in front of the cabin was dead, not a single leaf on any of the bushes. If she lived here, it would stay that way—plants preferred not to thrive around her. Since, apparently, one of her "curses" was to forget to water them…

A murder outside an old cabin where only a dead garden bloomed at the edge of a secluded woods might've been a bit morbid, but it only sparked her creativity.

Sadie pushed away from the cabin and trudged through the dirt to the truck her grandfather had left to her after he'd passed away a few years ago. The truck still smelled faintly of him—a hint of tobacco and spice.

Once inside, she finished off a water bottle, the liquid too warm as it slid down her throat, before she started the engine. The drive took about fifteen minutes, venturing down curved streets with dilapidated houses, until she reached the secluded cemetery. Something about a place that housed death could always draw a few lines from her, like the Phantom of the Opera getting inspiration from Christine's alluring voice.

She stepped out of the truck and walked past rows of graves—some headstones were new with fresh flowers, others cracked and crumbling, their vases empty. Holding up her phone, Sadie snapped a few photographs when the camera angled on two teenage girls farther ahead. They knelt before two faded headstones, rubbing wax over paper, creating gravestone rubbings. She took a picture, knowing she probably shouldn't have, but their expressions were so serene, focused, something she could possibly add to a future story.

Sadie glanced one more time at the two girls, and even though she wasn't much older, high school felt like a lifetime ago when there were fewer worries and dreams, or brilliant nightmares, seemed within reach.

Besides the teenage girls, the rest of the cemetery was empty, quiet, and only the dead were listening. A faded cement bench on the opposite side of the cemetery caught her attention, and she sat in front of a stranger's grave. Part of the headstone was cracked off and missing, the edges jagged. Some of the words were eroded, but not the person's name. *Stephen Forrest.*

"Hello, Stephen. I hope everything is splendid where you are." Sadie smiled and sent River a text with a picture of the headstone. *You're missing out on lunch with the dead.*

At some point, after he came across her words, she knew he would roll his eyes and message her back something sarcastic. Once she wrapped up here, she would head home to get ready for their date with a film. Eighties slasher boys was what she was in the mood for.

Fishing out the notebook from her backpack, Sadie wrote down words with ease. A spirit haunted the cemetery, wearing a billowing white ankle-length nightgown while carrying a candelabra, longing for her loved ones and stealing the life of anyone who came too close when she couldn't take over their bodies. It didn't matter if what she penned down at the moment was garbage—some of it would be salvageable, something for the short story she needed to write for an anthology if it didn't go well with the screenplay.

As the sunlight started to fade, Sadie jerked her head up. "Of course I'm late." She hadn't realized she'd been at the cemetery for *hours*. River wouldn't mind her being late, but it was their date night, and it mattered to her. On the other hand, her sister would be irritated—she was supposed to have called Charlie earlier. Sadie still didn't know how to prepare a meal to save her life, and Charlie insisted she needed to learn for when she had babies one day. It was always plural with the "babies"—Sadie only wanted one, which could happen sooner rather than later. She rubbed her stomach, thinking about the night before between her and River. They hadn't used protection the past month, knowing that whatever happened—or didn't—was meant to be. But she hoped…

Sadie gathered her things and hurried through the cemetery. She found Charlie's missed call on her phone and rang her sister back just as she hopped into her truck. It took a few rings before Charlie answered with a huff. "I called."

"Sorry, my phone was on silent while I was writing," Sadie said, backing out of the cemetery.

"You're spending too much time doing that."

Sadie rolled her eyes. "It's not going to write itself."

"Are these places paying you enough for all your hours? You're worth more than pennies from these tightwads."

"It is what it is." With all the time she put into the stories and articles, it didn't add up to that much if she were to break it down into hours spent on them. But it was experience.

Charlie groaned, changing the subject. "I have night shift at the hospital, so we don't have time to discuss the meatloaf recipe."

"Next week, we'll prepare two meals then," Sadie drawled.

"Hey, I'm not the one who wants to learn how to cook here."

"Don't be like that, Charlie." Sadie knew when her sister was irked, and she was reaching that point now. After their grandfather passed away, their parents had moved to the west coast, saying they wanted to live near a prettier beach, but they hadn't kept in touch with either of them much since leaving. So grumpy or not, Sadie loved her sister and would fight to the death to protect her.

"Fine, but be serious this time. I could've been doing other things."

"Like thinking about Skyler?" Sadie sang.

"Don't mention that name. He's dead to me."

Such a liar. Sadie knew Charlie wasn't over Skyler, and she wished her sister would just talk to him already.

Sadie chatted with Charlie a little longer, mentioning what happened at the party the night before. Needless to say, her sister wasn't as enthused as Sadie had been about it.

Since there wasn't time to prepare a fancy meal or dessert for indoor date night, Sadie swung by the bakery, grabbing a container of red velvet cupcakes. River's favorite. Or maybe, more so, hers.

She glanced at her phone—still no text from River. This usually happened when he found himself wrapped up in one of his art pieces, especially the sculptures, just as she did when enthralled in a story.

Sadie cranked up the radio while driving back to her house, but she was in the mood for nostalgia, per usual. A collection of her grandfather's vintage cassettes rested inside the arm storage, and she drew one out, then pushed it into the radio slot. The singer's deep baritone filled the truck, her fingers drumming against the wheel to the song.

She allowed the lyrics to drift through her head while trying to piece her new scenes together. There needed to be more than trees filled with blood and beating hearts. She needed a *story*, for the monsters to do *something*.

As she focused on the road, her gaze connected to familiar pine and oak trees in front of bricked homes. Sometimes she wondered how she didn't find herself on a date with death from a car wreck while her mind was on autopilot. It was as if she'd been visiting an alternate dimension, then returned to reality.

River's car was still parked in the driveway, and the neighbor's daughter was laying out on the lawn on top of a beach towel, even though the sun had already set. Sadie avoided talking to neighbors whenever possible and booked it inside once she turned off the engine. River was the outgoing one, while she was the recluse, the introvert, and she didn't mind it one bit.

"I'm home," Sadie called as she shut the door behind her. "And as you could've guessed, I don't have time to make dinner. *But* I brought you something even better!"

A cream sheet of paper lay folded on the table, her name written across it in River's perfectly sloppy handwriting. Her chest swelled at the sight. With a smile, she set the cupcakes on the table and picked up the note. More of River's paint bottles and brushes cluttered the living room. Various monstrous sculptures were sprawled across the coffee table, mostly complete. An unfinished canvas with the woods and a night sky sat atop the easel. Her framed insect collection and animal skulls covered nearly the entirety of the walls.

Unfolding the letter, Sadie stepped over the paint supplies and walked down the hall. Her smile grew as she pored over the words River had written to her.

Sadie,

I love you, but I can't. I'm sorry, my sweet nightmare.

Love you even after our bodies become dust,
River

And then there was silence.

"All right, River," Sadie called with a grin. "You got me. If you keep doing tricks like these, I don't think we'll ever leave the bed." She walked into their open bedroom, her attention catching on a shadow in the corner.

Sadie flipped on the light and her heart picked up, thrashing wildly in her chest, so much so she couldn't breathe, the room tipping sideways. Blood rushed in her ears and her hands trembled. Her lips parted, the note falling from her grasp.

Hanging from one of the wooden beams was River's lithe body. His arms hung limp—everything about him was still, and his head rested at an unnatural angle. Her husband's dark hair blocked half of his beautiful face, the other half exposing his unblinking bloodshot eye.

An ear-piercing scream poured from Sadie so loud that it could've shattered glass. She yanked the chair from the desk as hot tears flooded from her eyes, then rushed toward River to get him down and try to pump air back into his lungs. But she already knew it was too late, that the piece of him she loved was no longer inside his shell.

Gone forever.

3

"Memories are a part of us, what drives us."

"Aww, look at you looking all … bloody." River laughed, wearing nothing but his black boxer briefs, his bare chest speckled with yellow and orange paint from working on a beastly portrait.

Grinning, Sadie rolled her eyes and gave him a playful shove on the arm. "Sometimes one has to get into character."

"A beautiful *character," he purred, leaning against the wall, his arms folded. "So, this is your inspiration for the screenplay?"*

"It is." She shifted forward, inhaling his honey and sandalwood scent, and pressed her lips to his warm neck, tasting the salt of his skin. "But I also need to get into character with a seductive *romance storyline."*

River didn't hesitate to capture her mouth in a deep kiss, his arms lifting her so her legs circled his waist. And she didn't even care if the bed would be covered in fake blood as she made love to him.

He brought Sadie to the mattress, then hiked up her dress and freed himself from his boxers before hovering over her and caging her in. A lock of dark hair fell over a gray eye as he smiled wickedly at her. "It looks as if the bed is covered in real blood now."

A piercing pain shot through Sadie, ripping across her flesh. She trembled, peering down at herself, the fake blood turning real as it seeped out from every inch of her body.

"It should've been you hanging yourself instead of me," River cooed, his eyes bloodshot, his lips a pale blue.

He cut off her scream by pressing his cold, dead lips to hers.

Sadie jolted from sleep, her chest heaving as she checked her body for any sign of blood. Sweat trickled down her forehead, and her hair was soaked, matted to her cheeks and neck. She searched around the cluttered room, praying to find River. Nightmare or not, she wanted him there. But she hadn't seen him alive in three months, not since he'd hung himself. Every passing day she asked herself why he'd done it.

"Are you all right?" Charlie called, bursting into the room, her brown hair pulled back into a ponytail, never a strand out of place.

"I'm fine," Sadie rushed the words out, leaning against the headboard, her breathing becoming even. "Just another nightmare." But it had felt so real, and she wished desperately that it was, no matter how different her husband had seemed in her nightmare. Not once had he ever been cruel to her or anyone else.

Charlie sighed and sat on the edge of the bed, resting a warm hand on Sadie's. Her sister's nurse scrubs didn't have a single wrinkle on them, always ironed and neatly pressed for work. "You might want to talk to someone about the nightmares you've been having since they're becoming more frequent."

Sadie frowned, her lips turning into a tight line. "It's not as if a counselor can magically make nightmares disappear. I did that already and nothing changed. Besides, I talk to you about them."

"I mean … some meds." Charlie's hazel eyes held hers. "It might be time for that."

Sadie tugged her hand from her sister's grasp. "No. It's only been three months. Ask me again in a year." Truthfully, she was worried that if she took the meds, they would strip River away from her, pull him from her dreams—the only place where she could still see and meet with him.

Her sister blew out a long breath, then forced a smile as she asked, "White or brown chocolate?"

Sadie relaxed and cocked her head, pretending to mull it over. "That's quite the conundrum."

"Happy Birthday, little sister." Charlie ruffled Sadie's hair as she always used to do when they were younger.

"Right… That. The big twenty-four now." Sadie bit the inside of her cheek. Charlie was only a year older than her, but the gap in age between them always seemed like more. Maybe because she'd always taken care of Sadie in a sense, had stood up for her during their school days when everyone would ask why her younger sister didn't talk much, why she looked sullen all the time when it was just Sadie's natural expression. "How about both, as usual."

"I knew that would be your answer." Charlie smiled. "Just wanted to see if you might choose differently this time, though. Meet me in the kitchen when you're ready." She patted Sadie's shoulder, then stood from the bed, leaving her alone in her room. It wasn't really *her* room, but one Sadie was staying in until she found a place, even though she hadn't started looking yet. After River's death, she'd sold their house and moved in with her sister—she just hadn't been ready to live alone.

For the past three months, Sadie had become more of a recluse, only venturing out of her sister's house when she deemed it necessary. Usually by going to the store for groceries or the post office to pick up her mail. Even then, it was always a quick in and out, never meeting the eyes of anyone.

Sadie stared at her laptop and notebook on the desk in the corner of the room—she hadn't touched either of them to work on her screenplay, only to write pointless articles for online magazines or short stories for collections that had been due. However, those had been forced, lacking passion, the words coming out robotic.

It wasn't just three months give or take a day—it was three months to the *day* that River had hung himself. His limp body wouldn't vanish from her mind, her nightmares. That was the vision of River she wished she could forget. He'd still been warm to the touch when she'd taken him down from the beam, pressed her mouth to his to try and revive him, get him to *breathe* at all. What haunted her the most was that if she'd come home sooner, if she hadn't stayed so long at the cemetery, then maybe she could've saved him. Maybe he would've made a different choice.

But she hadn't been there. Not in his final moments.

She had so many unanswered questions. They'd been so happy, or at least, she thought they'd been. He would get into moods with himself when he was working on his art sometimes, as if he was putting himself in the place of the things he was creating. But never had there been an instance where she would even think to worry about him taking his own life. As silly as it was, since they hadn't been using protection, she wished she would've been pregnant. Because then she would've had a piece of him still. But she wasn't.

Tears pricked Sadie's eyes, and she wiped them away as she pushed up from the bed. Unopened boxes of her and some of River's things were stacked around the room. All her framed insects and skulls remained in boxes too, smothering inside, just as she seemed to be, even while being out in the open. She used to be more organized like her sister, but she didn't care anymore.

Sadie didn't bother to get dressed before heading into the kitchen, where blue and purple balloons were scattered across the tile floor. Polka dot streamers hung across the edge of the granite counter with a colorful *Happy Birthday* sign in the center. Above the decorations, the steaming mugs of hot chocolates rested beside a pristine circular birthday cake with white frosting.

"I woke up early and baked it for you," Charlie said, sliding the two hot chocolates toward Sadie.

"It's perfect." Sadie sank down on a bar stool, taking the two warm mugs and sipping from them both, relishing their flavors. If Charlie had known the underlying reason why Sadie drank two each day, she wouldn't have made them. It was a ritual, a most likely unhealthy obsession that Sadie continued to take part in, because each morning with River, she had made the different flavors and they would take turns drinking the opposite one, day after day. But now, it was only her …

drinking them both.

"I need to head to work." Charlie clipped her name badge to the front of her uniform. "I'm going to be late."

Sadie rolled her eyes. "You're going to arrive twenty minutes early instead of thirty."

"Exactly." Her sister smiled, grabbing her sack lunch and purse. "At least brush your hair today. Please."

"Fine." Sadie ran a hand through her tangled strands and watched as her sister closed the front door to the apartment.

She polished off the mugs and tapped her fingers along the counter. It had been a couple of weeks since she'd gone to the post office to check her PO Box, and she probably needed to do that. It could be her birthday *excitement* for now, a way for her to try and avoid the fact that it was also the three-month anniversary of River's death.

After rinsing the mugs and placing them in the dishwasher, since her sister said keeping anything in the sink was a no-no, Sadie grabbed her purse to go to the post office. She hadn't bothered to change out of her pajamas … or properly brush her hair. By the time her sister came home from work, she would make sure to do those things for her—it was the least she could do after Charlie had done so much.

Sadie hopped into her truck and pushed in a cassette, letting an old sixties song play. She cranked the music up as she drove the short distance to the post office. Sprinkles dotted the windshield, and her phone dinged as soon as she pulled into a parking spot.

She fished out her phone from her purse while walking to the door. Three missed texts. One from Skyler wishing her a happy birthday, the others from her mom and Coral. Her stomach sank at seeing them because she'd barely talked to anyone. That had been the norm with her parents, but Coral had invited Sadie to stay with her and Gabe, yet she just couldn't do that—the memories would've been overbearing. As for Skyler, she'd been an awful friend, mostly one-word replies from her end, but that hadn't stopped him from checking in on her.

Texting them all back a quick thank you, she walked inside the post office where only a couple of people stood in line to mail off packages. She passed rows of PO Boxes until she reached hers. A large stack of mail rested inside, and she took out the envelopes and catalogs.

Once she returned to her truck, Sadie flipped through the stack. *Trash, trash, trash...* Her fingers halted on a bright purple envelope, her eyes widening at the familiar sloppy handwriting, her throat growing dry. Everything about the day of River's death came crashing back—finding the letter he'd written for her, then discovering his... She shook away the painful image. But now an envelope was addressed to her, months later, in his same handwriting. *How?* Her hands trembled as her breaths came out ragged. It couldn't be his handwriting. She knew it couldn't be. Because her husband was dead. Yet that glimmer of hope burned within her, wondering if it had all been a nightmare and maybe, just maybe, she hadn't really found him gone.

Drawing in a deep breath, she peered down at the envelope again. No return address, only her name and PO Box written across the front.

Sadie slowly peeled open the envelope and pulled out

a folded sheet of cream paper, the same color as his last letter.

Sadie,

I scheduled to have this mailed near your birthday, even though I've been aching to tell you about it for months. Every time you complained about the cabin in the woods being purchased, I almost confessed it all. You know how terrible I am at keeping secrets from you. Figured we both might get better artistic inspiration living there together. We always did want to live in a place that was supposedly haunted, am I right? Your next step is to go to my parents' house to collect the keys from my mother, then you'll receive the following step there. Here's looking to the future, and Happy Birthday, my sweet nightmare.

Love you even after our bodies become dust,
River

Sadie's body trembled as she shoved the letter into the glove compartment, wanting to get it away from her. It was the way he always signed off on his notes or letters to her, but now his body was really ash.

No, she wasn't going to accept the cabin. She wasn't going to live there. She couldn't take more steps backward. Drinking two hot chocolates every morning was one thing, wishing for her nightmares of River to be real was another, but this, this… *No*. She needed to force herself to tell her husband goodbye, let the dream she'd always had of them living together in that cabin go, because he was gone and never coming back.

4

"Once a heart ceases beating, it isn't necessarily the end."

Sadie stood on Coral's front porch, rubbing her clammy palms against her jeans. Once she left the post office, she'd driven home to build up her nerve to come here since she wasn't the only one who'd lost River. Someone had to have mailed the envelope, and she assumed it was Coral. It wouldn't have seemed right for her to ask Coral in a text message, so she'd gotten cleaned up, brushed her hair.

Hands shaking, Sadie pressed her finger to the doorbell, the sound like solemn church bells, loud in her ears as it rang throughout the house. She hadn't been here since after the funeral, even though River's parents had invited her to dinner on several occasions. River hadn't wanted to be buried, to rot alone beneath the ground, rest as a skeleton inside a coffin for all eternity, so his wish had been to be cremated, then have his ashes spread. Which she had yet to do the final task…

Valentina swung the door wide, a white apron tied at her waist, and her smile was sad as her warm brown eyes met Sadie's. "It's good to see you," she said in her Spanish accent.

"You too. Is Coral home?" Sadie whispered, her heart thundering beneath her rib cage. A part of her didn't want to go inside to face not only reminders of the funeral, but all the wonderful memories of the time she'd shared in this home, memories that would surely rip Sadie's chest open again.

Valentina motioned her into the house, and Sadie took a breath, stepping past her onto the marble floor. The maid led Sadie through the living room and up the curving staircase. While walking down the hallway filled with framed photographs, a hint of a smile crossed her lips as she looked at them. Some were of River when he was younger—riding a bike, at the beach, dressed as Yorick from *Hamlet* and holding a skull he'd sculpted. Others were of him and his parents, or only of Coral and Gabe posing with one another.

Valentina brought Sadie to the sitting room, the doors wide open, where Coral was seated on the leather couch, drawing on a notepad. A desk rested in the corner, stacked with at least twenty sketchbooks, and two high-backed chairs sat across from the leather couch over an ornate red and gold rug. The French doors, cloaked with see-through white curtains, led to a luxurious balcony that looked out to the sparkling blue pool.

"Sadie is here as expected," Valentina said.

"Thank you." Coral smiled, setting her drawing tools beside an open pack of cigarettes on the glass table in front of her. The sketchpad lay open to several striped and polka-dotted dresses she'd designed. With the flare of their skirts and tight bodices, it gave them a vintage yet modern style. Coral's long dark hair was draped over one shoulder, curled at the ends, and she looked relaxed in a silky blouse tucked into tan pants, her feet bare. But her eyes were what gave her melancholic emotion away—they were red-rimmed as if she'd been crying earlier.

Valentina turned to leave, shutting the doors behind her. Relief washed over Sadie that she hadn't been led to the dining room where she'd been seated next to River when they'd been there together last.

"Hello, dear," Coral said as Sadie stepped farther into the room. "I took the week off from going into the office since I thought you might be coming, give or take a day or two, but I wasn't certain. Besides, I needed the break anyway." New paintings of beautiful gowns hung on the beige walls, replacing the ones that were there before. Coral was always changing out the designs in the room for creative expression.

"You knew about this?" Sadie took out River's letter from her purse, her fingers shaking.

Coral's lips tilted up slightly, her eyes turning glassy as she studied the cream paper. "I did. You were to meet him at the cabin after picking up the keys from me. And you know how River always planned things well in advance—such an impatient boy." She paused, letting out a breath. "He gave me the letter and the extra set of keys about five months ago. I didn't know if it was right or wrong to hold onto this last gift of his, but I thought if I mailed it to you as my son had planned, then it would be fulfilling his final wish in a sense."

Tears sprung to Sadie's eyes, her life with River coming back like wildfire consuming everything, licking its way through her mind. Their first kiss at the novelty store in a dark corner, their first date at an awful café with overcooked food, their first time making love in his car in the woods, skin to skin, clumsy yet perfect, the small Halloween-inspired wedding in her parents' backyard, the way he would paint beside her as she wrote. *Stop.* She tucked the lovely images away for now, but it wasn't soon enough. More tears fell, turning into a waterfall.

"Thank you," Sadie murmured, sinking down beside Coral and inhaling a hint of vanilla and nicotine.

"Come here," Coral said, circling an arm around her. They sat in silence, tears streaming from their eyes, until Coral drew back to hand Sadie a tissue. "You're not going to accept his gift, are you?"

Sadie bit her lip and shook her head, her heart drawn to the idea, yet she didn't want it to sink farther than it already had. "I can't."

Coral ran a hand through her hair and leaned forward. "I don't know what I would do if I were in your shoes, but don't decide until you've at least stepped inside the cabin, then make your choice. River told me over and over how much you loved that damn old cabin even though I wished he would've built a new one somewhere else, since we all know what happened in those woods."

"Then it wouldn't be the same." Sadie lifted her head and smiled.

"That's precisely what he said." Coral laughed,

opening the table drawer and producing a silver key. She placed the cool metal in Sadie's palm, closing her fingers over it. "Happy Birthday, dear."

Sadie sat in her truck for a moment, catching her breath in Coral's driveway. Before coming here, she'd planned on selling the cabin, but after the discussion with Coral, she yearned to see it again since River had put so much thought into this. Not only that, she finally decided on where she would release his ashes. The woods were where they would go for walks, spend time together, the place where she used to write. Near the cabin, that didn't belong to someone else as she'd thought, but to *her*.

She finally pulled out onto the road and stopped by her sister's apartment to collect the silver urn of River's ashes from the back of her closet, where they'd been hidden for far too long. It was time—she shouldn't have selfishly held onto them for so long.

After resting the urn beside her in the truck, she drove toward the cabin. The last time she'd gone there was the day River had hung himself, when she'd been consumed by writing. This was what she should've done before, not left him tucked away in her closet. But if she couldn't see the urn, then she could believe that he was out there somewhere still, that there was a chance she could run into him again.

Sadie's heart raced, her blood burning through her veins like lava as she pulled up to the cabin. *Her* cabin.

She lingered in the truck for a long moment, her hands tight on the steering wheel. With a shaky breath, she glanced at River's urn. "We're home," she whispered. "You're safe now. *Free.* But please, don't leave my dreams when I sleep."

Taking River's ashes, she trudged past the cabin and into the woods. Birds chirped high in the trees, and a strong gust of cool wind carried a piney scent as it brushed past her, ruffling her hair. The sun shone down, its rays warming her slightly beneath her thin jacket.

Once she stumbled on the old oak that always gave her a wonderful alive feeling, its branches gnarled and twisted, the ideal tree for a gothic horror film, she halted in front of the trunk. Setting River's urn before it, she took the pocket knife from her purse and carved her and River's names into its bark. Her chest swelled as she etched in the last letter, then she pressed her hand over their names, wondering if there was a ghost of a heartbeat beneath her palm, and she just couldn't feel it.

Sadie picked up the urn and surveyed the woods—less than half of the trees were still without their leaves, while most had never shed theirs. Removing the silver lid, she emptied the urn in front of the oak tree, allowing the wind to perform its duty and collect the ashes, spreading them around the woods.

"I love you, River." She sighed once his ashes were no longer drifting through the air.

Sadie didn't want to leave him, but she took the urn and trekked back toward the cabin. The house was still the way she'd always dreamed, with its dead garden and chipped paint on the outside. Nothing here would've ever made her guess that two murder-suicides had taken place in these woods years ago.

She stepped onto the porch, the planks groaning, and her stupid heart raced again. After she opened the door, she wished that River would magically appear alive and well, as he was meant to be. But she knew he wouldn't—the ashes she'd set free were proof of that.

Releasing a slow breath, Sadie slid the key into the lock and turned it. She flipped the switch beside the door inside, and warm ceiling lights illuminated the empty living room. Coral had turned on the utilities, but Sadie would have them transferred to her, regardless if she decided to stay in the cabin or sell it.

The refurbished wooden floorboards creaked as she walked across them, the sound like a beautiful haunt to her ears. A musty smell didn't linger inside—instead, a vanilla scent mixed with pine did. Her chest tightened—she knew Coral had been here recently, making sure the place would be clean if Sadie came to visit. Not if, *when*, because Coral had known Sadie would give into curiosity, temptation.

Rumor was that even though the deaths hadn't occurred inside the cabin, it was still haunted. There wasn't a hint that it could be, not a chill in the air, nor eerie sounds that could be her muse. If she closed her eyes, she could imagine a tinge of dark atmosphere calling to her, though.

She walked into the living room, peering at the wooden walls, the black-painted ceiling, the cozy kitchen at the back of the cabin. Biting her lip, she trailed a fingertip across the onyx mantel over the fireplace, and moths swarmed in her stomach. She didn't know what on earth to do—she was falling in love with the cabin, these woods, all over again.

River had bought her this home because he believed in her, in *them*. And even if she failed at writing the perfect screenplay, even if that wasn't what she was meant to do, she wanted to write one last story, for him, for her. Then maybe she would take another path if the writing didn't pan out—she could work on more articles, become a teacher, do the mundane thing.

"Dammit, River, you knew I would never say no to this, didn't you?" A small smile tugged at her lips as if he were looking down on her right then.

"I still don't think it's healthy for you to move out there," Charlie said as they loaded the last of Sadie's boxes into the bed of her truck. Over the past few days, she'd purchased new furniture and had started moving her belongings into the cabin.

"Is it any healthier for me to stay here?" Sadie cocked her head, thinking about how every day her sister got on her about not brushing her hair. "I want an escape, to work on writing."

Charlie frowned. "You can do that here. You can do that anywhere. Maybe it's time to use your degree and teach or do something else with it," her sister said the last part gently.

"Who am I hurting, Charlie? I don't *need* money. Whether you support me or not, I'm going to do this. I *will* finish this screenplay, and whatever happens after that, we'll see."

Charlie's shoulders fell, her expression softening. "I believe in you, Sadie. I do. But I don't like the idea of you alone in those woods. And what if the rumors are true about the cabin being haunted?"

"That's what I'm hoping for." Sadie grinned.

"You're so odd sometimes." Charlie rolled her eyes and wrapped her arms around Sadie, pulling her into a tight hug. "But I wouldn't take my little sister any other way."

"Hmm, I think I would make you less overprotective. Only a fraction, though." Sadie laughed, the first to step back. "I'll text you later."

"You better. I need to get to work now anyway. Patients to help save and all." Charlie started to turn, then spun back around. "Oh, I still owe you a birthday gift. I'm taking you to that gothic haunted house you've been fantasizing over. I'll get back to you on the day and time."

"Seriously? This is amazing." Sadie beamed. It was a new year-round attraction in the city, and it wasn't the Halloween standard bloody and gory haunted house, but the more gothic eerie style.

As Sadie started the truck, she pushed in one of her grandfather's old cassettes, letting the music ignite a new drive inside her. It took her a moment to realize what it was since she'd been without it for three months.

Determination.

5

"The night watches over us, whether we are wicked or not."

After putting her last black T-shirt away in the closet, Sadie had spent most of the day unpacking boxes, catching remnants of River's scent from the items inside. She arranged her movie collection alphabetically, filling up most of the shelves in the bedroom. She'd called the internet provider before moving in to see about setting up Wi-Fi. However, it wasn't available in her location yet, which was fine because she could still use her phone data for research and take her laptop to a coffee shop when she needed to submit one of her magazine articles or short stories.

Sadie finished hanging her framed insect collection on the walls, placing a few of the animal skulls between each of the moths. The other beetles, butterflies, and mantises were scattered about. Her favorite amongst all of River's art pieces, a painting of deep reds, umber, black shadows, and mysterious grays, depicting a werewolf carrying a savage mermaid back to the water, their love everlasting despite their monstrous states, she'd rested above the fireplace mantel. Some of his art she'd given to his mom, but the remainder she couldn't part with. They were just too alluring and as selfish as it might be, she didn't want anyone else to have them.

She couldn't part with River's vintage stereo or his records either. If she'd let those go, that would mean completely letting go of him. Same as when she'd kept her grandfather's cassettes—they were an important piece that she wanted to remember him by, listen to them when the need was there. So she'd set the stereo and records up in her bedroom beside her movie collection.

Yawning, she checked the time on her phone, and midnight was approaching soon. She took a water bottle from the fridge, ready to crash on the futon, when a loud creak echoed from the porch outside.

Her brow furrowed, and Sadie shrugged it off as she drank a few sips of water. Then it sounded again.

She set the bottle on the counter and grabbed a butcher knife from the collection of utensils before slowly tiptoeing to the door. Curiosity, unease, and giddiness filled her at once. Holding her breath, she drew back the black lacy curtains a sliver and peeked out the window, the porch light illuminating the area slightly. She could vaguely make out the outline of the road and the trees.

Shadows danced along the ground, but they were only a reflection from the moon shining down on the rustling trees as the wind blew.

Her shoulders sagged, realizing it was only the wind creaking the planks outside. Even though she gripped the knife still, she was more curious about uncovering a possible supernatural presence. Another night, when she wasn't too exhausted, she would explore the darkened woods. She lingered a few more minutes, staring out the window, hoping to catch a glimpse of the paranormal.

But nothing otherworldly showed itself.

Sadie tucked the curtains back around the glass and placed the knife on the table in case she did need it. She then lay on the velvety futon, drawing a fleece blanket up to her chin—she couldn't sleep in the bed just yet since it would've been where she and River would've slept. One step at a time.

As she closed her eyes, falling deeper and deeper into a blackened space of oblivion, the wind outside picked up, rattling the windows, and she could've sworn a gentle musical sound purred through the air, calling to her.

A slight headache pulsed above Sadie's right eye as she peeled open her lids. She'd slept like the dead, literally. It had been her first night's sleep over the past three months where she didn't remember dreaming. A knot formed inside her rib cage at the thought. It should feel like progress, only it didn't.

Pulling back the blanket, she wiped the sleep from her eyes and headed into the kitchen. This was the first time she'd ever lived alone. Before her sister and River, she had only lived in her parents' home.

Sadie tugged the ends of her hair and sighed as she prepared the hot chocolates to get her day started. She took her notebook and laptop from the desk and brought them with her to the futon.

Tapping the pencil against her lips, she flipped through the pages of her notebook, scanning over the things she'd written before River died. She contemplated whether to start fresh, but she shot the idea down—she wanted to add to the scenes that she'd created after the party at his parents' house. The ideas that had formed because of River.

Sadie jotted down a few lines about a haunted hotel, then erased them. Another line about a farmhouse where something insidious was lurking about, doing nefarious things with the livestock. "Too cliché," she grunted and erased that as well. An anxious feeling churned in her stomach, and she tightened her grip on the pencil, writing one single sentence, or more like three lonely words. *This is appalling.* And to strengthen it, she scratched out the first word and changed it to *Life is appalling.*

"Dammit," she whispered, tossing the notebook aside. She leaned forward and pressed her face into her palms, then wiped away the tears that had started to fall. Why couldn't she do this? Why couldn't she at least write a single sentence for River? A start. Even if she didn't submit it to anyone, she just wanted to *write* it, maybe even bury it in the woods where she'd spread his ashes. *Something.*

Sadie relaxed against the back of the futon and stared up at the midnight-black ceiling. "If only I could be a part of your dark depths, just for a moment, to absorb that desire, that grim strength to write this." But of course the ceiling didn't answer back.

She lifted her second mug and took a sip of the brown chocolate, letting the rich flavor coat her tongue as she attempted to think of *words*. For the time being, she worked on her laptop, typing up an article that was due soon, then she transferred what she did have in her notebook for the screenplay to a file, followed by creating a page of what she imagined the characters would look like. As she closed her eyes, she focused on the main characters, and the only images that came to mind were … her and River…

The phone rang and Sadie jolted, snatching the cell from the coffee table. Her sister.

"Hey," Sadie answered. "You're not on shift?"

"No, my schedule got moved around yesterday," Charlie said. "You didn't text me."

"I'm still alive and kicking. No sign of hauntings besides some shadowy tree limbs and the porch making glorious creaking noises from the wind."

"That's good." Something in her sister's voice was different, nervous.

"What is it? You don't sound like yourself."

It took a moment for Charlie to answer before she sighed. "I saw Skyler at the grocery store this morning."

"Uh oh." Sadie grinned, resting her elbows on her knees as she leaned forward. "That's what you get for going to the store so early. You know his routine." She would have to text Skyler later—he knew she was moving out of her sister's place, but she hadn't told him where just yet. It was going to be a surprise.

"It's fine," Charlie rushed the words out. "I turned around and left after he spotted me."

"Without finishing your grocery shopping?" Sadie laughed.

"I mean, I'm going back later to do it."

Sadie rolled her eyes. "I think you need to talk to him. It's clear you still have feelings for him and Skyler is one of the nicest guys ever."

"Of course, you're—" Charlie's voice cut off and the call dropped. Sadie tried to ring her sister back, but the phone signal was down. No Wi-Fi for the laptop, no phone—it was as if she was completely cut off from society.

Her gaze locked on River's painting above the fireplace. "You would've liked this if you were here, my vicious dream," she murmured.

Biting her lip, Sadie stared at the laptop one more time before deciding on a distraction. She polished off the hot chocolate, then slipped on her boots and headed out the door.

The sun sat bright in the sky, its rays piercing through the trees. The porch creaked as she went down the steps onto the sparse grass. Besides her footsteps, the world was quiet, so quiet, the woods still. The wind remained dead and not even the buzzing of insects stirred. Only the silence. It wasn't like this the day or night before when the woods had been alive.

Sadie stared out at a tall pine tree, a vine dangling from it … like a noose. Her heart lodged in her throat as she inched closer. The image of River drifted through her mind, his dead body hanging not from the ceiling beam in their old home, but here in this vine, swinging.

Hand shaking, she wrapped her fingers around the vine. Even though it wasn't made of rope and there wasn't a noose at the end of it, she still yanked the vine down. That desperate emotion crawled through her, where she blamed herself for what she hadn't done, how she hadn't been there for him… Sometimes she wished she could've shaken his dead body for answers, a feeling she'd kept to herself.

Tangling her fingers in her hair and tugging, she lowered herself in front of the tree. "Stop it," Sadie whispered to herself. She wasn't the only one to have ever lost someone they loved more than life itself, to have lost someone in such a grim way. But it hurt. It hurt like fucking hell. And she didn't think these catastrophic waves of emotions crashing inside her would ever stop. Tears beaded her lashes, and she shoved them away.

He's gone, and he isn't ever coming back.

Sadie pushed off the ground and went back to the cabin to try and do something productive. Instead, she paced inside, outside, then sat on the porch in her new swing chair, only venturing into the cabin a few times to grab something to eat. She couldn't think and just wanted to sit outside and stare at the woods, to pretend as if everything was all right. Her sister and Skyler had messaged her, and even though her phone signal was working again, she couldn't bring herself to text them back. She didn't want to talk to anyone.

A gust of wind rustled the leaves, caressing its invisible hands across the branches, the first sound she'd heard since being outdoors. Sadie opened her eyes, taking a deep breath. At some point, she must've drifted off. The sun was no longer glowing but, instead, was replaced by the night—the stars freckled the dark sky, and a werewolf moon shone brightly above. If River were beside her, he would've howled at that moment. As though hearing her thoughts, a wolf howled in the distance.

The chilly night air blew, making her shiver. She tucked her hands into her jacket and listened for more sounds. Not too far away, a dark silhouette glided from one of the trunks toward her. As it crept closer, she gasped, squinting to get a better view.

"Hello?" Sadie called, standing from the swing chair. "Good one. Call a vicious animal to your cabin."

But then the silhouette sunk into the ground, vanishing. Or maybe it was a ghost…

With wide eyes, she stepped to the edge of her porch, peering at where the silhouette had been. Floorboards creaked behind her, and she whirled around, her gaze meeting nothing but darkness. Her heart pounded, and even though she would've liked the adrenaline rush on any other day, she still wasn't in the right mental state.

It's all right to be a coward sometimes. Sadie darted inside the cabin, slamming the door behind her and locking it. She looked through the window and past the light from the porch—only nothing was there, not even shadows from the trees.

Sadie grabbed the knife and brought it to the bedroom, where she put on a record from River's collection, letting the music calm her nerves. As the music drifted through the space, she sifted through the DVDs, contemplating which one to watch to get her out of this strange mood. No matter how many times she'd seen them, they always helped, even if only temporarily. They weren't just for pleasure but also research, mostly guiding her to decide what not to do in a story. In this case, not go out into the woods tonight, even if her curiosity blossomed.

After she found a 1930s film she hadn't seen in a while, Sadie started the movie on her laptop in the living room. She settled onto the futon and drew the blanket to her chin as she watched the black and white screen. Halfway through the film, when the man was terrorizing people in his invisible form, her eyes fell shut. She started to slip away when she could've sworn footsteps sounded near the front door.

Sadie jerked up, sweeping her gaze across the small area and finding no one but herself. It might've been the movie still playing, her imagination, or … maybe the rumors were coming to fruition, and the haunted gateway of the woods was starting to open.

6

"And then the quiet of the woods came to life."

Thick fog cloaked the woods as Sadie left her cabin and trekked through it, clutching the container of red velvet cupcakes to her chest. With each step, the fog grew heavier, and she was unable to make out any of the trees, only the cloud of white surrounding her.

Chilly water droplets collected on her bare arms, and she shivered while continuing to walk, searching.

"River!" Sadie called out, her voice echoing, his name never ceasing. "You didn't eat your cupcakes." His name fell from her lips again, repeating until the sound of her voice morphed into something else. Multiple voices shouting his name, the word becoming more drawn out, slower, deeper, the sound not of this world.

Through the fog, spots of white darkened to swirling black until shadows began to form, crawling forward, horns curving from their elongated heads, their details obscured.

The shadows crept on all fours along the ground, their silhouettes hunched, crooked, inching toward her. Hands trembling, Sadie gripped the cupcake container, the plastic crackling, and took a step back just as the cool blade of a knife dug into her throat. Hot breath crawled up her neck, and a chest pressed to her back. Then screeching came from everywhere, piercing enough to shatter her eardrums.

Sadie jerked forward, searching around the room, her gaze meeting a framed death's-head moth. She was inside the cabin on the futon, waking from a nightmare… Only one night without them, and they'd returned, but this one didn't feel like the others. Goosebumps covered her arms, and the chill slowly dissipated like a cold blanket lifting away from her. She ran her fingertips across her throat, where the blade had dug in. It had seemed so real… And why the hell had she been so desperate to cling to those cupcakes? If she'd found something unruly like that in the woods at this very moment, she would've thrown the desserts and darted away. But she understood why the cupcakes were there—they were symbolic in a sense. River had never gotten to eat them and never would.

Sometimes nightmares could be a proper antidote, even though they drove fear through her. But sometimes fear was necessary to survive. She sighed, her chest heaving as she picked up her notebook from the coffee table.

The nightmare was already starting to fade, but she scribbled down the parts about the shadows slinking toward her, their horns, the inhuman shape of their heads, the cool steel blade pressed into her flesh, then the heinous screeching. If River were around to hear about the nightmare, he would've wanted her to describe the shadows thoroughly so he could sculpt them. A hint of a smile played on her lips as she thought about the memories of his skilled hands molding the clay.

Sadie turned on the laptop and opened the screenplay document. She briefly scanned over what she had so far, starting with the party, then the husband's death, the struggling wife, her desperate need to see him again…

There was more she could add—truthful things. The story was taking a different turn than what she'd originally planned, but maybe that was for the better. She typed a short scene of the wife spreading her husband's ashes in the woods, moving into a cabin, the quiet surrounding the place during the day, the nightmare she'd faced. And that was where she ended the work in progress for now—what would come next was still unknown, but it was there, brewing inside of her. A darkness eager to unleash itself, to sate her dark appetite. But she wouldn't force the story as she had in the past—something told her to *wait*.

A knock pounded on the front door, and Sadie startled. She pursed her lips, knowing it could most likely only be one person, as she went to the window and looked out. Her sister stood on the porch, wearing her blue scrubs and backpack, her hair pulled into a neat bun at the base of her neck.

Sadie drew open the door and leaned on the frame. "You didn't tell me you were coming by."

"Figured you needed a visitor." Eyebrow arched, Charlie clicked her tongue as she scanned Sadie up and down. "And possibly a shower."

"Let me guess," Sadie drawled, shutting the door once her sister stepped over the threshold. "You came here because you can't stop thinking about Skyler."

Charlie glared at Sadie. "How about we stop mentioning his name?"

That wasn't a no, yet she would play along, pretend her sister wasn't still in love with him. Charlie was too proud to give in so easily. But all in due time.

"Do you want me to pour you a bowl of cereal? I have fruit in there if you prefer that." She motioned at the bowl on the counter, brimming with apples, bananas, and oranges.

"No, I brought your favorite." Charlie unzipped her backpack and handed Sadie a white paper bag. "Glazed donuts."

"Ah, just what I needed. Why do you keep lugging that huge backpack everywhere you go lately?" Sadie asked, digging her hand straight into the paper bag.

"If there's an emergency, you'll be glad I have it," Charlie pointed out. "Besides, I've seen too many disturbing circumstances at the hospital *not* to carry one."

"Touché," Sadie said, thinking of the horror stories her sister had told her. Body parts hacked off, flesh burned down to the bone, bloated corpses… "I was planning on brainstorming for a bit if you have time before you go to work."

Charlie tilted her head to the side, her mouth set in a tight line, clearly unimpressed. "So, you mean a *horror* movie, right?"

"Yes, your fantasy stuff won't work for this. And it has to be one of my DVDs since I can only stream on my phone at the moment. Wi-Fi doesn't approve of me being out in these woods." Even then, she wasn't fond of most new horror movies. It took her watching a truckload of awful films to get to one that she considered mediocre, and if she was lucky, decent.

"Fine, I have about four hours to kill, but I'm not

going to watch any of those gross slasher movies," Charlie pointed out as she set her backpack on the floor and plopped down on the futon. "You still decided not to get a new TV?"

"It's unnecessary at the moment." Sadie finished her donut, then thumbed through the DVDs in her bedroom until she settled on a classic one with ghosts. As she slid the movie into her laptop, she noticed Charlie glancing at her hand several times. "Why do you keep looking at my hand strangely?"

Charlie bit her lip. "It's nothing."

"It's something." She frowned.

"Do you plan on eventually taking the ring off?" Charlie asked softly. "I'm only curious is all."

Sadie's chest tightened as she peered down at the white gold ring with a sapphire in its center that never left her finger. "I haven't thought about it," she whispered. "I've always believed vows aren't only until death do us part, that they belong even after."

"You and I finally agree on something." The edges of Charlie's lips tilted up. "But even if you decide to take it off, the vows are within your heart forever, Sadie."

Sadie continued to study the ring, remembering the day River slipped it on her finger, how she'd worn the crimson gown and he'd donned a vintage suit and a dark cape for their Halloween-themed wedding. Her chest warmed at the memory. "It doesn't feel right to take it off."

"You don't ever have to. I only wanted you to know that no one would fault you for it."

Sadie rotated the ring around her finger. "Thanks, Charlie."

"All right, let's see what horrendous movie you picked out." Charlie waggled her brows, changing the subject to lighter things. "Are we going with supernatural vibes? The slow serial killer? The poor misunderstood monster? The person who doesn't know they are the murderer?"

"You know more about these movies than you pretend to, but you'll find out." Sadie laughed and pressed play, then snuggled close to her sister.

Sadie could feel Charlie rolling her eyes or huffing about how the main character was making poor choices, but less than she normally did. Once the film's credits rolled, Charlie put on her backpack and turned to Sadie. "That movie was a bit iffy but better than the ones you normally pick out. I *suppose*."

"I think you might be turning to the horror side. *Finally*," Sadie cooed, walking her sister to the door.

"Also, if tomorrow is a good time for the haunted house, I can pick you up for it."

Sadie nodded. "Sounds perfect. Message me before you head my way."

After her sister left, Sadie took the movie back to her room. She stopped in her tracks when she caught the scent of honey combined with sandalwood. *River*. The smell enveloped her, stronger than it had been when she'd opened the boxes of his things. Fear had struck her in the heart that his comforting smell would eventually fade, but this was stronger, not fading…

Sadie squeezed her eyes shut, knowing her mind was playing tricks on her. "You got this," she said, opening her lids as she slowly backed out of the bedroom to go and bathe.

As she peeled off her clothes and stepped into the

warm shower, her stare didn't waver from her wedding ring. *Should I take it off?* Even for a little while? Why was it a struggle to decide what to do? Maybe she should've taken it off after she released River's ashes. Yet she still didn't want to give up her dreams of him. He hadn't been there the past two nights and the thought worried her.

Once she finished attempting to drown her thoughts while cleaning herself, she draped a towel around her body, then slipped off the ring, resting it on the sink counter.

A hollow feeling traveled through her, screaming at her to put the ring back on. It was anger inside her that she'd never felt before, unnerving her slightly. She shoved the ring on her finger and sighed as she came back to herself.

After getting ready, Sadie collected her notebook and headed outside for fresh air. She stopped in her tracks at the edge of the porch, listening. Same as the day before, quiet echoed around her, owning every inch of the woods.

She trekked through the trees, gazing around her. Not a single sound besides what was coming from her. Her feet snapping twigs, her breaths, the rustling of the notebook.

Sadie caught sight of a dead finch on the ground farther away, her stomach sinking at the sight of it, but decided to let nature take its course with the bird. She found herself stopping at a rotting tree stump and lowered herself to the dirt in front of it to outline the two short stories she needed to work on for separate articles.

She'd gone to the cabin a few times throughout the day but always returned to the same spot. And when the night started to descend, Sadie closed her notebook, peering up at the sky until the stars shone brightly. A cool breeze trickled in, rustling the branches, followed by an owl hooting in the distance. It was as if the quiet had waited until night cloaked the woods to speak.

As she stood, her gaze caught on movement in the distance. A dark silhouette slid from one of the trees and bolted deeper into the woods.

Sadie's eyes widened—her heart raced. It was too far away to tell if it was an animal or a person, yet she was leaning toward the supernatural... She thought the previous night had been a trick of the eye, but maybe it *was* a spirit that had vanished into the ground. What did she have to lose that she hadn't already? She turned on the phone's flashlight and followed in the direction the silhouette had gone, the breeze picking up, the branches rustling harder. Sadie was about to turn around when another—or the same?—silhouette leapt from the oak tree that she'd carved into, twigs snapping as it took off.

"What's *happening*?" Sadie was about to lunge for the shadowy figure but cursed herself for not having some sort of weapon besides a phone. But then, a familiar scent struck her nose, so very familiar. Sandalwood and honey. Just like it had been in the cabin's bedroom, in River's things. *His* scent.

As foolish as it was, she called out his name. "River?" But of course no one answered. No one came running toward her. Fear tore through her—not of who it could be, but of who it wouldn't be.

So she fled for the safety of her home, locking the door behind her. River's scent permeated the air again, filling the cabin. Her body shook as she slowly walked into her bedroom, the smell growing more potent. Hand trembling, she lifted one of the pillows and inhaled. Sandalwood and honey.

Taking a deep swallow, she looked around the space as if he would slip out from the closet or beneath the bed, turn on the vintage stereo system and sit in the chair with his headphones on.

Sadie twisted her wedding ring round and round her finger, her breaths quick. She didn't want to call Charlie—her sister would tell Sadie she was unstable without saying the word. Maybe she was. But there was Skyler—she could always call him. Besides that, he was also a police officer…

The phone rang several times, and she was about to end the call when he answered, "Sadie? Are you *finally* inviting me to your new mysterious place?"

"Skyler, can you come over in the morning?" Her words came out in a rush. "Not on police duty, but to check out something in the woods for me."

"Woods?" He chuckled. "What are you up to?"

"Living in the woods, apparently. You know, in the cabin I've been bewitched by for years."

There was a long pause before he spoke. "I can't believe you didn't tell me you moved out there. Do you want me to come now? You sound a little off."

"No, I'm fine. Just come in the morning."

"All right. If you need me sooner, I'm there."

"Thanks, Skyler." Sadie clutched her phone at her side after ending the call.

She needed to release the words yelling within her, so she went into the living room, writing inside her notebook what had happened in the woods. The story was becoming disjointed, but eventually, she would stitch it all together. Dr. Sadie Frankenstein. *Idiot.*

She lay on the futon wide awake until sleep took over, traveling through her bloodstream, opening to the starlit woods. As though welcoming her into its darkness, an alluring melody stirred to life, filled with stringed instruments and flutes, roaring with the wind, followed by the sound of bugs buzzing inside her ears.

Black forms, hidden in shadows, peeked out from behind the trunks. They beckoned her forward, and her heart sang, aching to join them. But then the ground disappeared beneath her feet, and she fell and fell into a pit of darkness.

7

"During the day we stay quiet, then at night we take."

A warm hand cradled Sadie's face, and lips brushed softly against hers. *His* hand. *His* lips.

Sadie opened her eyes to morning pushing out the night as bright light illuminated the curtains. She was alone, no one there but her. She inhaled a sharp breath, drinking in as much oxygen as she could while her heart beat wildly in her chest, so much so that she thought it would burst. Her fingers touched her lips, where she'd imagined River's whisper of a kiss had been. Even though she'd pretended he'd been there, she could've sworn she smelled him in the room. It was unhealthy for her to be conjuring up these things, she knew.

She exhaled and looked at the time on her phone.

Since Skyler would be there soon, Sadie rinsed off in the shower, then prepared her mugs of hot chocolate while nibbling at a bagel.

Taking a sip from the white hot chocolate, she opened her notebook and scrawled a single sentence: *And the quiet of the woods came to life.*

Sadie thought about the dream that was coming back to her, where music trickled into the woods, and dark silhouettes watched her from behind the trees, beckoning her toward them. She'd wanted to go to them, follow wherever they led, but the ground had disappeared beneath her feet. All she could remember after that was falling, but no matter how long she fell, not once did she scream, not once had she been afraid. If anything happened after that, it was all a blur. To others, it might've been a nightmare, unsettling, but to her, it was something more… Yet she couldn't pinpoint what. She briefly sketched the images and wrote a few lines about how the silhouettes had enticed her until someone knocked on her door and she shut her notebook.

Skyler stood on the porch, his hand pressed to the doorframe, his head tilted to the side, and his golden-brown eyes meeting hers. He was dressed in his police uniform, his dark hair slicked back instead of the loose waves he wore when off duty.

Sadie arched a brow. "You didn't tell me you were going to come while on shift."

He rolled his eyes. "I'm not on duty yet, and you told me you were moving but not to the secluded cabin in the woods where at least two murder-suicides took place."

"Could you expect anything less of me?" She batted her lashes. "Besides, that was years ago."

Skyler smiled, his crooked incisor showing. "How's your sister?"

"Living the mundane life." *And secretly pining over you.* But it wasn't her business to tell. If Charlie wanted to talk to Skyler, she needed to own it and call him instead of fleeing like she had from the store.

"*So*"—his grin widened—"she's still single then?"

"Why don't you ask her yourself?" He was just as irritating when it came to her sister as he'd been in school. Back then, she had to practically force him to ask Charlie out so she wouldn't have to keep hearing about it. But Skyler was her closest friend, one of the few she would protect with her life. She'd missed seeing his face, hated that she hadn't talked to him as much over the past three months. That was her fault, though.

"Maybe I will. If she doesn't run away again." Skyler chuckled softly. "We're getting off-topic. I can't believe you moved here. *Or* maybe I should because I know how infatuated you've always been with these woods."

Before she met River, she'd brought Skyler here a few times to see if they could find anything haunted. He wasn't into it like she was, but he'd come with her nonetheless. As her heart lodged in her throat, she stepped forward, throwing her arms around him. "You're the only other person who understands me besides Charlie." Only the two of them … because River was dead.

Skyler held her, his comforting woodsy scent pulling her back from the madness. When she'd called the police after discovering River's lifeless body, Skyler was one of the first responders. He'd seen it all, seen River on the floor after she'd taken him down from the ceiling beam, seen her sobbing uncontrollably as she tried to get him to breathe.

"River bought you this cabin, didn't he?" Skyler asked gently as he held her.

Sadie nodded into his chest. "He was the buyer. When I complained to you about the cabin being sold, all along, it was him."

"I should've guessed that. No one else would've wanted to buy this place," he said, a hint of humor in his voice to lighten the moment.

She smiled, wiping away tears as she pulled back from him. "Untrue, plenty of people would."

He blinked and cocked his head. "Name one."

"Me," she said.

"That doesn't count. You two were a…" he trailed off.

"I know you don't believe in ghosts, and you always say that people see what they want to. But I saw something last night in the woods. Dark silhouettes of some sort. One ran deeper into the woods, then another dropped from a tree."

"Sadie." Skyler sobered, his expression slipping from playful to serious, the way it was when he was on police duty. "You saw someone, possibly *multiple* someones, in the woods where you live *alone,* and you had me wait until the morning to come out?"

"I have a gun … and knives." Sadie straightened. "Besides, it's supernatural. I said silhouettes, not people."

Skyler sighed, closing his eyes briefly.

"If I really believed it was an axe-wielding murderer, I would've happily told your ass to come out last night. But they were shadows. *Shadows,*" she repeated the last word for emphasis.

"People can look like shadows in the dark, Sadie."

She tightened her fists, her nails digging crescent moons into her flesh. "I smelled River's scent, all right? I smelled it in the woods, then when I came inside it was there, too, stronger than it should've been, as if he'd been *here*." She'd meant to keep that part to herself, but she needed to confide in someone she trusted, even if there would be pity in his eyes like there was now.

"Sadie…"

She waved a hand in the air and brushed past him, barefoot down the creaking steps and onto the sparse grass. "Listen."

He furrowed his brow and craned his neck. "What am I listening to?"

"It's quiet! For the past few days, it's been quiet out here, then at night, it comes."

"What comes?"

"Loud sounds!" she shouted.

"You do realize you're in the woods," Skyler drawled. "There's bound to be bugs, wind. Maybe even a wolf or ten."

"Skyler!" Sadie hissed.

He rested his hands on her shoulders, his gaze meeting hers. "Look, I know you're at the cabin because you love this area and writing out here. Maybe for other reasons, too. I get it, and I'm on your side, all right?"

"All right," she said, tamping her emotions down.

"Can you show me what tree you saw the silhouette in?" he asked.

"Let me get my shoes first."

She grabbed a pair of sneakers from inside, then led

him through the thick brush. The leaves crunched beneath her feet, the only other sound besides their breathing. Her gaze drifted to the spot where the dead bird had been the day before but was now gone, most likely a meal for another animal.

Sadie stopped in front of the oak tree and pressed her palm against its bark. "This is where I saw the second one for sure."

Skyler's face softened as he looked from the carved names to the ground. He pointed at a footprint in the dirt. "This is yours."

"Why yes, I can see how you were destined to become a police officer," she said sarcastically.

Skylar pinched the bridge of his nose, ignoring her comment even though he fought a smile. He then motioned at the muddy area. "The ground is soft over here, so if this was a person and they jumped out of the tree like you said, there would be prints."

"So, something supernatural as I said, right?" She bit her lip. "Besides the two people outside the cabin, two others died directly in these woods, and I saw two forms…"

Skyler rubbed the back of his neck, the way he did when he was mulling something over. "If it's all right, I'll swing by tonight after work to check things out since you saw them after dark."

"I have this haunted house to go to with Charlie," Sadie said with nonchalance. "You could stop by around ten."

The edges of his lips curled upward. "Will she be with you when you come back?"

"Maybe," Sadie drawled.

"You're not going to tell her I'll be here, are you?"

"Nope. I suppose she'll find out, then you two can stop beating around the bush and talk already." Sadie smiled. "You're two grown adults here."

"I fucked up, Sadie." Skyler let out a heavy breath. "If I could marry her today, I would. I don't know what I was waiting for."

"You were being a human, unsure of the future. My sister can be a hard ass sometimes."

"I never told her the real reason why I wanted to wait."

She wrinkled her nose. "Something you didn't tell me either?"

"Because it's ridiculous. I see death all the time, each day, and I was afraid of losing her. I couldn't tell her because she sees the same at the hospital, and yet, she didn't give up wanting to marry me, knowing that I could lose my life in an instant."

Charlie would've understood that, and she would've given him a break if he'd needed it. "Tell her this, Skyler. Tell her tonight. I know how quickly we can lose someone, but it's worth it. It's all worth it." She paused, wringing her hands together. "You helped me today, so now I'm helping you with a fated meeting in exchange."

"Fated meeting, huh?" He chuckled. "I really do wish you could've been my sister."

"We don't need a marriage for that. You're already like a brother to me."

"I'm going to look around a little more, but I'll see you later tonight, Sadie." He hugged her one more time, and it felt as if months hadn't gone by since she'd seen him.

Sadie headed back toward the cabin, the world still quiet as she trekked through the foliage. Her attention caught on a dead squirrel and another fallen bird. She frowned at them for a moment, wondering what could've happened to them but shook it off and continued home.

Once inside, Sadie took out her phone and lowered herself to the futon. She tapped through the pictures until she reached the last one she'd taken of River. Her heart lurched at the sight of him. His hair tucked behind his ears as he sculpted a horned figure, a line of yellow paint on his left cheek. Sometimes she felt she was forgetting what he looked like and needed to remind herself she wasn't.

Sadie scrolled through the rest of her pictures. Christmas with River's parents. The beach with Charlie and Skyler. When they'd dressed up as eighties slashers one Halloween, then another where he was a giant crow while she was the screaming heroine.

After a long while, Sadie brought her notebook outside, the woods silent and Skyler's car already gone.

As she walked through the trees, movement along the ground caught her attention, and she halted, glancing down. Shadows weaved and slithered across the dirt, and she looked up at the trees. Their branches weren't swaying—the wind wasn't blowing… Squinting, she dropped to her knees, running her hands over the dark silhouettes, feeling nothing but dirt. She blinked, her throat dry. How was this happening? Was the trick of the light somehow causing the movement even though the branches didn't stir? Or was it *something* else…? She took a few pictures with her phone, then recorded a video of the shadows and the unmoving branches.

A tickling sensation crawled up the back of her neck, and the hair on her arms stood on end. She whirled around to find it was still only her, but it didn't feel that way—it felt like she was in a crowded room with hundreds of people *watching* her.

"If you're there," she shouted to the woods, "just come out. I can try to help you."

Only silence answered.

"Are you ready for a good haunt?" Sadie asked, standing beside her sister as they looked up at the haunted house attraction. It was a gothic-styled Victorian mansion with an obsidian roof and off-white paint covering the pleated walls. A wide porch rested in the center, an iron gate surrounding it. On the left side, a tower loomed, its top a deep blood red.

"Nope," Charlie said, folding her arms. "I'm only doing this for *you*."

"It's not like the last one we went to years ago." Sadie laughed. "There won't be clowns."

"I did my research beforehand."

Sadie rolled her eyes. "Of course you did." The last one they'd gone to wasn't even scary, yet her sister swore she hadn't slept for days after a clown touched her arm.

As they entered the building, only one other couple was there, about to be led into the attraction. Sadie assumed it was busier on the weekends and near Halloween.

Cracked doll heads lined the walls, some without eyes, others blacked out or only containing one, and Sadie couldn't take her gaze off their different melancholic or blank expressions. Charlie showed the middle-aged woman, dressed in a lacy black gothic dress with a dipping V-neck line, at the front desk their tickets on her phone. The woman told them not to touch anyone and to wait for the door to open.

Just as Sadie thought nothing would happen, an entrance hidden behind the green wallpaper opened. Charlie groaned beside her, and Sadie grabbed her sister by the wrist, pulling her into a small space where slow and deep organ music crackled from vintage speakers. Fake flames burned a brilliant orange and red inside a fireplace beside a cream velvet settee. More dolls were there, resting on shelves, some of their bodies tipped to the side. Only these weren't cracked but old with chipped paint.

Another door creaked open and Sadie stepped inside, leading the way while Charlie clasped the back of her shirt, her sister's hand shaking. Everything was dark as she ventured through, her fingers skimming the narrow walls. The organ music turned to violins, accompanied by squeaking and ghoulish sounds. As the music grew louder it reminded Sadie of the song she'd heard in her sleep, but not quite as alluring.

Dim light illuminated the next room, showcasing antique furniture and a massive bookshelf cloaked in spiderwebs. Charlie released Sadie's shirt, seeming to grow a bit bolder. Sadie smiled as she walked into another area decorated with Ouija boards, candles, antique mirrors, and coffins. Faded portraits hung across the walls of people missing their eyes, their mouths twisted in fear.

As she turned into the next room, the smile dropped from her face when she stared up at the body hanging from a noose. She froze. River. *River*…

"It's not him. Don't look at it," Charlie whispered, wrapping her arm around Sadie and guiding her into the next room.

But the giddiness had left Sadie—all she could see was the body hanging from a noose. She'd watched movies with death just fine since River's passing, even hangings. But for some reason, being in the same room with a body like that, even a mannequin, brought her back to the moment she'd lost her other half.

Once they reached the exit, Sadie put on a false expression that made it seem like nothing had been wrong at all.

"I'm never going to a haunted house again," Charlie said, walking past bushes cloaked in fake cobwebs and black flowers. "Next year, I'll take you to Cirque du Soleil or something."

"I mean, this was your idea," Sadie pointed out. "I would've been completely satisfied with Cirque."

"I brought this on myself then." Charlie laughed, her expression sobering. "Are you all right though? Back there…"

"I'm perfectly peachy." But she knew her sister could tell otherwise, could see straight through her lie, even though Charlie nodded.

Sadie stayed quiet for most of the car ride home, wishing they were in her truck so she could turn on one of their grandfather's cassettes. As if knowing, Charlie put the radio on a station that played older music. Sadie's shoulders relaxed as the strum of the acoustic guitar comforted her for the remainder of the ride.

"Why is there a police car in your driveway?" Charlie asked, squinting as she pulled up to the cabin. "Skyler's *here*!"

Sadie gave Charlie her most innocent look while perking up in her seat. "I *might* have forgotten to mention that Skyler would be here. He's helping me find something in the woods."

"What the hell?" Charlie parked the car and unzipped her purse. "I should disown you."

"Then why are you putting on lipstick?" Sadie laughed.

"You're still a pest," Charlie grumbled as she applied the scarlet color to her lips that she only ever wore around Skyler.

"No one said you needed to stay. You can drop me off and leave." Sadie grinned while stepping out of the car.

Charlie glared daggers at her and opened the door.

"Hey, the woods look clear, and so does the area around the property and shed." Skyler slipped out from the side of the cabin, carrying a flashlight. His gaze shifted from Sadie to her sister, locking on her. "Charlie, it was nice seeing you that brief moment at the store the other day."

Charlie held up a finger. "Don't start with me about that. And what do you mean the woods look clear?"

"Sadie saw something out here last night," Skyler said.

"Something supernatural," Sadie clarified.

"I told you not to move out here!" Charlie shrieked, her expression horrified.

"Lots of people live with spirits in their homes."

Charlie pursed her lips, seeming to try and calm herself. "Who the hell would intentionally want to do that, other than you? Besides that, I don't really believe these woods are haunted. And if they were, what would you do? Call out a priest? You're coming home with me."

"Calm down, *Mom.* You do realize I'm twenty-four years old."

Charlie seethed, hating when Sadie called her that, but she needed to realize that she had to let her go. She'd been married, lived with River for several years, but as soon as she moved back in with her, she stepped into the overprotective sister she'd been when they were younger.

"Sadie, I don't care if you're fifty." She cast a glance at Skyler. "Talk some sense into her. You're a police officer!"

He scratched the back of his neck, clearly not wanting to get in the middle of things. "There hasn't been anything suspicious in these woods since, well, the last murder-suicide. Honestly, there's more violence in the city."

"That's because *more* people live there," Charlie snapped.

Sadie drew out her phone to show them the pictures and video she'd taken earlier. "You see how the shadows are moving on the ground? Nothing else was."

Skyler arched a brow. "If that's what you consider haunted, you might want to consider watching more movies or documentaries."

Sadie rolled her eyes. "What about the woods? It's not quiet anymore."

"It's nighttime, things tend to get louder." Skyler

shrugged.

"Do I need to stay here with you for a bit?" Charlie asked, her voice soft.

The conversation was getting nowhere, and Sadie wanted her sister and Skyler to be alone together to face their past, especially after what he'd confessed. Life was too short, and someone could disappear from one's life at any moment. She knew that better than anyone.

"I wouldn't get any work done if you did that. But I love you, and I'll text you tomorrow. Same goes for you, Skyler. Thank you for coming out." Unable to hold back a smile, Sadie hurried to the front door and knew without a doubt that Charlie was throwing invisible weapons at her back.

At about a quarter to midnight, the engines of both cars purred from outside as Charlie and Skyler finally left.

Sadie focused back on the nostalgic film she'd turned on while lying on the fur rug in front of the unlit fireplace. She drew her blanket tighter, too tired to move to the futon. Her eyelids became heavy, and they fell shut as the movie continued to play. When she used to do this, River's fingers would stroke her hair, skim down her neck, across her jaw. She missed that touch. Instead, it was imaginary fingers caressing her.

But then, a honey and sandalwood scent tickled her nose and real fingers trailed along her cheek, her lips. And she knew that touch. She gasped, cracking open her lids for a moment. Only no one was there, but *his smell* was.

As though under a spell, her limbs were too heavy with exhaustion to search the cabin, and her eyes closed. She fell into his scent, wishing to feel his touch once more. The sounds of the film faded, replaced by gentle music—like a dark lullaby—outside as a dream tugged at her.

Sadie finally forced herself to stand, the world swaying, the walls closing in on her while she walked toward the door. She opened it to the night sky, and an orange light shone in the woods to her right.

A silhouette slipped out from behind a wide tree trunk, beckoning her forward. Only a single form this time. She caught sight of alabaster horns curling from what looked to be a goat skull, like the ones she collected.

Sadie's lips parted, and her heart sped. She stretched her arm out when walking toward the creature, hoping she would reach it this time. But then the world opened below her feet, and she fell into darkness as a swarm of moths flew above her.

8

"Make a wish. Any wish."

"Will you marry me?" River knelt on one knee, his fingers laced with Sadie's.

She cocked her head, fighting a smile, her heart booming with thunderous excitement. "Will I marry you? Hmm…"

"I can entice you if you wish." River's hooded gaze pinned to hers while he held up the white gold ring, a brilliant sapphire in the middle.

"I suppose *I'll spend the rest of my life with you," Sadie drawled. She couldn't hold the serious expression for another second and beamed, sinking down in front of him so they were both on their knees, her lips capturing his. No longer would she be Sadie Smith, but Sadie Hawkins.*

The sweet kiss became needy, desperate, their hands exploring, and she didn't ever want to stop touching him—her future husband.

"Now, I'm taking you to the bedroom." He grinned as he pulled

back from her mouth, his lips swollen. "Till death do us part, my sweet nightmare."

"Till death do us part, my vicious dream," Sadie whispered now, her legs tucked to her chest as she studied her wedding ring, reliving the proposal, that perfect moment. She thought about the way she'd inhaled River's scent the night before, the way she'd sworn his fingers had caressed her flesh. It could've been part of the dream that had come after, where she'd experienced the delirium, the skulled creature in the woods, the falling, the moths… But she'd smelled River on several occasions when awake.

The phone rang, jolting Sadie from her thoughts. She snatched the cell from the table and looked at the name, her chest tightening. River's mom.

"Hi, Coral." Sadie pressed her back against the coffee table.

"Hello, dear. I was checking in to see how you're settling in at the cabin," Coral said, a smile in her voice.

"It's perfect, and frankly, it was just what I needed." If it came down to it, Sadie could reveal what was happening at the cabin—River's smell, his touch, the strange dreams luring her into the woods, the quiet outside, the shadows—with Skyler and her sister. But she couldn't tell Coral that she might or might not be smelling her dead son in places.

"I was wondering if you'd like to have lunch at my home today? If you're free, that is."

"Of course." A part of her wanted to say no, linger here, but she wanted to thank Coral for following through with River's wish for her birthday. Sadie had only texted her to say she'd decided to move into the cabin—she should've at least called her, stopped by in person.

Sadie ended the call and collected her clothes on the way to the bathroom. She halted in her tracks, inhaling sharply, as the strong scent of River filled the air around her. There was no denying his distinct smell. Closing her eyes, she whispered, "If you're here, show yourself."

When she opened her lids, Sadie was alone. Except... A shadow stretched across the floor. A shadow that wasn't her own. Sadie fell to her knees, her fingers tracing its outline, feeling only the oak floorboards.

"River," she murmured. And then the shadow sank through the floor, vanishing from sight, the same as she'd seen a silhouette do the other night outside.

Hands trembling, Sadie stood and gripped the counter while studying herself in the mirror, the dark circles beneath her brown eyes, the hair a little below mid-neck that was in desperate need of a trim. She thought about the rumors of the woods being haunted—the silhouettes she'd seen. It could be other paranormal entities playing tricks, *manipulating* her. "Or you're imagining it all," she said softly.

But no, Skyler had heard the quiet of the woods, too, even if he believed it was normal. Never once had it ever been like that when she'd come to these woods to work on her stories.

Stripping away her pajamas, she let the shower temporarily wash everything away. The hot water pelted her back as she shut her eyes. In a supernatural film, if she were to open her eyes, a ghost would be standing before her in the shower. But she remained alone.

Sadie finished getting ready, then grabbed her purse and laptop before heading to Coral's house. She turned up the radio, letting the music blare even though the distraction of the instruments couldn't stop her thoughts from turning to how she'd smelled River, seen a shadow in the bathroom with her. Then to the dream of the creature in the woods, where part of its silhouette had been an animal skull. She hadn't caught a glimpse of the rest of the figure before falling. Desperation to find out more clawed inside of her…

Sadie drove onto Coral's street and parked in the long driveway. Only Coral's SUV and Valentina's car were there. She opened her laptop and used Coral's Wi-Fi to email one of her finished articles to the horror magazine publisher. Once sent, she closed the laptop and went to ring the doorbell.

Valentina answered, her hair braided back, a radiant smile on her face. "You look good."

Sadie didn't feel that way in the least. Her jeans were still a little loose, but she'd been eating like she used to since moving into the cabin.

"So do you," Sadie said.

"The weather's lovely, and Coral thought it would be nice if you joined her out on the patio."

"That would be great." Relief washed over her again that she wouldn't have to eat at the dining table, but somehow, she thought Coral might've known she wouldn't have wanted to.

Valentina led her through the living room and past the kitchen. Iron art pieces decorated the walls of the back of the house, and a row of leather barstools was tucked beneath the high countertop.

Sadie stepped out into the warmth as Valentina held open the door. One day it was chilly, and the next, it wasn't—the usual weather in this part of Texas. The sun's rays glistened off the pool, and Coral sat in front of a dark iron table, sketching in her large drawing pad as she smoked a cigarette.

She glanced up, putting out the cigarette in the ashtray, and motioned Sadie forward. "I'm glad you decided to come—take a seat."

"It's a pretty day." Sadie sank down in a padded chair just as Valentina came out to serve them both glasses of ice water.

"Are sandwiches fine with you?" Coral asked.

"You know I can't ever turn down a sandwich." Sadie laughed softly. They were always her favorite—simple, yet versatile.

"I've been working more than usual." Coral sighed. "Some days are better. Some aren't. But as long as I'm designing, I can escape."

"I understand that." Except Sadie had done nothing for three months. Maybe if she'd dived into writing for pleasure, or *anything* really, it would've helped a little.

"So, you're really doing all right out there in the woods?" Coral sipped from her glass.

The small things in the woods, during the day and at night, were adding up. And River… She shook the last part away. "It's been good, different."

Coral leaned back in her seat, studying her. "Nothing out of the ordinary, then?"

Sadie blinked, knowing she still couldn't tell her everything, but maybe she could find out something. "Did you see anything when you went out to the woods?"

"Besides getting bitten by insects? No. It just felt too far away from everyone for me. But I'm a needy individual. I can't even stay alone at my own home without Valentina here."

Sadie smiled. "Maybe you should try it then."

"Wouldn't that put Valentina out of a job?" Coral grinned as Valentina came out, carrying plates displaying two turkey sandwiches stacked high with condiments that looked as if they'd come from a fancy restaurant.

"Are you two discussing me?" she asked, the edges of her lips tilting up.

"You know I would never let you go. I was just explaining to Sadie my neediness."

"It keeps me busy and away from my husband." Valentina laughed, the sound high-pitched.

"Don't let Mario hear you say that," Coral snickered.

As the door closed behind Valentina, Coral lifted her sandwich. "So, nothing at the cabin, then?"

Sadie shrugged and rested her elbows on the table. "I don't know. This might sound like I'm hallucinating, but I swear I've seen shadowy forms. Not only that, but the woods are unusually quiet during the day, then at night they aren't. Yet nothing like beds levitating or objects mysteriously floating through the air."

"Hmm." Coral ran the tip of her finger across her lips. "If you're curious, my friend Kalina owns a metaphysical shop downtown called Crow Moon. They have all sorts of things there. I buy candles from her, but I've never been into the supernatural or the occult."

"I've never been."

"River used to go there all the time with me when he was younger." Coral took a breath, her eyes growing distant as she seemed to fall into a memory for a moment. "Tell Kalina I sent you—she'll help you find anything you need."

Sadie nodded, then her shoulders fell as she looked out at the pool, remembering the times she would come and swim here with River. "I miss him."

"We always will." Coral folded her hand over Sadie's, squeezing gently. "How about we do lunch again soon?"

"I'd like that." Maybe not all the time, but again would be nice.

Coral then showed her some of the gowns she'd been sketching in her drawing pad—they were darker than her other designs, gorgeous blacks and flowing skirts. Sadie finished her sandwich and they chatted a long while before she knew she needed to get home.

After she left Coral's, the anxious feeling grew stronger, pulling at her to get back to the cabin, to see if the shadow that had smelled of River would be in the woods, so she sped on the empty road. When she was almost there, her phone rang, startling her. Charlie.

"So," Sadie drawled, disguising the restlessness inside her, "you talked awfully late with Skyler last night."

"It was ridiculous how you bolted inside like that."

Sadie's brow rose. "We both know you didn't mind or you would've banged on the door."

"God, you're so frustrating."

"You're going to hang out with him, aren't you? Or did you two go somewhere after you left my place," Sadie purred.

"Seriously, shut up." Charlie laughed.

"You *so* did!"

"Anyway," Charlie said. "Are you sure you don't want me to come out there?"

"Look, if things got really brutal out here, I would

crawl back to you in a bloody little heartbeat."

"No, you wouldn't! You would still stay there and say it isn't so bad."

"I mean, it would create a miraculous story. And if I'm not worried, then you don't need to be worried, big sister." This was the lightness she needed, but as she pulled in front of the cabin, the desperate desire filled her to get off the phone and go into the woods.

"You're doing great, Sadie. But if anything changes, and I mean *anything*, I'll be there in a nanosecond," Charlie said, her words sincere as always.

"Will do. Love you."

"Love you, too."

Stepping out of the truck, Sadie trekked through the woods, not finding a single moving shadow. She came to the oak tree where she'd released River's ashes and had seen the silhouette. She breathed deeply, hoping to catch River's scent, but it was only pine. With a sigh, she knelt in front of its trunk and pressed her back against the bark.

"I'm sorry I locked your ashes away before freeing them, but I selfishly didn't want to let you go," she whispered. "And then I knew I had to, yet now, it's as though you're here sometimes. I want you to hear me because then that would mean you haven't left, that maybe you were in the bathroom with me, that you did touch me last night. Not my imagination. But that could just be wishful thinking, right? Since you've been gone, I've loved you, hated you, missed you like crazy. I don't know why you hung yourself, why you left me. I don't know if it was something I did. If I could've done more… I just wish you were here so I could slap you, then hug you, dammit." Hot tears spilled from her eyes, and she curled against the leaves and dirt, sobbing for what felt like hours. Until there weren't any tears left, and her throat was dry from crying.

Sadie stared up at the sky, listening to the silence accompanied by her heavy breathing. Movement caught her attention along the ground near the tree across from her. Shadows. But no other scent besides the woods. She started to crawl toward them and froze as her gaze fell on a pile of dead beetles littering the dirt. It wasn't only beetles that surrounded the area, though. Butterflies, spiders, ants…

What is this?

The shadows crept toward her, more drifting across the ground from behind trees. They seemed to dance and entwine with one another as they formed a circle around her, inching closer. She held her arm out where the shadows should have reflected on her skin, blocking it from the dirt. But they didn't. Her breath caught. It was like the shadows were trapped along the ground. Or *inside* it? She thought about the shadow in the bathroom disappearing into the floor, then the one outside during the night. Digging her fingers into the dirt, she peeled away layer after layer. Yet the silhouettes remained, swirling between one another. There was still no scent coming from them.

"Who are you?" she asked. But no words escaped them.

Sadie needed to dig farther, and she needed something more than her bare hands to get answers. That desperation clawed at her once more.

Leaving her position, she snatched a shovel from the shed, returned to the oak tree, and slammed it into the dirt. Digging. And digging. And digging. Creating a gaping hole.

Wiping the perspiration from her forehead, Sadie watched the shadows swim within the dirt, following her downward.

So she continued to dig.

9

"I would follow you anywhere."

Sadie dug farther into the dirt, only taking breaks to drink water. She imagined digging her way into this deep abyss to find rib cages holding bloody hearts or skulls with fresh eyes still in their sockets. Yet there were the shadows that swirled in the dirt around her, never stopping, not even as nightfall descended and the quiet shifted into nature's noise and vibrato once more.

The hole grew wider, and the flashlights shone above her where she'd set them out around the edge of the dirt. It was as if she was standing inside her own grave.

Her muscles cramped, her fingers locking as she tossed out one final clump of dirt. The chilly night air blew down on her, and she dropped the shovel, her body swaying. Reaching up, she grabbed a flashlight and the sack of food she'd brought from inside the cabin, finally taking a break to eat dinner. Dirt and sweat covered most of her body, but she was too exhausted to care. The digging was getting nowhere, and really, how far should she keep going? To the center of the Earth? Dig through to the other side of the world to see if the shadows would still follow? If she knew she could get answers, she would dig forever. Too tired to climb out, she sank to the ground, leaning against the dirt wall so she wouldn't collapse.

Sadie inhaled deeply, catching her breath as she flexed aching, blistered fingers. She lifted the flashlight, watching as the shadows moved around the dirt.

"Can you tell me why I've smelled River several times now?" she whispered.

Taking out an apple from inside the plastic bag, she pierced its skin with her teeth, the sweet flavor bringing a hint of strength back to her. She checked her phone, seeing missed texts from Skyler and Charlie. It was almost midnight, and she would message them both back in the morning. She didn't know if they had an early shift or were together, and she sure as hell didn't want to interrupt them having sex.

Sadie finished the apple and tossed the core into the plastic bag. Exhaustion washed over her, and she didn't think her aching limbs could lift her from the hole.

She was about to push herself up and collapse on the porch swing with a heavy blanket to sleep, since she was too tired to shower, when honey and sandalwood invaded the small space. With a gasp, she pointed the flashlight around the hole, but it was empty. Not even a single shadow slid against the dirt. Only River's heavenly scent, becoming stronger, intoxicating.

Pressing a hand to the dirt, Sadie murmured, "Are you in here?" Were River's ashes somehow speaking to her in this manner?

Her eyes fluttered shut momentarily as she waited when a light stirring filled the air, the wind blowing stronger, making her teeth chatter. A tinkling entangled with a soft melody that grew louder, bolder. It was the same dark song as in her dreams. Or was she dreaming now? She had to be awake, her heart dancing inside her rib cage, harder, fiercer. But if she wasn't, she would find a way not to fall through the darkness.

Shoving herself from the ground, Sadie gripped the hole's edges and pulled herself out. Her chest heaved while she took in breaths on all fours before relaxing to her knees.

Swishing sounded from behind her, and she whirled in its direction. She grabbed one of the flashlights, pointing its light around the woods.

"Are you there?" Sadie called into the darkness. "Whoever you are, just show yourself to me. If it's help you want, I can try to do that." Although she wasn't sure what she could even do to help anyone, but if it was River… She swore to herself if it was him, she would follow him wherever he led her. It didn't matter if it was to a bottomless pit of flames, she would. And then she could find out why he left, why he couldn't confess to her his hidden truth.

Only the deep and alluring melody of the wind continued to speak, to sing, violins and flutes melding into one. Strange clicking sounds reverberated through the trees, seeming to come from *everywhere*. Hand trembling, she lifted the light to the oak tree, the carved names on the trunk were *moving*. Her eyes widened—not only the names but the entirety of the trunk. When she peered around, it was *all* of the trees. Their bodies expanded and deflated as if they were breathing. The noise was coming from *inside* the trees.

"What's happening?" she breathed, goosebumps collecting along her flesh, the hairs at the back of her neck rising.

As another gust of breeze blew past her, it seemed to whisper, "My sweet nightmare, follow them."

Sadie stumbled, her back slamming into a tree, its bark rising and falling against her. She pushed away from it, and in the distance, two bright white orbs caught her attention. Flashing, then remaining lit.

Covering her mouth, she squinted as more lights appeared. Follow was what she was supposed to do. Follow was what she had wanted to do the past two nights. So far, the ground stayed whole, not vanishing below her feet. These otherworldly occurrences didn't frighten her—instead, they called to her very heart, her being.

She stepped forward as unintelligible whispering echoed, the trees seeming to discuss with one another in a secret language.

Sadie walked toward the lights, but the closer she came to them, the farther they went back, making it appear as though she'd never catch up.

She squeezed the flashlight while skirting around trees, the whispering unfurling inside her ears. As her desperation grew, the orbs of light halted, and as they finally allowed her to catch up, the white glowed a brilliant orange inside of lanterns. Behind them, more flickered to life, the light inside swaying in the same direction, guiding her to where they wanted her to go.

Charlie's voice shouted in Sadie's head for her to turn back, to leave the cabin and woods behind. But she couldn't, *wouldn't*. Not when whatever she was following could possibly lead her to River's spirit. It wasn't only his scent she'd smelled, but the name he'd called her had drifted with the wind. An inkling coursed through her that she was about to uncover something, and there would be no turning back.

Ducking below several low-hanging branches, she followed the eerie glow of the lanterns, casting their wavering shadows. Up in the trees, hundreds of white moths rested, their wings unmoving as if they were studying her. They were the ones she'd seen above her the previous night when she'd fallen. Beneath the silvery light of the moon, silhouettes glided along the trees, the ground. Her heart beat rapidly, fighting to break out of her chest.

And then, a dark form stepped from behind a trunk. As the light caught on it, the creature edged toward her. It was the same one that had been in her last dream. Dark fur covered its muscular body, and two sets of alabaster horns spiraled atop its goat skull. Its hands and feet were skeletal, pure bone. The creature lifted an alabaster digit, motioning her forward as it had before, this time through an area where vines hung like a curtain.

But this creature wasn't alone—from the trees, figures slinked out as shadows, then changed into whole forms. The shadows were these creatures… Their heads were various animal skulls. Antelope, cows, deer, horses, and others she couldn't name. Their hands and feet were all human bone, the rest of their bodies furred except for their skeletal tails. Perspiration dotted her brow and upper lip, her heart pounding faster when they each pointed in the same direction as the first creature, their heads bowed.

Sadie didn't dare close her eyes, for fear everything before her would vanish, that the melody would halt its enchanting sound. Something about these creatures reminded her of the sculptures River would make, as if he were speaking through them somehow.

"Thank you," Sadie said to them, even though she wasn't sure what she would uncover. She pushed the hanging vines aside and slipped through.

The trees on the other side formed a circle, their trunks gently moving, inhaling, exhaling. Lit lanterns dangled from their limbs. And then, as if by dark magic, a fire ignited in the middle of the space, its flames black and orange, licking across the logs to highlight a circular opening in the ground.

The goat-skulled creature stepped out from behind her, the flames illuminating the hollow black spaces of its sockets.

"Why did you lead me to this spot? Is River here? Or is it someone else?" she asked, unable to read anything from the creature's neutral expression.

It didn't shake its head or nod, only pointed toward the opening in the ground.

"Is this a trick?" Sadie asked, somehow able to remain calm, but something felt strange inside her, and she couldn't draw an answer as to what it was exactly.

The creature only bowed its head at her, then nudged her toward the opening. It didn't follow her as she stopped along the edge, where a stone staircase led farther down. Sadie glanced back, and the other creatures now stood there, waiting for her to descend the steps. Her throat grew dry, in desperate need of water. But she forced down the lump in her throat and took the first step onto a stone stair—she would risk whatever she came upon.

As she slowly ventured down the steps, the air smelled of freshly-dug earth. She held up the flashlight, the soft light guiding her through the darkness. Glistening white stones covered the walls with strange markings etched in. She skated her fingers across the swirling patterns while going down the path that led to a wall.

Sadie reached the bottom, studying the massive wall before her, carved with bird and eye symbols and what looked to be a man and woman standing by a bonfire in the center. Skulls and lifeless bodies surrounded them. Another staircase curving downward rested to Sadie's left, a soft orangish light flickering from its depths.

The air shifted, the earthiness becoming less heavy, and a new scent took shape. Sadie inhaled, breathing in honey and sandalwood. She silently begged any entity above to hear her prayers, let this curving staircase lead to her husband. But she didn't know if the steps would only bring her to another staircase, to more otherworldly creatures, or maybe even the spirits of the ones who'd died in these woods, or something else … insidious.

At the end of the stairs was a short foyer or passage covered in more symbols, these triangular with eyes circling each one. The passage opened to a small square area where, at the center of the room, stood a man, facing away from her, his dark hair brushing his nape. He wore a black T-shirt and jeans, dark boots covering his feet, just like the day he'd died... Only, in his right hand rested a glistening, obsidian dagger.

His body stood still, frozen, and it had to be him. It had to be. Yet a part of her was too afraid to look in case it wasn't.

Sadie trembled as she inched forward. The room held six doors with lanterns hanging from each one, different insect symbols carved above them.

"River?" she whispered, her gaze never leaving the dagger in his fist as she pressed her hand to his shoulder.

The figure inhaled, the dagger crashing to the floor, and he started to turn. Before Sadie caught sight of his face, she was no longer in the room but somewhere else surrounded by dirt. Her eyes adjusted to the morning light spilling into the hole she'd dug.

It had been a *dream*. Following mystical lanterns through the woods, the mysterious creatures who'd led her to a man whose face she hadn't gotten to see. But Sadie knew, without a doubt, it was River. The scent, his build, his hair color. The only thing that had been different was the black dagger in his hand.

But maybe, just maybe…

Sadie ignored the burn in her arms as she hoisted herself out from below ground and ran down the path where she'd gone in her sleep. The branches… The trees… They were all how they'd been in her dream—only they weren't moving or whispering. Instead of wind carrying music or creatures luring her in through the darkness, quiet filled the air, and shadows swarmed like bees along the ground, folding around her.

Her eyes widened as she stood before a curtain of

vines hanging from a long, curving branch. And when she pushed them aside, the trees still formed a closed-in circle, yet there were no hanging lanterns, no fire, and no entrance in the ground that could lead to her husband.

10

"Sometimes you have to wake."

As Sadie stared at the weed-covered dirt, it should've come as no surprise that an underground pathway wasn't there, that she'd been dreaming after all. But it was more than a fantasy—everything that led her to this spot in the woods had been the same as in her dream, only the hole and the fire from the bare logs were missing. She hadn't been out in these parts of the woods in months, and she didn't remember there ever being trees aligned in a circle, hidden behind lush vines.

Temptation barreled through Sadie, urging her to collect the shovel and dig once more. No matter that her arms ached or that hunger stirred within her. Sadie needed to quell her curiosities and find out exactly what was happening. When she'd pressed her hand to the figure's shoulder in her dream, she had *felt* him. Had felt the muscle and bone that she knew belonged to River.

Sadie retrieved her shovel and hurried back to the place of her dreams. Tucking a lock of greasy hair behind her ear, she buried the shovel into the ground as the shadows formed around her, not leaving her side.

She dug for an hour, second-guessing herself as she uncovered only dirt. "Something is down there," she whispered to the shadows. "You being here is proof of that, so why won't you let me see it?"

None of the silhouettes answered her, and she needed to be doing something different.... Maybe she needed something more powerful to open this gateway—she thought about Coral, how she'd mentioned the metaphysical shop. Taking out her phone from her back pocket, she called Skyler.

"Sorry I didn't message you back yesterday," Sadie said after he answered. "Are you still off work today?"

"I am. Why?" he asked slowly. "You have that *sound* in your voice."

"If you're referring to the time I dragged you to the abandoned movie theater and you broke your arm, it's not like that. Anyway, remember when we first met, and you told me your house was haunted after I did an essay on ghosts?"

"I lied."

She snorted. "I know this because you made that confession the same day. But before the admission, you showed me the dowsing rods that supposedly detect spirits."

"Right." He chuckled. "And if you recall, they moved zero, so I ended up saying fuck it, then told you I lied and didn't believe in ghosts."

"Your parents wouldn't still have them, would they?" She hadn't been to his parents' home in years since Skyler moved out right after high school.

"No, they never worked for them either, so they got rid of them."

"That's fine, I have an alternative. Can you swing by in an hour?"

"Sure, but I don't like the sound of this," Skyler groaned.

She should've done this yesterday instead of wasting so much time digging a hole. If nothing worked, then maybe that night, she would find a way to the secret opening again. Even if she had to shatter the woods to get to it, she would.

"So what do you need?" Skyler asked when Sadie opened the front door. "You were incredibly vague, but I can put the pieces together since you asked about the dowsing rods. You want to go ghost hunting, am I right?"

"In a sense," Sadie said, running a hand through her still-wet hair. "There's a friend of Coral's who owns a metaphysical shop downtown."

"Crow moon?" He arched a brow.

"That's the one. I want to purchase a few things there and have you watch me use them. If they work, then I won't wonder if it's me falling down a mad hole." Imagining River…

"You didn't ask Charlie?"

Sadie cocked her head. "Why? So she could say just being in the store would summon demons?"

He chuckled. "She would still go, though."

"And complain the whole time." She shut the door and motioned to her truck. "Just hop in, you don't even have to use any gas."

"That right there makes it worth it," he said sarcastically.

"I'll buy you a bundle of sage then." Sadie waggled her brows.

"I can think of better things I'd rather have. How have you been sleeping?" he asked as she backed out onto the main road.

"Are you asking as a friend, or are you testing whether I need to see a shrink?"

Skyler's face softened as he studied her. "When I'm with you, I'm your friend, not an officer. You know that."

"Unless I'm doing something naughty." She paused before sighing. "I'm not having nightmares like I did before moving here." Instead, she was having something else, something she wanted to have more of…

"That's a good sign."

Sadie would tell him the rest once they returned to the cabin. She didn't want his good mood to sour, for him to become concerned like her sister would have.

"From how Charlie's acting, you must've told her the real reason you ended the engagement," she said, changing the subject.

"I did." He grinned.

"Good." Sadie smiled, not needing to know any more details than that. They then chatted about mostly mundane things until she pulled up in front of a small shopping center.

A comic book store and an antique shop rested on either side of Crow Moon. They approached the gray brick building, the blue paint faded and peeling along its roof. In front of the metaphysical shop sat several black cauldrons beside crimson-painted skulls.

"As expected," Skyler said, his gaze drifting from the outside decorations to the comic book store.

Sadie folded her arms, knowing he'd discovered one of his weaknesses. "Go check out the comic books and meet me back here. I don't need you to hold my hand for this part."

"Are you sure?" Skyler was already leaning toward the other store.

"Go. I know you can't control yourself when it comes to heroes and villains. Plus, I want to be able to think in here."

"Fine, but if you need me, text me, and I'll come right back with my cape." He grinned and walked to the comic book place while Sadie opened the glass door to Crow Moon.

A soft bell dinged as she entered, accompanied by a strong citrusy scent. Hanging above Sadie were two brass spherical incense burners. To her right, stood a charcoal desk and white counter. Behind it, a middle-aged woman with long dark hair, wearing jeweled bracelets along both arms, rang up a customer. Beside the desk, connected to the wall, was a plastic gate, behind which sat a large rottweiler, panting, its beady eyes fixed on her.

"Don't mind him—he won't come out," the woman said, gesturing at the dog with a welcoming smile. "Can I help you with anything?"

Sadie scanned the shop—the wooden shelves, the glass cabinets, the baskets of small items, not sure where to begin. "Do you know what I can use to call on spirits?"

"Sure." The woman pointed behind Sadie as another customer walked up to the counter. "Just go through those red curtains to the back room, and if you can't find what you're looking for, let me know."

"Thanks." Sadie took a wicker shopping basket, then walked past rows of bookshelves and tables cluttered with crystals and colorful stones. Several glass cabinets held mystical figurines, while others contained unique taxidermy. Her gaze stayed fastened on a deep auburn fox, its skull protruding from its open jaws, spine, and ribs breaking free of its torso. Flowers and vines bloomed from within its bones, the beauty of life and death entwined.

Sadie pushed back the red curtains and stepped into a small room where Charlie would've been performing the sign of the cross. But something about this place made her feel at home. Shelves of black and white candles lined one of the walls. Some in jars, others in plastic wrappers, all various sizes. Another shelf held an assortment of Ouija boards. And not like the ones she used to see in the game section at the store when she was younger—these looked to be the real thing, regardless if they could call on a spirit or not.

Another shelf filled with books hugged a corner, mostly black spines as if they had to be that color to draw a supernatural entity. She took out one of the tomes on the middle shelf about how the dead listened. As she flipped through a couple of pages she wasn't impressed, but then her gaze fell to a paragraph about spirits searching for the broken-hearted or someone in sorrow. Her breath caught—that was her… She continued to pore over the words, turning pages. Some spirits were malevolent, manipulating and bending people to their will, which she knew. Sadie bit the inside of her cheek—she'd seen so many ghost movies that she'd lost count, and she needed to remind herself to keep her eyes wide open, not seeing only what she wanted to see.

There was an assortment of ways to call upon a spirit. *But be warned, certain spirits will feed off fear.* Some of the items that could be used were electronics, mirrors, music, incense sticks, candles, Ouija boards… Her gaze drifted to the planchettes and boards. Sadie's fingers skimmed over the different surfaces, some showcasing beautiful dark and elaborate drawings, others simpler with only the alphabet. A few planchettes were without a board, single holes resting near each of their pointed tips. She picked one up, inspecting the smooth black surface and the wheeled casters beneath. It was meant to be written with instead of sliding across a board to point at letters.

Sadie smiled to herself—this was perfect. She thought about the figure below ground, how he'd stood so still until she'd pressed her hand to him. Why had he been like that? If this planchette worked, she could find out if River's spirit was in the woods, if the writing matched his. And if not, she would see if someone was choosing to look like him, *smell* like him.

She scanned over the other objects in the room—pentagrams, crystal balls, and ornate handheld mirrors. Nothing good ever came from those in films, but she could say the same for the Ouija boards. Still, she passed over those items and tucked the book she'd been reading under her arm. Sets of dowsing rods were stuffed inside a red barrel, and she grabbed a pair, along with a few candles and three bundles of sage that she put into the small basket before making her way to the front counter.

A couple of customers lingered in parts of the store, but the counter was clear as she approached the woman.

"Sadie?" the woman asked after she set the basket on top of the counter.

Her eyes widened. "My guess is you're a fortune teller?"

"Sometimes," she answered coyly, typing in the price of the planchette. "Coral used to show me pictures of you and River when she would come in." Her expression softened. "I'm sorry about River."

Sadie gave a solemn nod, her chest tightening. "Kalina?"

"That's me," she said as she wrapped the planchette in brown paper. "Coral also told me you might show up here. Told me that you've been staying in the woods."

"Have you ever been out there before? Felt anything?" Maybe she would know more than Sadie did and could possibly give her advice.

"When I was your age, I used to go out there to see if I could, but I never felt a presence." She shrugged. "But that doesn't mean you won't be able to."

She hoped so, to find out if River was really out there… Trapped…

Kalina paused on placing a candle inside a bag, her face lighting up. "Did you know River used to sell his pieces here when he was younger?"

Sadie blinked, surprised. "No, I didn't."

"This was actually the first place he started selling."

She pointed to a glass curio cabinet. "Right over there."

Sadie's heart swelled as she learned something new about her husband. She imagined a younger version of him placing his sculptures in the cabinet, not yet knowing how in demand they would one day be. "I didn't know that."

"He was such a charming boy." Kalina furrowed her brow. "But sometimes, I felt a touch of darkness inside him. Yet his was different than the piece that most of us have. It's the same thing I feel in you right now."

Sadie stilled, a strange feeling washing over her. "What is it?"

"I never could put my finger on it, and I still can't. Perhaps you'll book an appointment for a tarot reading with me sometime?"

Sadie wanted to roll her eyes, wondering if Kalina was just trying to feed off her emotions to get money for a tarot reading. But Kalina was Coral's friend, so she would keep her mouth shut about it and discuss something else. "How do you know if a dream is real or not?"

"Maybe we're all in a dream right now, just part of someone else's world," Kalina said slowly.

"Sounds like a movie I've seen before." Sadie's lips curved up.

Kalina laughed and replaced the four candles with different ones, then added a pack of black tealight candles. "These work more consistently if you want to call on a spirit."

A ding sounded as the door opened, and Skyler stepped in, his hands in his pockets as his eyes met hers. "Did you find anything good?" he asked, hovering near the door while picking up a jar of herbs.

"I suppose we'll find out, won't we?" Sadie smiled.

"He's got a good aura about him," Kalina said as she handed Sadie the bags.

"He does," she agreed. "Let's hope my sister keeps him."

After they got back into the truck, Sadie handed Skyler the bags so she could start the engine.

"That's it?" he asked, incredulous, as he riffled through the plastic. "You didn't get as much as I thought you would've."

"Only the most important things, and hey, Charlie would be proud because no pentagrams." She laughed.

"You really got dowsing rods?" he scoffed, rolling them over in his hands. "And you have a planchette but no board?"

"You don't need one for this beautiful little thing." She pointed at its tip. "A pen goes through the hole, and if a spirit answers, it will move the planchette."

Skyler's lips pursed, his expression turning serious. "You want to see if the handwriting is familiar."

She didn't answer.

"I don't think you're going to get what you're searching for," he said, his voice low.

Sadie sighed. "I might not, but something is out there." If there was a chance she didn't find anything and she was slowly losing her mind, then she would let that drive the scenes in her story for River.

Once they got back to the cabin, she grabbed the dowsing rods as she stepped out of the truck. "Will you walk with me into the woods?" she asked Skyler, already heading toward the cluster of trees.

"Of course," he said, catching up to her.

Sadie glanced at Skyler as he shivered. She frowned, a strange feeling traveling through her veins while she watched him. She wasn't cold at all...

"Skyler?" Sadie whispered, tugging him by the arm.

"Why are you looking at me like you're seeing a ghost." He paused. "Are you?"

"No." She moistened her lips. "Do you feel the wind?"

He wrinkled his nose. "Yeah? What about it?"

She surveyed the branches above, and nothing rustled, not even an inch, not a brush or lick of wind against her flesh.

"When you look at the branches, are any moving at all?" Her voice rose, her breaths increasing.

"Yes?" He stepped back, the line between his brows becoming deeper. "What's going on?"

"What do you hear?" She didn't let go of his arm, her fingers pressing harder.

"At the moment, I hear you asking me a question."

"Seriously." She dropped his arm, her patience growing thin. "What else do you hear?"

Skyler tilted his head and listened. "I don't know? A few insects, some birds. There's a finch chirping above you."

Sadie wasn't hearing that, not *any* of it. She slowly lifted her head, finding only an empty branch. As she searched the ground, she froze. A dead crow rested there with shadows swirling around its limp feathered form.

Eyes widening, she stumbled back. "I don't see it. I don't hear it. I don't hear *anything*. I told you the woods have been quiet during the day."

"You said quiet. Not that it was silent as if you

couldn't hear anything at all." She could see the fear in Skyler's eyes, but his face remained neutral, the way he knew how to do when on police duty.

"I hear you, though, and I hear any sounds I make." Her voice shook. "I see a dead crow on the ground and shadows surrounding it."

"There's no bird there, Sadie," Skyler said slowly as if he might spook her. "The shadows are from the tree branches."

Her heart sank to the pit of her stomach—something was wrong. Very wrong. She hadn't believed she was the only one hearing the quiet.

Sadie took out her phone and messaged Charlie. *When you were here, did you feel a breeze? Hear birds or insects outside?*

A second later, her phone dinged. *I don't know about the wind. I remember hearing and seeing a woodpecker, though. Why?*

Just wondering.

So it was only her then... She wasn't ready to hear Skyler's opinion on what that meant for her mental state or his sympathy.

But Skyler seemed to notice something and left her side, walking farther past her to the oak tree, then stopped in front of the hole she'd dug. "Did you do this?"

She caught up with him, running a hand through her hair. "I did. I was trying to get to the shadows. I know how this is sounding. And please don't look at me like I need a straitjacket."

Brushing past him, she headed toward where she'd been the night before in her dream, where she'd started to dig a second hole that morning.

"Sadie!" Skyler called as she hurried down the path.

"You can go home if you want," Sadie shouted over

her shoulder, gripping the dowsing rods. "Don't worry about me." She prayed something would happen, to show herself that this was real, that she wasn't imagining any of it.

Skyler caught up with her, wrapping his arm around her shoulders as he walked beside her. "I'm not going home."

She nodded, holding back the dam that wanted to burst inside of her as they reached the area with the trees in a circular formation.

"You dug another hole here?" Skyler asked, lifting his arm from her shoulders to kneel in front of it.

"I had a dream last night, and something was here—something supernatural. I know you want me to tell you it was just a dream, but it's more than that. I was led to this hole in the ground with stairs and symbols etched into the walls. And I think I found *him*, but then I woke up." Sadie confessed everything to Skyler in thorough detail, the dreams she'd had before that, River's scent, the shadow in her bathroom vanishing through the floor.

Skyler slowly ran a hand down his face. "I don't know—"

"You don't have to believe me. I just needed you to listen is all. For right now, that's all I need, Skyler." Sadie lifted the rods, steady and determined as she walked around the space. Neither one of the rods moved. It should've been expected, but she begged them to do something, *anything*.

As she approached the partially dug hole, a shadow slinked up from the ground, traveling against her body. She couldn't feel it, not even when it folded a hand around hers. It didn't have a scent, so it wasn't River, yet she knew it was one of the creatures from her dreams. The shadow slowly moved the rod to the other, making her gasp. Skyler might believe she'd hit a water source or that she'd done it herself, but her hands had remained perfectly still. And then the shadow moved the rod again, slow at first, then faster and faster.

"Are you seeing this, Skyler? A shadow is doing it!" she shouted, giddiness thriving inside her.

"I see the rod moving, but not a shadow doing it." His eyes widened. "Can I see them?"

Sadie handed him the rods, the shadow slipping down her body before sinking back into the dirt. As Skyler held them up in the precise spot where she'd been, they didn't budge a millimeter. The silhouettes didn't crawl up Skyler, only stayed closer to her.

"You think I was doing it myself, don't you?" she breathed, her gaze trained on the shadows.

"No, I was watching your hands. I've seen videos of people using the rods before and none are ever like that. I don't believe in ghosts, but I believe in you, and something isn't right here."

"It isn't." Sadie picked up the shovel, but before she could resume digging, Skyler took it from her hands.

"Let me help," he said.

11

"They listen to us."

Skyler grunted, wiping the sweat above his brow away. "I believe you, Sadie. I believe what I saw with the dowsing rods. But I think we need to give the digging a rest."

He was right. They weren't uncovering anything otherworldly—they weren't reaching the staircase she'd seen in her dreams. In her *dreams*... And that was why ... it had come while she wasn't awake, just as the silhouettes had become the creatures.

"We should," Sadie agreed. "Let's go inside, and I'll make you something to drink."

"I need a beer or two." He blew out a breath, raking a hand through his damp hair.

Sadie smiled. "Hot chocolate it is."

"You and your damn hot chocolate," he mumbled as

he walked beside her toward the cabin.

Sadie said nothing about the dead birds and squirrels littering the ground before her, knowing Skyler couldn't see them. She didn't understand why she was seeing dead things, why the shadows continued to follow her, or what they even were exactly. Demons? Spirits?

After collecting the bags from Crow Moon out of her truck, they headed inside the cabin. Sadie halted as that enticing honey and sandalwood scent wafted through the air. She inhaled deeply, searching around the living room.

"River again?" Skyler asked.

"You don't smell honey or sandalwood?"

He shook his head. "Mostly pine. Maybe a hint of lavender."

With a sigh, she sank down on the futon. "Don't tell Charlie about any of this yet. I don't want her to worry."

"It's not my place to tell her, but I think maybe you should stay with Charlie for a few days." He lowered himself beside her, resting his elbows on his knees.

Charlie would know something was wrong and would worry too much. "No, I came here to write, and I'm going to continue."

"But writing isn't your top priority anymore, is it?"

It wasn't—not in the least. "Something is here, and whether it has to do with River or not, my plan was always to come to this cabin, knowing that this place could be haunted. But my gut instinct is saying that River has some sort of unfinished business." She paused, running a hand through her hair. "Anyway, even if I did go to Charlie's, what makes you think something wouldn't follow me there?"

"You've seen too many ghost movies." Skyler sighed.

"If it were me, I would've already gotten the hell out of these woods."

Sadie cocked her head and folded her arms across her chest. "No, you wouldn't have. You became a police officer for a reason. It would nag at you too much to uncover what was going on. You're just saying that so I'll leave."

"Fine, you got me." He chuckled softly, then immediately sobered. "Even though I'm worried about you, I'm not going to carry you out of here unless you ask me to."

"If I get attacked by a spirit and end up having bloody gashes all over me, I'll gladly ask you to," Sadie said as she pulled the planchette from the plastic bag.

Skyler pinched the bridge of his nose. "You're going to try that now?"

"After I make us something to drink."

He skimmed his fingers across the casters of the planchette as she took a large drawing pad and permanent marker from the desk. She opened the notebook to a blank page and rested it on the coffee table, then tossed Skyler the permanent marker for the planchette.

Sadie prepared two mugs of regular hot chocolate since it would've been too close to her routine with River to do otherwise. Skyler didn't even blow on his while drinking it down as if he were tossing back whiskey.

"You're meant to savor the taste." She grinned, lightly blowing on hers, the brown liquid rippling.

"I think this only made me thirstier," he said, clucking his tongue against the roof of his mouth.

Sadie rolled her eyes. "There's cold water in the fridge."

"I probably should've started with that," Skyler said with a grin while going to grab a water.

Sadie lit two of the black candles, unsure if she needed to perform a special chant or only have the flame ignited. As Skyler settled back beside her, she placed her fingers at the bottom of the planchette, praying it would move across the notepad.

Taking a breath, Sadie tried to relax her mind, focus on what she wanted to ask. "Hello?" she whispered. "Is anyone here?" *River?* Her heart pounded, and her fingers trembled in anticipation as she waited. But the planchette remained still. No shadows seeped into the room to brush the triangular piece, and no invisible hands either.

Sadie fired off question after question. "Are you River?" No response. "Are you one of the people who died in the woods?" The planchette didn't budge. "Why are the woods quiet during the day? Why am I seeing dead animals? Why did the dowsing rods move?" Nothing. Nothing. Nothing. "Are you going to answer me?" Her voice shook, pleading for something, *anything*, to answer her. A feeling rested inside of her that she didn't understand—anger, wanting to unleash itself.

Before she could ask another question, Skyler gently pressed his hand to hers. "Stop for now."

"No," Sadie said between clenched teeth.

"You can always try again later."

Sadie took several breaths, reeling the anger back in, even though she ached to demand answers until she received one. She needed to understand why she could see these things.

"I can stay a little longer if you need me to," he continued. "You can put on one of your movies unless you prefer to focus on your screenplay. I don't have to meet Charlie until later."

"Stay. A movie sounds good. Then you can keep Charlie off my back while I figure things out."

He chuckled. "Ease up on her."

"I'm only kidding." She smiled. "For the most part." But really, she didn't want to be alone right then and if Charlie wasn't working, Sadie would've begged her sister to come over. Something about how she was the only one experiencing these things was bothering her more than anything. And she needed to know why. It would still be hours before she could dream again—if she could force herself to fall asleep now, she would.

Once Sadie turned on a psychological horror film for Skyler, she started working more on her screenplay to distract herself until she could fall asleep. She glanced over at Skyler, thinking about how she used to do this same thing beside him when they were in high school. Those moments weren't that many years ago, but on some days they felt like a lifetime. As wonderful as it was that Skyler had Charlie back, Sadie didn't have River. Only the possibility that a remnant of him was here, maybe even his spirit.

She jotted everything down in her notebook that had happened in the last few days, trying to piece things together as Skyler finished the movie. Only there were more questions than answers.

"If you need me, call me," he said as she let him out onto the porch. "But at least give me enough time to shower. I smell like shit from digging. Honestly, I'm not sure how you sat beside me the whole movie."

"I don't care if you smell like a barn." Sadie smiled,

wrapping her arms around him and resting her head on his shoulder. "Thank you." She then shoved him away. "Now go entertain my sister."

As soon as Sadie shut the door, she eyed the planchette, coming up with an alternative. She collected it along with the notebook and candles, then took off into the woods. The quiet pounded in her ears, seeming louder than anything she'd ever heard before, like a haunting sound within itself. She stopped in the center of the circular formation of trees, directly beside the hole where Skyler had dug.

Sadie placed the two candles next to her, lighting the wicks of both. Their flames didn't flicker, only stood still, reaching toward the sky as if there was no breeze at all. But she knew there was, hidden in a place where she assumed everyone else could feel it except for her.

Resting the notebook before her, she set the planchette atop it. "I'm alone now," she called. "Maybe that's what you wanted. Maybe now you'll answer me if you're here."

Along the ground, shadows wove between one another, running their lithe forms up the trees, but not a single one trailed their fingertips over the planchette.

"River?" she asked, praying, tears pricking her eyes.

When she sighed, about to go back inside, *his* scent returned, and two shadowy hands ran up her thighs to her arms, and she couldn't feel a single thing. But oh, how she wished she could, her body trembling for it. The darkened fingertips fell beside hers to the planchette. And she waited while holding her breath for the triangular piece to move, for words to form.

But then the shadowy fingers drifted away, the page

remaining blank. "Why can't you just write a single word?" she murmured. "*Why*?" Her voice grew louder as the shadow left her, disappearing into the ground before she could even try to run after it.

Sadie's shoulders fell, and she scooted to a nearby tree, pressing her back against the trunk. The silhouettes didn't leave—they lingered around her as they'd started to do when she was in the woods.

She decided to stay out there until the night captured the day, when the sounds of the woods escaped their silent prisons. To see if maybe there would be a spark of the place from her dreams.

The sky darkened from blue to gray as though facing the same mood she was currently in. Sprinkles fell, the raindrops becoming heavier, pelting her skin. But she couldn't hear their sounds, couldn't hear the thunder boom after the bolt of lightning lit up the sky.

"All right, maybe I'll budge for now." She snapped up her things from the ground and booked it for the cabin. The shadows followed her, and she caught glimpses of the dead animals along the ground once again, her stomach churning at what it could mean. By the time she broke through the woods, her clothes were soaked, her wet hair sticking to her chin and neck.

Sadie halted in front of her home, the silhouettes clinging to the cabin, roaming across one another over the outside walls like snakes.

Even though her eyes widened, even though her heart pounded a tad bit more, fear didn't course through her. Nothing had hurt her. Yet.

As she stepped onto the porch, she skimmed her finger over the wood, tracing a silhouette but only feeling the hardness of the boards.

The night started to descend, the noises of the woods sneaking out, the rain's music singing. Sadie opened the door—not a single shadow followed her inside, only the smell of River greeting her.

"Stop disappearing!" she shouted, but no shadow came forth.

Water dripped from her body as she peeled off her wet clothes. She put on a fresh pair of pajamas, then lit a few logs in the fireplace.

The notebook she'd brought was ruined, so she grabbed another and placed it on the coffee table with the planchette atop it. Once the rain stopped, she would return to the woods and try one more time to have a spirit or shadow answer her.

But the rain didn't let up, even when it was close to midnight, so Sadie sat on the swing chair outside beneath the overhang, waiting, the planchette and notebook in her lap. She'd tried to sleep, to enter that place, yet she couldn't.

Sadie's eyes finally became heavy, and she closed them briefly until movement beneath her fingertips roused her. She opened her eyes to find the planchette sliding across the paper. As shadowy digits wrote, she remained still, black letters forming against the white sheet.

Meet him.

Sadie took a deep swallow, panic lacing its way through her heart—it wasn't River's handwriting. And she didn't know if the "him" was meant to be River or someone else… But for the chance that it was him, she would cross oceans, worlds.

Lanterns illuminated in the trees near her home, the

rain no longer coming down. An assortment of moths swarmed around the lights, the trees whispering. She walked toward them, plucking a lantern from a limb before allowing it to guide her down the path.

The low song of the wind played a new melody that rose within the woods. It grew in tempo, wicked and enticing, as it folded around her.

Out from behind trunks, the shadows slinked, their forms shifting, becoming skeletal and furred creatures. They lifted their alabaster hands, pointing her onward—not one sound escaped their animal skulls.

As she reached the vines, the goat-skulled creature waited, bowing its head and holding the foliage back for her to duck beneath.

"Hello again," she said, her gaze scanning its long, bony fingers.

The fire flickered to life, not seeming to burn the logs, and the area that had been dug out was no longer a hole with dirt walls—an entrance rested there, just as it had the night before when she'd been dreaming. Last time it hadn't felt like a dream, and neither did this, but dream or not, she wanted to remain there.

She walked down the staircase, holding up the lantern to guide her way, the light illuminating the symbols on the walls. As she descended the next set of steps, her pulse thrummed, and she tried to hold her lantern steady while moving closer to the dim light spilling into the area from below.

Sadie's feet touched the dark stone of the foyer, and when she entered the main room, same as before, the male form in its center stood facing away from her, his dark hair just past his chin. The black dagger was in his hand, no longer on the stone floor.

Sadie didn't want to waste time, didn't want to disappear from this place before she confirmed that it was, in fact, River. She darted around him, her gaze meeting gray irises, and she choked on a sob. It was River. The angles of his face, the shapely lips, his aristocratic nose. She dared not whisper his name, still afraid she would wake from this lovely dream or that he might vanish from her sight.

He didn't move—he was still as a statue. Then she remembered when she'd been here last, how when she'd touched him, he'd shifted. Unable to resist temptation, she shakily pressed a hand to his soft cheek, his skin cool to the touch.

River inhaled, his chest rising, the blade clacking against the floor as he dropped it. His gray gaze fell to hers, blinking. "You came, my sweet nightmare," he rasped.

"Is this real?" she asked, her trembling palm not leaving his face—only his cool skin was now warm.

"Yes." His hand captured hers, his other arm cradling her waist.

"You were frozen," she murmured. "Is it really you?"

"It is."

But wouldn't an evil spirit answer the same? An entity of that nature could possibly take the form of something else—she'd known that, so she needed to make certain. "When did we get married?"

"October thirteenth." His forehead kissed hers, their breaths mingling.

"What did you say when I asked you out on a date?" She held back the urge to press her lips to his, to kiss him until death came for her.

"*I* asked you out, and you said not in this life."

Sadie laughed, tears sliding down her cheeks. As the image of him hanging from the ceiling slithered into her mind, the smile slipped from her face. "Why did you kill yourself?"

"I had to." His throat bobbed. "Dance with me."

"That's not an explanation, River," she said. "Was it something I did?"

"Never." He drew her closer, her breasts brushing his chest. "Now dance with me."

She furrowed her brow. "Dance? I don't even know how to dance."

"You do." His fingers dug into her waist, his hand gently squeezing hers. And before she could argue, he spun her around the room, her feet somehow not tripping over themselves.

It was only the two of them, the light glowing from the doors. As he continued to move with her, his warm body against hers, she didn't want to stop—she only wanted to be closer.

"Why did you leave?" she asked again. "Was something going on inside you that you couldn't talk about?"

"All in due time, but for now, please just dance with me," he whispered in her ear. "That's all I ask, my sweet nightmare."

Something in his voice made her not press the matter, at least not yet, to give him time. She rested her head against his shoulder, letting him lead her, her body seeming as if it was floating, the feel of his hard muscles keeping her grounded.

He lifted her chin, his mouth so close to touching hers. Then he shut his eyes, taking a step back. "You need to stay away from me," he growled through clenched teeth.

Sadie furrowed her brow. "River, what's going on?" When she reached for him, she jolted forward, her eyes flying open. She blinked several times as the morning light spilled in across the woods.

Her body swung softly in the swing, the planchette and notebook in her lap. The paper beneath the triangular piece was blank. No letters spelling out, *meet him.*

And then Sadie screamed, her voice echoing through the quiet, shattering it.

12

"There is nowhere else to go but back."

Sadie screamed until her throat was raw, until she could barely drink in breaths of air. Balling her hands into tight fists, she stormed her way through the woods with the shadows gliding around her.

She couldn't be imagining any of this—it all felt too real. His touch, his words, the strangeness of it all. The shadows circled her as she reached the area where the opening had been, but it was empty. *Again.*

Letting out a raspy screech, she grabbed the shovel and slammed it against the logs in the center. "Let me in!" She struck the ground over and over until her arms lost strength. Dropping to her knees, she sobbed. "Please, just let me in."

The shadows along the ground flocked closer to her, their hands falling across her legs and arms, comforting her. "I need answers. I know you're the creatures of the night," she whispered. Night… That was what she needed to come again, for night to cloak its obsidian wings around her.

Sadie peeled herself from the dirt, needing to distance herself from here for now. As she headed back toward the cabin, something large on the ground caught her attention, stopping her in her tracks. Small, dead animals were one thing, but this was a stag, its long antlers beautifully tipped toward her. She knelt beside the fallen animal, trailing her fingers across one of its antlers. A gasp left her mouth when the stag's chest rose and fell as if in a deep slumber.

"Hello," she said, lightly shaking the animal, prepared to leap back if it bucked awake. But the stag remained there, sleeping. A piece of the puzzle found its partner as a thought crossed her mind. What if the animals she'd been seeing—the birds, the squirrels, the bugs, weren't really dead but in some sort of strange sleep? Yet at night, that was when the sounds of the animals and bugs came out, when they might possibly wake again… Unless they disappeared instead…

Sadie couldn't linger by the stag's side all day, waiting until nightfall—she would drive herself crazy. She needed to explore more, but first she needed to strengthen herself.

Casting one last look at the stag, she bolted to the cabin, where shadows still crawled across the wood and roof. Once inside, she quickly made herself something to eat. Her mind spun as she downed two cups of hot chocolate while taking out her aggression inside her notebook. Sadie dug her pen into the paper, almost ripping through the pages. The story was welcoming the dialogue and scenes, but why was all of this happening? Why hadn't River answered her questions thoroughly? Why wait and dance? Why wasn't he coming now, even as a shadow?

Anxiety crawled into her heart, expanding the organ until it might burst if she didn't return. That desperation screamed for the night to fall so she could go to him and ask why he wanted her to stay away from him. Sadie thought about how Kalina had mentioned a touch of darkness within River, the same within her.

Sadie finished her last bite of toast and sprinted back into the woods. The deer lay in its same position, its chest still rising and falling. Focusing on her surroundings, the shadows drawing nearer to her, she scouted out more of the area until she came across a fallen raven. She crept up to the black bird and scooped its fragile body into her hands, only it wasn't lifeless. Its chest moved, the same as the stag's. Something was happening, both extraordinary and disturbing.

Resting the bird back on the ground, Sadie skirted around the trees, searching for more fallen animals. Bugs lay everywhere, unmoving, but if they were like the others, then they hadn't succumbed to death. Two squirrels were sprawled on their sides, and when she pressed her fingers to their chests, they were alive. So were the other birds, rabbits, and foxes she stumbled on.

If she didn't get out of there now, she would continue to walk through the entire woods, looking for every single animal that was asleep. And with that, she would still have no answers, only her mind spinning with questions that ached to be answered. So, for now, she needed to leave the quiet of the woods and test out another theory.

Grabbing her purse and the dowsing rods from inside the cabin, she got into her truck. She cranked up the song as soon as the engine roared to life. Her grandfather's cassette soothed her, and it might not have been him singing or playing the instruments, but she remembered riding with him in this truck with Charlie, him humming along with the music.

Sadie drove until she ended up at the cemetery, where nature's sounds were in motion. She took the dowsing rods and paced up and down the grass between headstones like a crazed person, trying to see if they would spin here or if a shadow might make them move. The rods didn't budge, and none of the shadows were here besides the ones reflected from something. A worm seemed to crawl into her head, whispering to her that she could be imagining everything.

Steadying her breathing, she called River's mom—Skyler and Charlie were both at work, and she needed a distraction until nightfall.

"Hi, Sadie," Coral said.

"Are you busy?" she asked.

"Only for the next half hour. Why?"

"I didn't know if it was too soon to get together for lunch again. My treat." She could hear the begging in her voice, but she hoped Coral didn't notice.

"Sure. How about the Mexican place on Fifth Street? I can be there in an hour."

"Perfect. See you then." Sadie ended the call and lingered with the shells of the dead. If their souls had moved on, then no one was really listening when people visited their loved ones. But maybe they were listening from somewhere else. If River was trapped in the woods, would he be able to hear her now?

Sadie wrote down the things she'd seen this morning in the woods on a scratch sheet of paper, then headed to meet Coral. She waited maybe five minutes in front of the small Mexican restaurant before Coral pulled up, stepping out in a crisp white pantsuit that Sadie didn't know how she even kept clean. Sadie would be the first to spill something on herself if she wore clothing so light.

"Is everything all right?" Coral asked.

"Um, it's different," she said slowly.

Coral studied Sadie, her gaze trying to read her. "Different?"

"I went to Crow Moon yesterday and bought a few things."

"How about we find a table, and we can talk more about it." Coral guided Sadie inside, where a sign read to seat themselves. They took one of the small booths tucked into the back corner, and as soon as they sat down, an older woman with gray hair took their drink order. "So, you bought some items from Kalina's shop, and I take it something happened?"

Sadie fidgeted with the edge of her black T-shirt. "The dowsing rods I bought moved." Even though she'd seen the shadow spinning it.

Sadie still couldn't tell Coral that River might be a shadow in places, that somehow she'd seen him the past few nights, spoken with him. When she lived with Charlie, her nightmares had felt real, but never like this, never this vivid.

Coral nodded. "I've never seen anything supernatural, and I already told you I didn't spot anything in those woods, but I still believe in it. Just because I didn't see anything doesn't mean you can't. I don't know what's out there and whether the rumors people have said are true or not, but you seem to have experienced something. Not only that, but you might need to protect yourself. Kalina told me in the past that some spirits will feed off of emotions. You could always do a reading with her."

"Maybe." Most people would think she was being foolish, but Sadie's heart told her it was River, even as a voice seemed to whisper in her ear that these could be tricks of the mind, that she could be going insane.

"If you ever need an escape from the cabin, my door is always open. That will never change."

"Thank you, Coral."

"Of course, you've always been like a daughter to me." Coral smiled, tears beading her lashes when she squeezed Sadie's hand.

Sadie smiled in return just as the waitress came to the table with their drinks.

After finishing their meals, they parted ways, and Sadie's anxious feeling came back to her in a rush as she drove back to the woods. She wondered if the animals would still be there, waiting, breathing.

When she arrived home, she gathered her laptop from the cabin and trekked to where the stag rested, the shadows slipping by her side. A single shadow lingered farther away, traveling up a tree as if watching her. Sadie wondered if it was River, and if it was, she would let him approach her if he chose to.

She sat beside the graceful animal and watched it in wonder. As she waited for night to fall, she worked on a magazine article that was due soon. Yet every few moments she would lose focus, glancing at the deer, thinking the stag's eyes would be open and watching her. Only, it remained as it was.

Sadie wrote the last sentence of the article, then read through it several times, but she would have to wait and go another day to the coffee shop or library to use their Wi-Fi. It was a bit tedious, but at least it was keeping her busy until she could sleep.

As the sun started to set, she kept her gaze trained on the stag. Darkness rolled in and the wind started to blow. Just when she was about to chalk it up to the stag being locked in eternal sleep, the animal jolted, its eyes slowly opening, as if it was being pulled out of an enchanted slumber.

Sadie sat still to not frighten it, but as soon as the stag's gaze fell on her, it shakily stood, then darted away from her through the trees, twigs snapping below its hooves. She cursed herself for not being ready to film it, but the whole occurrence had been too beautiful not to watch.

Sadie thought about the daily rotation of time. Silence in the morning. Sound at night. Music at … midnight… That was it.

Taking her laptop, she dropped it off at the cabin before heading to the secret place behind the vines in the woods. She watched as the shadows moved—something had to connect it all. She needed midnight to arrive, for the music to call to her, for River to be waiting for her below ground.

Sadie rested against a tree, continuously checking the time on her phone. Skyler and Charlie had both texted her earlier, but the conversations had been brief, nonchalant.

As the numbers on the phone changed to midnight, Sadie's body grew limp, exhausted, her eyes closing of their own accord. But she forced them open to lit lanterns, the small fire, and a deep and low melody entwined with the wind. It was just the same as the previous nights—she would feel tired, forced to close her eyes, then the music would stir.

Ivory moths rose from the whispering trees, hovering above the circular opening in the ground. The creatures slipped out from behind their trunks, standing beneath the bobbing flames of the lanterns. They lifted their arms, their skeletal fingers pointing toward the entrance. The goat-skulled creature stepped through the vines, bowing its head, motioning her forward.

Sadie didn't wait to ask if River was here—she knew they wouldn't speak, and she *craved* what was to come. So she plucked a lantern from a tree, then raced down both flights of stone stairs until she found River in the center of the room, as he'd been the previous two nights. When she pressed her fingers to his cool skin, he warmed, just like before, coming to life, as if she'd woken her prince from death. The dagger fell from his hand, and he gazed intently at her.

"River." She smiled with a sigh.

"I thought I told you to stay away from me," he said in a gruff voice, yet folded his arms around her and pulled her to him.

"Talk to me," she pleaded, her voice shaky. "Tell me what's happening in these woods."

He traced his fingers up her spine, brushing the tip of his nose against hers. "I want to, but it's not time." His fingers skimmed down her side and grasped her hand like before. "Dance with me once more."

She blinked, staring at him as if he'd lost his mind. "We can't just dance and not talk about anything."

"For now, I think we can," he purred and nudged her forward.

As if under a hypnotic spell, she gave in, following his steps like they'd done this a thousand times, spinning round and round until the room disappeared in a blur.

But then she remembered the other nights, not having much time. Before forgetting where she was, that this was a dream of sorts, she halted her movements, holding River by the arms. "What is this place? What are the symbols on the walls? Why are you frozen when I come down here? Why are you a shadow during the day? Why did you hang yourself, River?"

"Mmm." His lips tilted up at the edges. "All good questions. Ones you may not like the answers to."

"Stop it!" she shouted. "I know what you're doing, and I don't like it. Stop toying with me. If you think this is going to prevent me from coming back here, it isn't."

"Is that what you think I'm doing?" River arched a brow, a grin spreading across his face.

Sadie scowled, peering around the room. "What's behind these doors? Can you tell me that?"

"Now that I will do, my sweet nightmare." He licked his lower lip, then motioned with a finger for her to follow him.

He opened one of the doors, and she stilled as she gazed inside. A strong metal smell filled the air. Blood, so much blood.

Crimson drops splashed to the floor, while others

rose from the small puddles to something Sadie would've only imagined in the stories she wrote. Hearts, sewn together in a ruby web across the entire ceiling, gleamed in the candlelight. The organs lived, beating like drums, blood spilling from them.

"What is this?" Her voice wavered as she stepped away from the door.

River turned to her, his fingers twitching, a nervous habit of his. He slowly backed her against a wall, his knuckles grazing her cheek as he leaned in close, his hot breath tickling her skin while he murmured in her ear, "I can't decide if I want to kiss you or kill you, and that's why you need to stay away from me. Now run and don't return, my sweet nightmare."

Sadie shoved him away—anger coursing through her. "Why would you say that?"

"Run." His neutral expression turned to one of fear. "Now."

River's fingers twitched again, his nostrils flaring while bending to pick up the dagger from the floor. He seemed to war with himself about something as his hand folded around the blade. Even though Sadie wanted to fight it, she chose to listen as his pleading eyes turned hollow, an emotion she'd never seen in him. So, clenching her teeth, she hurled herself up the steps and hated herself for it.

As soon as she hit fresh air, she halted—the trees had woven together, locking her inside its circle barrier as thick fog seeped in, preventing her from leaving.

13

"I wouldn't ever want another. Only you."

Heavy footsteps pounded against the steps, and Sadie slammed her shoulder against the seam between two trees to break through, but of course it didn't budge. Dark stitching lined the seam as if something had sewn the trunks together.

The lanterns and fire flickered out just as she leapt to a gnarled branch, the trees whispering. Though Sadie climbed, grasping branch after branch in the moonlight, she remained along the tree's first limb, as if some magical force held her in place. River growled, his deep voice echoing beneath the ground, drawing closer. But the fog was too thick to see through.

The soft brush of wings kissed her skin, and when she looked down at herself, white moths coated her entirely, blending her with the fog. Through a small gap between the trees, the goat-skulled creature pressed a skeletal finger over its mouth, shaking its head and hushing her. Protecting her?

Sadie listened, keeping her breaths even, but there was nowhere to go. Just as a hand wrapped around her waist, she jolted. Her eyelids flicked open to blinding bright sunshine pouring in around her. It took a moment for her to adjust to the light, the rays bursting through the trees—trees that were no longer woven together. No fog. No white moths cloaking her.

She crawled forward to where the opening should be, no longer a pathway leading to an underground paradise … or hell. At this point, she wasn't certain. The dances with River … the room with anatomical hearts bleeding blood like rain, how red droplets rose to refill them. River confessing how he didn't know if he wanted to kiss or kill her, then telling her to run. Which she had after he'd picked up the dagger, though there seemed to be a struggle within him. Something or someone was doing this to him. And she wouldn't run again, even if she had to grab the dagger first.

"If you can hear me, River," she shouted, her chest heaving. "Here I am. And I promise I will keep coming back. I will always come back. No matter what you do or say, whether I'm awake, or even if it's only in my dreams at midnight. Something's going on with you, and I will always help you, just as you would for me."

Shadows along the ground swarmed around her, forming a circle as if they didn't want her to leave. But even if she stayed or took a bottle of pills to fall asleep, she somehow knew she needed to wait for midnight to arrive. Besides, pills might not take her to the place she wanted to go.

As Sadie trudged back to the cabin, the silhouettes followed her, never once breaking their circle. Sleeping rabbits and birds sparsely covered the ground, more than usual. If it were the same as before, they would wake when night cast down its darkness.

Sadie slumped on the porch steps, pressing her face to her hands, thinking about River, his struggle, him wanting to hurt her. Over the years, when she'd come to the woods, there hadn't ever been a sign of anything supernatural. In the past, she'd stayed in the woods at night on several occasions, camping with River, and there was no paranormal activity then. Yet when she moved in, this had all begun. Her moving in couldn't be the trigger, could it? She hadn't been to the woods in three months and … she covered her mouth. The answer was so simple. When she first returned here, she'd spread River's *ashes.* And then the first night she stayed in the cabin, the music came to her at midnight.

It was the ashes—they somehow triggered something when she'd set them free, opening a gateway to what felt like another world, yet still in these same woods. Sadie's mind reeled, focusing on all the films she'd watched over the years—the ones where the protagonist was imagining *everything.*

Skyler had seen the dowsing rod move in her hand, but not the shadow… Her mind wasn't inventing these things. She wasn't *imagining this.*

As she went inside, she took out her phone and called Skyler.

"Hey, I was just about to call you," he said. "You had your one-word message replies yesterday, which, with you, means something is going on."

She did do that when she was trying to concentrate on something or in a mood. "I know what triggered this entire thing. It's because I spread River's ashes here in the woods, and—"

"You didn't tell me you spread his ashes," Charlie interrupted.

Sadie groaned, briefly squeezing her eyes shut. "You didn't tell me my sister was with you."

"She came over last night worried about you." He sighed.

"Don't be sneaky," Charlie said softly. "Just tell me what's going on. I already know you and Skyler were up to something the other day. He might know how to hide the truth because of his job, but not with this. I know you two didn't go to the mall. You hate the mall."

"We went to a metaphysical shop, all right?" Sadie huffed. "Not that I have to tell you where I go. I know how you get around things like that or I would've asked you to come."

"It's not that I fear the things in those types of shops, but it's hard to explain how they make me feel. I could've easily gotten some sage and lit it at home after, though," Charlie grunted, and Sadie rolled her eyes. "I'm not going to push, but I want you to confide in me."

Sometimes, even when Sadie knew she could do things on her own, she still needed her sister. "Fine. After spreading River's ashes in the woods, I've been experiencing these lifelike dreams, then the past few days I've found … River there. I know what you're going to say, and you don't have to believe me if you don't want to, but I'm choosing to believe. It's not only that … other things have been happening to me here." She then confessed to her sister what she'd been experiencing during the day. The shadows, the animals, the silence, the rousing of sound, the dowsing rods. Even if she were conjuring up these things, she was functioning just fine. She wasn't going off the rails, wandering the streets while shouting for River to come home to her. This was in her woods, her cabin, her home. It didn't matter if any of it was a hallucination—it was her decision.

For a beat of a second, there was silence before Charlie spoke in a rush, "I'm taking off work and coming over."

"Do not do that," Sadie bit out. "I told you the truth, trusting that you weren't going to treat me like a child. Mom and Dad don't even do that." She hadn't talked to her parents about any of this, only checking in on them and telling them she moved out of Charlie's place and into the woods.

"They stopped doing that when we became teenagers." Charlie sighed. "And I'm not treating you like a younger sister—I only want to know if you need me to come to the cabin."

Sadie mulled it over, and maybe she would've asked Charlie to swing by, to take off of work, if she were able to see the things she was. But she couldn't. And even if she could, this was her needing to unravel the secrets with River.

"I'm all right. But if anything else happens, I'll confide in you, Charlie. I promise."

"All right, Sadie. I don't care if I'm at work, call me if you need me. This is me treating you as an adult and not hurling myself over there," Charlie said.

"I bet that was hard for you to say." Sadie smiled. "I love you."

"I love you, too. How about we get together on my next day off, at least? We can watch a movie of your choosing."

"I'd like that. Tell Skyler I said bye." Sadie set the phone on the counter, then placed frozen pancakes in the microwave before making hot chocolates.

To pass the time until midnight after getting ready for the day, Sadie took her laptop to the library, where only a few people were milling about. She submitted her magazine article, and since she was there, she glanced at the horror book section, yet nothing called to her. When she was younger, she used to read books all the time, but then she started veering away from them and falling in love with films more.

Sadie fidgeted with a corner of a tattered spine, the draw to get home to the woods pulling at her. She'd planned to stay out a long while—however, her mind was turning elsewhere, unable to concentrate on anything else. Gathering her things, she left the library in a rush.

Back at the cabin, she didn't find another stag or doe close to her home, only a small brown rabbit and woodpecker. She wondered if this was the same woodpecker her sister had seen.

Sadie scooped up the rabbit, its chest gently rising and falling, and rested it near the woodpecker—all the while the shadows lingered on the ground near her. A little before sunset, she would return to see if they would stir as the stag had.

The group of shadows didn't follow her back to the cabin, except for one that halted near her truck. Even though she couldn't see the eyes hidden in its dark depths, she knew they were pinned to her.

"I know it's you, River," she said. "You might as well just come in the cabin."

With that, she went inside, yet he didn't follow. To keep herself busy, she worked on a short story that was due soon, but she had to stop as her mind continued to spin. So she took out her screenplay and listed more things that had occurred. River and the dagger, the bleeding hearts, the stitched trees, the cloak of moths, the goat-skulled creature warning her.

Sadie put on a seventies vampire film to play in the background for a bit of noise until daylight was about to end. She then went back outside to where the rabbit and woodpecker still rested. Sinking to the dirt, she waited with the shadows as company.

The sun seemed to take forever to dip down into its slumber. Sadie held up her phone, and as the sky darkened, she started to record. A few moments later, the sleeping animals' eyes cracked open, their small heads perking up, then the bird darted into the trees, and the rabbit hopped away as if they hadn't been in a forced sleep.

Sadie cut the beginning of the video, focusing on when the animals woke, then she sent it to Skyler and Charlie. *What do you see?*

After a couple of minutes, Charlie texted back. *A tree trunk and grass?*

Sadie frowned, rewatching the video again. She was still seeing the wildlife rouse. She then headed inside the cabin when Skyler messaged her. *What am I supposed to be seeing?*

A shiver ran up her spine. Why weren't they seeing these things? She didn't have the strength to wait in the woods until midnight. Besides, did it matter where she lingered? Each time, whether outside in the swing, inside the cabin, or near the opening leading underground, she found herself in that eerie night world of the woods.

As midnight neared, and she started to fidget, Sadie changed her mind, taking a flashlight and darting into the woods. Even though the shadows hadn't spoken to her, she wanted their company again, wanted them beside her as she waited.

Sadie settled inside the circle of trees, the shadows rising from the ground, their silhouettes taking shape. No longer flat and connected to the dirt, but like the ones she'd seen leap from the trees, only she hadn't seen them this clearly. Her eyes widened, her gaze fixed on the horns sprouting on their dark heads. The one nearest her, she believed, was the goat-skulled creature by the shape of its horns.

"Is River with you?" She hadn't smelled his scent that day at all, even though she knew it had been him hovering by her truck. The creature didn't answer, only bowed its head.

In the distance, a wolf howled, and it most likely wasn't the safest thing to be out here, but her eyes unwillingly fell shut. She forced them open and gasped—the creatures surrounding her were no longer silhouettes, but in their true forms. Skeletal and furred.

"Why do you follow me around?" Sadie asked, her gaze fastened to the empty sockets of the goat-skulled form.

It only lifted its arm, pointing at the opening in the

ground, then slowly backed away from her to the others, who were all pointing to the same place. Their empty eye sockets rested on her, and she watched as the moths lifted from the trees, swirling around the entrance in the dirt, the lanterns' light illuminating their ivory color.

A scuffing sounded around her, and Sadie gave pause, staring in horror as the trees expanded, enfolding themselves together, trapping her in like she'd been the night before. The trunks exhaled and inhaled, whispering louder and louder until it resembled hoarse screams.

Sadie stumbled backward, her grip tightening on her flashlight. She turned from the creatures, slowly moving toward her, forcing her to descend the stairs.

Heart pounding, she rushed down the steps and glanced over her shoulder, but the creatures didn't follow. Sadie hadn't been afraid of them, but now, she wondered if they could be the ones keeping River trapped here.

As soon as her gaze fell on River, she touched the back of his neck and watched as he took a breath. The dagger fell from his hand, and she snatched it, pointing it toward him.

"You came back," he rasped, not shying away from her, even though she held up a dagger. "I told you not to. Last night I had you, and if you hadn't woken up..."

"Then what?" She scowled, motioning around the room. "You're not saying anything. Only slivers of things. You're not saying why there are creatures with animal skull faces above us and if they are the ones keeping you here, why the trees move and breathe, why you always have this dagger in your hand, why your eyes went hollow last night, why the woods are quiet during the day, and the animals sleep. When I released your ashes here, it created all of this, am I right?"

River's throat bobbed as he nodded. "The ashes did open this."

Was that the only question he was going to answer? The blood in her veins roared and she squeezed the dagger. "You said you didn't know if you wanted to kiss me or kill me. Why?"

"My heart yearns to do both," he said between gritted teeth. "That should make you want to leave me here."

"Stop being vague!" she shouted, her voice echoing off the walls. "Why did you kill yourself?"

River stepped toward her, his hand wrapping around her wrist that was holding the dagger. He gently brought it to her side, and with his other hand, he pushed a lock of hair behind her ear. "To protect you," he whispered, his gray eyes pinned to hers.

"Protect me from what? Are those creatures doing this to you?"

"No, the fiends do not cause harm. Let me show you something." River arched a brow as he turned away from her, pressing his fingers to a door handle.

"The last time you opened a door, the room led to bleeding hearts," Sadie spat.

"If that bothered you, then I suggest leaving the other doors shut."

"Why are you talking differently? You wouldn't have used 'harm' or 'suggest' before."

The edges of his lips tilted up as if this was all a trick. "There's plenty you have left to uncover, but I *suggest* you don't. If you do, keep the dagger close."

Sadie glared before saying, "Show me." Her heart lodged in her throat as the door opened. Taking a deep breath, she followed him inside the candlelit room, expecting something more ominous, bloody.

Instead, it was a bedroom of sorts—a bit gothic in style. Two glass boxes, like coffins, rested in the center of the room on top of a black fur rug. The walls were a glistening obsidian—an oval mirror hung on one side and abstract portraits, painted with a deep crimson, that might have been *blood*, on the other.

Two large onyx wardrobes hugged opposite corners, and a black desk with a quill and stacks of paper sat in between. The flooring was the same stone that was in the main room, and the scent of sage surrounded her.

River led her to another door at the back of the room. Inside was an antique clawfoot tub and a mirror framed with bones.

"All right, you've officially shown me scenes from a horror film," she said, trying to sound light, yet her voice came out anything but that. "Is the bath going to fill with blood next? Are bones going to protrude from the walls?"

River sat on the edge of the bathtub, running his hand along the porcelain as he stared at her, his eyes hooded. "This is our room, our bathing chamber. Welcome."

Sadie's brows rose up her forehead, and she blinked at him. "Sleep in glass coffins? Like we're vampires?" At any other time, the thought would've amused her, but not now, not when she didn't have answers.

River pinched the bridge of his nose, his other hand starting to shake, the expression he'd tried to hold twisted into something more like him. "As you've discovered, you're not wholly here, but your essence is. At the stroke of midnight, that's when the veil drops, opening to us all."

"Like Cinderella?" She scowled. "Instead of a magical

carriage turning back into a pumpkin at the stroke of midnight, my magical bloody palace appears underground?"

"Precisely." He stood from the edge of the tub, his hungry gaze meeting hers as he brushed his finger across her lips. "It took you a few real dreams entwined with the veil to get to me."

She remembered her first clear dream. The cupcakes. The blade to her throat that now had to have been held by him, only not really him. Her conscience conjuring it up while linked to some sort of veil.

"I shouldn't have come to you during the day," he continued. "I should've left you alone. I *should* leave you alone now. But I don't want to."

"During the day, you're a shadow like the fiends. When you're close to me, I can smell your scent..."

He moistened his lips, his finger trailing across her collarbone. "You're getting warmer."

"And when night rolls in, you're still a shadow, but you can choose for your form to get more prominent, like the others. How the animals are asleep during the day, then rouse at the same time."

"Even warmer." His nose brushed hers, his fingers wrapping around the back of her neck. A warmth spread through her, and her breath caught.

"Then at midnight, when this veil drops, the fiends' true forms slip out, just as yours does, only you're trapped down here until I wake you. And none of you can leave the woods, no matter the time of day."

"Mmm, so warm." River's arms drew her closer to him, his lips featherlight against hers, making her eyes flutter. "Perhaps hotter, I should say."

He lifted his head from hers, his gaze looking past her. Even though his expression didn't change, she knew something was there—behind her.

Sadie whirled around, only to find the oval mirror staring back at her, yet she wasn't wearing jeans and a T-shirt. Reflecting inside the glass was an image of her upper body in a much older style lacy black dress with a high collar, while River's outfit was different too. A long sweeping black jacket, the white collar of his shirt folded atop the other. Neither of the faces belonged to them. They were maybe around the same age, the woman's jet-black hair curled to her waist. The man's red hair swept back in a low ponytail just past his shoulders.

Eyes wide, Sadie peered down at herself, finding she was still dressed in her regular clothes, and so was River. "Who are they?" she asked, her voice rising.

"I don't think you want to keep digging." River's fingers softly brushed her throat, and he leaned closer, whispering in her ear, "Now, listen to me. If you keep coming back, things will only become more wicked, my sweet nightmare."

"How so?" Sadie's body shivered beneath his touch as he gripped her waist, his fingers digging in.

He pressed his mouth to hers, his delicious tongue sweeping across the seam of her lips. "No matter how hard I try to resist, my blade will eventually pierce your heart."

"What's doing this to you?" Sadie asked, grasping the front of his shirt. When he didn't answer, she shoved him away and stormed out to the room where she'd woken him to gather herself for a moment. His footsteps sounded, and just as she turned, her body jolted forward, her eyes flying open. The woods surrounded her, the morning sun shining across the foliage.

River's words rang in her ears as she remembered his kiss. *My blade will eventually pierce your heart.*

"River!" Sadie shouted. "Confide in me the rest, and I'll save you from this."

A shadow broke from the trees where the other silhouettes of the fiends lingered. It slinked, along the ground, the scent of honey and sandalwood carried with it. One of River's shadowy fingers moved across the dirt, spelling out words. If she'd been unsure if this was him before, she now had her answer. His handwriting was just the same.

Leave the woods.

14

"They should have listened."

"River!" Sadie shouted as his shadow slinked away past the other silhouettes. But he didn't stop, didn't turn around, didn't write anything else in the dirt. "You can't just write that and leave! Do you think I really care if things get more wicked? You can't say you want to pierce my heart with a blade and act like that's the end of it." She paused, tightening her fists. "Well, you know what? Tonight, I'll see you again. And I'll keep coming back because that's what we do. Why is it that you skulk around me during the day here? I might not catch you every time, but I know you are. We can't leave each other. Even in death."

River had hung himself to protect her, just as he was pushing her away now—something inside him had the desire to kill her. He knew exactly what it was yet refused to tell her … another way of protecting her. But from what? She didn't want to be protected—she didn't want to leave the woods and be safe—she wanted to know what was going on with her husband and how she could save him.

But sometimes, I felt a touch of darkness inside him. Yet his was different than the piece that most of us have. It's the same thing I feel in you right now. Kalina's words rang inside Sadie's skull. She'd believed the shop owner had said them to lure her back in for a tarot card reading, but now, maybe there was something more to that. Coral had also mentioned that Sadie might want to try a reading. What did she have to lose?

Sadie took a quick rinse in the shower and grabbed an apple before heading to Crow Moon. She blared her grandfather's cassette as she left the woods. Precisely what River wanted her to do, but she was only staying gone temporarily.

As she bit into the apple, Sadie thought about everything River had said. How at the stroke of midnight, something in the woods forces her to sleep and opens a veil. How he could move around as a shadow during the day and become a different silhouette form at night. He'd touched her that night in the cabin—she'd felt his hand. But then when the veil dropped, he wasn't like the other creatures—the fiends—he was sent below ground until Sadie's essence woke him with her touch.

There was still so much she hadn't uncovered, like the reflections lingering in the mirror, the images that weren't of her or River. Who were they? What did it even mean? River was a spirit of sorts with fiends that were trapped in the woods. He'd hung himself to protect her, but he hadn't shown any signs of a war going on within him. Unless he'd hidden it well or it had come about when she'd been gone that day.

As Sadie mulled it over, she took another bite of her juicy apple, chewing the fruit as though she were murdering it. A part of her thought that maybe she should give him space, let him come to her, but if she chose that path, she might be too late. She was already far too deep into whatever this mystery was. And then her mind turned back to the mirror reflection that wasn't them. Maybe they were the spirits doing this. But why?

Sadie pulled in front of Crow Moon and chugged her water bottle before tossing it and the apple core into the trash outside. The shop had just opened five minutes ago, and by the looks of the empty parking lot, not many customers, if any, would be inside.

The bell dinged and a citrusy scent filled the shop as light smoke curled out from the hanging incense holders when she walked inside. Sadie was the only one in the front area, and she skimmed her fingers across a few red and black book spines. Beside the desk, the rottweiler sat on the other side of the gate again, panting.

Sadie went to him and reached to pet his head, but the dog flinched from her touch, backing away as though afraid of her. She frowned—animals had never been afraid of her.

Kalina slipped out from behind the long black curtains, carrying a box of rattling jars. Her black and white striped skirt swished around her as her jeweled bracelets clanked against one another.

"You're back." Kalina smiled, resting the box on the countertop. She then glanced at her dog. "Don't mind him. He can be a big baby."

Something told Sadie it was more than that, though.

"Did you return for a tarot reading, or are you needing help with more items?" Kalina asked, taking out a few jars filled with herbs. "Spell jars." She winked, motioning her head at them.

"The tarot card reading. I know I didn't book an appointment, so I'm not sure if you have any openings. Sorry for the short notice."

"You're in luck," Kalina drawled, taking out a few more jars containing small stones. "I don't have any clients booked until this afternoon."

"It's my lucky day, then." Sadie forced a smile, even though a nervous feeling prickled inside her chest.

Kalina pushed her dark hair over her shoulder and glanced at the curtains behind her while shouting, "Jolie, put your phone down and come watch the counter. I have a client."

A few seconds later, a girl, appearing to be a younger version of Kalina, strolled out to the front, fiddling with her phone. She wore a dress of all black, lined in felt buttons down the front of it, a silver hoop through her septum, and both ears dotted with jeweled studs.

"What did I say?" Kalina frowned, plucking the phone from the girl's hands, then slipped it beneath the counter. "Not out here, Jolie. Only when you have nothing to do in the back. Finish unloading the box and put the spell jars up in alphabetical order, not just anywhere you please, like last time."

"Fine." Jolie huffed while collecting a few of the jars in her hands.

Kalina motioned Sadie forward and led her toward

the back of the shop. "Don't mind my daughter's attitude. Jolie helps around here when she isn't at the community college."

"She looks exactly like you," Sadie said, scanning a few of the new additions to the taxidermy section. A boned mermaid with a blooming flower for her skull had her itching to have it.

"Tell her that, and she'll get pissed." Kalina laughed, guiding Sadie through a couple more areas with various crystals and stones. But Sadie's attention was drawn to the framed bug collection like the ones she owned.

At the back of the room, between two glass curio cabinets, holding jeweled goblets, hung deep purple curtains. Kalina pushed them aside for Sadie to pass through.

The dimly lit room revealed a windowless space straight out of a film set. A round table draped in crimson velvet lingered beneath a ceiling painted like the night sky, and two antique high-backed chairs faced one another. Glass orbs of every color shone against black shelves, herbs and crystals, and countless candles of all shapes and sizes. On one side of the room sat a dresser filled with narrow drawers and deep purple stone knobs. And in the far back corner stood a classic Zoltar fortune-telling machine.

"I always loved those," Sadie said, knowing it must've cost a fortune.

"It's for when someone doesn't want a true reading." Kalina arched a brow. "But sometimes we need a little Zoltar in our lives."

"I'm afraid of what Zoltar would say to me at the moment." Sadie grinned, pulling out a velvet chair at the reading table and lowering herself onto the plush cushion. "How long have you been doing this?"

Kalina smiled in return, gathering a few white candles from one of the shelves. "I've always had an intuition about things. Sometimes I can see auras when I do palm readings. I'm letting you in on a secret because you're one of Coral's friends. I'm not always right, but I'm more right than not." She lit the candles, then placed them along the table's edges, atop brass stands, filling the closed space with the scents of citrus, ginger, and pepper. "Choose the deck that speaks to you." Taking three stacks of cards from a wicker box, she set them in front of Sadie before sitting across from her.

Sadie looked at the different decks, not knowing which one to choose. Angels and rainbows? Knights and swords? But the third stack, small and unassuming, hidden in the shadows of the candlelight, drew her gaze the most. If there was a deck created for her, that was the one. Forest animals decorated the tattered and worn box, their forms half skeletal, half whole, weeds and flowers twining around the edges. She pointed at the deck.

"Have you ever had a tarot reading before?" Kalina asked, pulling the cards from the box and resting them in front of her.

Sadie shook her head. "I've only had my palm read when my grandfather took me and my sister to a carnival once." She wasn't sure if she believed in tarot readings, but if it was real, what if the answer she uncovered was wicked like River had said?

"How was it?"

"I was told all my dreams would come true." Sadie peered down at one of the unlit candles. *But now, maybe it's my nightmares that are coming true.*

"Let's see what we can find out today, shall we? Inhale deeply and focus your mind and heart on your question," Kalina said, her oddly hypnotic voice startling Sadie as the woman closed her eyes. "Then shuffle the cards. Any way you like. When you feel it is time, choose three and place them here, here, and here." She indicated the center of the table.

Admiring the art across the back of the deck, Sadie inhaled slowly, then exhaled just the same. Her curiosity to see the drawings on the other sides grew as she spread the cards into a messy pile, thinking of River all the while, his arms around her, his skin warming beneath her touch. Finally, she chose three cards at random, placing them at the center of the table against the soft velvet.

Kalina opened her eyes and met Sadie's gaze while slowly turning over the first card, then the second and third. The woman's eyes widened as she looked down at the cards.

Sadie couldn't find anything horrifying on them—a beautiful stag, an owl, and a bear, their colors vibrant, their skeletal faces somehow majestic. "What do they mean?" she asked.

Kalina laughed then, shaking her head as if clearing images that only she could see away. "It's nothing. Just a practice round." She smiled sweetly, but the smile didn't quite reach her eyes. "Please. Shuffle the cards once more and choose again."

All right... Sadie wasn't sure what the point of that was, but she told herself it was all part of the act, to get customers wondering. She shuffled the cards once again, cutting the deck four times, gathering and fanning the cards out across the table like she'd seen dealers do in the movies. There weren't any specific cards calling to her, so she took out three random ones from the line.

As Kalina turned over the three cards she'd chosen, Sadie blinked, her lips parting. The exact same ones. A chill swept through her, seeping down to her bones. Coincidence or not, Kalina's face had paled, her fingers fidgeting with the cloth of the table.

"Past. Present. And future. Darkness is all I can see." Kalina lifted a shaky hand and reached toward Sadie. "May I see your palm? I won't charge for this."

Only darkness… There had to be something hidden in its dark depths. Biting the inside of her cheek, Sadie rested her arm on the table, and Kalina traced the lines along her palm with the tip of her finger.

"The darkness is clearer now. Your aura," Kalina whispered, her gaze latching onto Sadie's. "The black spot resides on your aura, as if it's marked."

Sadie forced down the lump in her throat when she swallowed, thinking about River's words once more. *If you keep coming back, things will only become more wicked, my sweet nightmare.* "Marked for what?"

Kalina gently lay Sadie's hand on the table. "I don't know. It looks like it's branded there with a symbol of an eye."

Below ground, after midnight, there were symbols etched across the walls. The eyes, so many of them... It had to be connected. Had River somehow marked her? Or was it something else…

"Before I told you we all have a bit of darkness inside us," Kalina continued. "But within you, deep down, there is a desire to relish it."

Relish it? That couldn't be right. It had to mean something else. "Do you think it has to do with my love of horror things, the macabre? I would never hurt anyone, have never hurt anyone, only in the things I write."

"Possibly. Did you use the items you bought already?" Kalina asked, quickly setting the tarot cards back into a pile as if she was in a hurry to leave the room.

"Mostly. Should I use something else?"

"No," Kalina rushed the words out. "Don't use them anymore." She stood from the chair and opened one of the dresser drawers. When she returned to Sadie's side, she pressed a bundle of sage into her palm, different from the ones she'd purchased. "In fact, you might want to ward things off instead of trying to bring them to you."

"Even if it's someone I love?" Sadie whispered.

Kalina's eyes softened, folding Sadie's fingers around the sage. "Especially if it's someone you love."

Before Sadie left Crow Moon, she'd asked Kalina not to mention any of this to Coral. Kalina had said what occurred between her and her clients was never discussed outside of the room. She'd also given Sadie a large bag of salt to ward off spirits and a few white candles, but she wouldn't use them.

To take up time, she spent a few hours at the coffee shop, finishing a mess of a short story and sending it in. She then wrote down more of the recent events in her notebook, the way she'd chosen the same tarot cards twice. Her theory about what was going on was blossoming into something dark after Kalina's words continued to echo in her head, that she was *marked.*

The images she'd seen in the mirror could be the spirits of one of the couples who'd died in the woods, or even before that based on the clothing. River might be possessed… But could a spirit even be possessed by another spirit? There were so many missing pieces, and a lot of it wasn't making sense. It wasn't a standard dead spirit haunting her… It was something much bigger.

She'd been too late to save River before, but she wouldn't be too late this time.

Sadie gathered her things, rushing out of the coffee shop and back to the woods. As she pulled to a stop in front of the cabin, her stomach sank when she looked out the window. At the *trees*…

She stepped out of the truck and surveyed the area around her, taking in each trunk, their location. They weren't where they were supposed to be—it was as if they'd been taken from the ground and buried somewhere else. Yet huge trees couldn't just be plucked from the dirt so easily. The trees had breaths within the veil at night, whispered, but this was strange, just as strange as the sleeping animals.

Along the ground, the shadows approached her, surging toward her, then away as if wanting her to follow them.

Casting another glance at the pine tree that should've been on the other side of the cabin, she trekked behind the shadows toward the woods. The silhouettes stopped in front of a small furry animal, and Sadie halted as her gaze fell to it. It wasn't a sleeping rabbit any longer, but something else... Its chest was ripped open with a beating heart beside the body, blood pooling around the organ. Even though the rabbit should be still, its chest rose and fell, somehow continuing to breathe. The quiet became louder, and she looked around her, finding more animals just like the rabbit. Horror churned within her at the sight. Horror, and something familiar. Something like satisfaction…

"No," Sadie whispered and ran back toward the cabin. She stopped just outside her home, where she couldn't see any animals.

That morning, River had written to her in the dirt, not needing a planchette or any other supernatural device to answer her. He might not be beside her, but she knew without a doubt he lingered nearby.

"River!" Sadie shouted. "What's happening?" Her hands trembled as she waited for him to respond, wondering if maybe the words he'd written that morning were the last she would ever get from him. "I am good at being calm, but I'm not now. Please answer me."

And then a single silhouette crept out from one of the trees, inching across the ground toward her, River's scent permeating the air. The other shadows stayed near her, resting still, as if they were paying attention to him too.

River's silhouette traveled up her body, his hand falling across hers, his other brushing along her cheek. She couldn't feel his touch, but he was there, and that was what she needed.

"You couldn't stay away from me, could you?" she murmured with a smile. "Now tell me, why are the animals like this now? Why are the trees moving?"

River glided down her body and back to the ground,

his fingertip crawling across the dirt, shaping letters into words.

If you come to me tonight, you will only learn of more wicked things.

She dropped to her knees, tracing the letters. "Am I really marked then?"

Yes, my sweet nightmare. We both are.

15

"They always want answers, don't they?"

Sadie sat in the porch swing, rocking back and forth, thinking of River's words. How they were both marked. He had disappeared into the woods when she'd told him she needed space to think, his shadowy form blending in with the others. Tonight she would discover what the wicked things he talked about really meant.

The sound of a car engine drew Sadie from her thoughts, and she looked up to see Skyler's police cruiser pulling up in front of the cabin. When he stepped out of the car, he wore his uniform and held a paper cup in his hand.

"Did you come all the way out here just to bring me a drink?" She forced a smile, pushing up from the chair.

"Just wanted to come and check on you since you haven't been sounding like yourself."

"It looks like you're on shift now. You're not supposed to be working?"

Skyler handed her the drink with a smile, the cup still warm. "I am, but you're a civilian, and I'm checking in on you." He glanced down at her fidgeting hands. "What happened?"

"Things that I'm sure only I can see." Sadie gestured at the foliage around the cabin. "The trees have moved around and aren't in the same places."

Skyler took a step back, scanning the area, his expression remaining neutral. "The trees are in the same spots they were in before. I mean, I don't know exactly where they belong, but nothing looks out of place."

"Hold on." Sadie set the cup on the porch, then walked to a nearby trunk that had shifted from the left side of the cabin to the right. She tapped the bark with her knuckles. "This one's pine and swapped places with the cedar that's now over there."

Skyler followed her gaze to the other tree, then ran a hand through his hair, shaking his head. "The one you're beside is cedar and the pine is the opposite one." He pursed his lips, seeming to mull something over. "Let me try something." Taking her hand, he glided it around the trunk. "I still see it going around perfectly."

"So do I." Even though the pine tree was thinner... "It's because I'm marked," she whispered.

He arched a brow. "Marked for what?"

Sadie leaned her back against the trunk, folding her arms and peering up at the sky, listening to the quiet for a few seconds before speaking. "I went to Crow Moon today and had a tarot reading."

Skyler groaned. "She was wanting your money."

"I initially thought so too. But that wasn't it. Kalina felt something inside me, and you could see it on her face. I know it's true because things have become different around here."

"What do you mean?"

"You won't see it, but follow me." Sadie led him down a grassy path, twigs snapping below her boots, until they came across the brown rabbit. It still lay on its side, its mouth parted, and its chest torn open. The heart continued to beat, and even though she couldn't hear it, she knew what it would sound like. *Thump, thump. Thump, thump.*

"You're seeing another sleeping animal here?" Skyler asked gently.

"A rabbit, only it's different than before," she breathed, lowering herself beside the bloody animal. "A heart is pounding outside its broken body, and its chest is still rising and falling."

Skyler knelt beside her, running his fingers across the blood on the ground, yet when his hand came up, red didn't stain his skin. "I don't see or feel anything." His gaze latched onto her, and she could see it, the unease, the worry. "I think it's time for you to maybe leave these woods. Things you're experiencing are sounding worse. Have you seen River again?"

Sadie stood, clenching her teeth. "You saw the dowsing rod spin, so don't start looking at me as if you think I'm going crazy."

"I don't think you're crazy, Sadie."

"One more thing. Just one more thing to show you." She hurried back toward the cabin to the place where River had left her the messages. She didn't think Skyler would see the words, but she would show him them anyway.

Sadie waved him closer, pointing at the messages. "Do you see them?"

Skyler's eyebrows knitted together, and he dropped to the balls of his feet. "If you come to me tonight, you will only learn of more wicked things? Yes, my sweet nightmare. We both are?"

"You see them!" Sadie covered her mouth, relief washing over her that he could see *something*. "In shadow form, River wrote these earlier. There's another message out in the woods that told me to leave here."

Skyler rubbed the back of his neck, staring at her hard, as if he was trying to read something inside her.

"It's his handwriting," she said, her voice shaking.

He sighed. "Handwriting can be mimicked if someone tries hard enough."

Sadie felt the color drain from her face. The thought crossing her mind briefly—what if she had? "I didn't write it!"

"I'm not saying *you* did." Skyler paused. "I saw the rod move in your hand, remember? But if something supernatural is warning you to leave, maybe you should listen. It's not healthy for you to do this to yourself. I'm telling you as a friend, not as a police officer."

Tears pricked her eyes, and she decided to confess the rest to him about what had happened at night the past few times, leaving out the part where River was struggling with urges to hold back from hurting her. That wouldn't go over well at all.

"Fiends with animal skull faces? River trapped below ground? A veil? And now you're seeing bloody animals and trees in new positions when you're not asleep? I honestly think this is something fucked, Sadie. And dark."

"And what if the dark things want to hurt River after marking him, marking me?" Sadie shouted. "If you lost Charlie in the same way I lost River, and this was happening to you, would you leave it alone? Let her spirit be trapped in these woods?"

Skyler's face softened, and he wrapped his arms around her, holding her close. "I would rip every tree out of the ground here to set Charlie's spirit free. But this isn't me—it's you, and I don't want you hurt."

"As a friend, I need you to support that I'm going to stay here," Sadie bit back, stepping away from him.

"And as a friend, I'm telling you that each day you've been here, the things that are slowly unfolding are becoming more sinister. What's going to come out of Pandora's box after tonight? After tomorrow? Once you unravel everything? I've seen enough horror in my life, both real and not, to know when it's time to get the hell out of a situation. I'm telling you, the time is now."

"If it's only affecting me, then why does it matter?" she whispered.

"What happens to you affects me, and it also affects your sister." He exhaled in exasperation. "I can tell you're stubborn as hell and aren't going to leave. You're an adult, and I can't force you to, but that doesn't mean I won't keep checking on you. Charlie too."

"You're right. I won't leave." Sadie folded her arms and bit the inside of her cheek. "Thank you, Skyler." She gave him another hug before walking him back to his car, asking him not to tell any of this to Charlie. If Sadie chose to, she wanted to be the one to tell her.

After Skyler left, she drank down the hot chocolate he'd brought, even though it had grown cold, the way the blood pulsing in her veins was starting to feel. Now that she was alone, she could only focus on Kalina's words once more. She was marked.

Sadie sat on the porch, catching glimpses of the shadows peeking out from the woods every so often.

She went inside, finally taking a hot shower, then filling up the bath to relax and not think for a little bit. Tears fell down her cheeks, and she drew her knees to her chest while her body racked with sobs, not knowing why she was even crying. But she felt something in her chest expand, as if it soon would crack open.

A shadow crept beneath the door, and Sadie's eyes widened when she inhaled River's scent. His silhouette slid up the wall to the mirror, his shadowy finger writing into the fog of the glass. *Follow me.*

Sadie frowned as his silhouette slipped back beneath the door. An anxious feeling pulsed in her, and she hurried to towel off before throwing on a T-shirt and black pants. She found River gliding across the floor in the living room as if he was pacing. He then passed through the wall leading outside.

Collecting the flashlight and her phone, she threw open the door and followed him into the woods, where only a little daylight remained. River stopped in front of the brown rabbit with its torn-out chest.

"What do you want me to see?" Sadie asked.

His finger slid across the dirt. *Wait.*

Sadie didn't know what she was waiting for, but she listened, standing there for about ten minutes when the sky started to darken, the wind blowing across her skin.

And then the sounds of the forest filled the gathering night. The beating of the rabbit's heart as she knew it would make. *Thump, thump. Thump, thump.* The thumps grew to a roar as the sounds of hearts beating thundered around her, from every fallen creature throughout the woods.

She gasped as the bloody heart sank into the ground and the rabbit's broken chest sealed itself shut. The animal roused, yet it didn't dart back into the trees like the ones had the previous nights. The rabbit's body quivered, as did the other animals around her that she could see. Their bodies shrunk in on themselves, withering, becoming smaller, their coloring turning to onyx. The fur on the rabbit changed to something else entirely.

Sadie's eyes widened—what rested in front of her was no longer a rabbit but a shadowy butterfly … no, a moth. The other animals had turned the same, flying up into the trees, their fragile wings fluttering. She had an inkling that once midnight arrived they would become ivory.

Sadie pointed her flashlight at the dirt until she found River's shadow. "By showing me this, you had to know it would only make me more curious."

River rose from the ground, his shadow taking shape. She gasped as he pressed his hand to her cheek, running his thumb across her bottom lip. He then knelt, writing in the dirt. *You wouldn't have left anyway, and selfishly, that pleases me.*

Sadie sat on the futon beside River's shadow, tapping her feet, waiting for midnight to arrive. After the bloody animals turned into moth silhouettes, and River's last message, she'd gone inside with him following behind her. He'd returned to his shadowy form, and although he hadn't written anything else, he lingered beside her on the futon as if it were a first date, too shy to touch one another. But she knew he was trying to distance himself still, even though he couldn't, just as she couldn't.

"It's almost time," Sadie said softly, wondering if once midnight came if he would vanish from here and appear below ground.

Her eyelids fell shut, then opened. River's form was no longer beside her, so she knew she was already sleeping.

Outside, the wind howled against the windows, the same haunting music as the other nights thrashed along with it. Grabbing her flashlight, she ventured into the night, the trees lit with lanterns, guiding her way. The whispering in the trees was even louder, the screams clearer, raspy.

She set aside any fear bursting within her and darted straight through the woods. The fiends slipped out from the trees as she ran—the white moths swarmed around her, more of them than before. And she knew why.

The goat-skulled fiend held the vines up for her so she could easily slip inside. "Hello, and thank you," Sadie said.

The fiend bowed its head, motioning her toward the entrance to River. As soon as she stepped to the edge of the opening, the trees whispered, folding together, creating a barrier once more. The fiends were no longer with her, and she couldn't see even a sliver of an opening this time.

But Sadie didn't hesitate before rushing down the steps. She glanced at the symbols, the engraving of the eye reminding her of what Kalina had said about Sadie's marking.

River stood, waiting for her, lifeless. As she skirted around him and reached to touch him, she wondered if he could hear in this state or if he was dead to the world.

His skin was cool to the touch—then it warmed as he took his first breath, his chest heaving as his gaze met hers. "I want you here, *badly*, even though I shouldn't," River said, handing her the dagger. "Keep it away from me."

"Whatever has us marked is making you want to do this to me."

He nodded, cupping her cheek before trailing his fingers down the crook of her neck. "You're getting *very* hot. I don't know everything, but I know why the animals became what they did. Are you certain you want to uncover the wickedness behind it?"

"No more vagueness. I want to know the truth." She grasped the front of his shirt.

"I haven't told you because I wanted you safe from this, and if you uncovered it, then it would've been on your own, not by my selfish words of wanting you here." He bit his lip. "Do you still want to know the truth? There is no turning back once it's done."

"Yes."

A look of concern crossed his face, yet he led her to the room with the glass boxes. She studied one of the mirrors on the wall, her image reflecting as it had in the bathroom the other night with the same woman from before. Only, instead of a black gown, she wore a crimson one with a high collar and buttons lining the front.

"Who is she?" Sadie asked.

"Come," River said, lifting a lid on one of the glass boxes, then motioned her inside.

Sadie shifted beside him, peering into the box. A black silk pillow rested inside, along with a matching black cushion to lay on. "You want me to go in there?" She wrinkled her nose. "Why can't you just tell me?"

"I can, but you won't understand unless you see it." He gestured at the box once more. "Go in and close your eyes. If you don't do it soon, you may wake again."

Sadie didn't know how much time she had left, so she would take the chance. Heart pounding, she stepped into the glass and lay back on the silk pillow. It was soft, so soft, but she forgot about the feel of it when River started to close the lid.

"Wait!" she shouted, pushing up. "What are you doing?"

"You're safer from me behind the glass. I love you, my sweet nightmare," he said softly. "I'm not even entirely certain this will work as it once did. Just focus on wanting to know the truth."

The lid fell shut, and she watched him leave her. An anxious feeling stirred within her as she stared at the obsidian ceiling through the glass. Dropping the dagger, she pressed her hands against the lid, then pushed—it didn't budge. She was sealed inside. Had she been that foolish? To trust so easily, to not even be forced inside a mysterious box.

"River! Let me out!" Sadie screamed, her fists pounding against the glass, and she expected it to shatter, *wanted* it to shatter as pure anger, so unlike her, stormed through her. Yet not a single marred line fractured it.

But then a blue light flickered on top of the glass, giving shape to something—two symbols that looked like eyes. And as the eyes closed, exhaustion swept over her, her arms falling limply to her sides, her lids closing. All she could do was think of River's last words, focusing on learning the truth.

Like a crack of lightning, the first vision struck.

16

"Vicious dreams or sweet nightmares ... which do you prefer?"

A world of black spun around Sadie as she fell through emptiness, hollowness, rage, melancholy, revenge, fear, love. She didn't think she would ever stop falling as she traveled through the darkness. But then a spark of light bloomed, and a woman with curly brown hair sat below her. Before she could make out any other features, Sadie crashed on top of her, or better yet, *inside* of her. Heather… Sadie could *feel* her, see into the young woman's mind as if she were flipping through a book at warp speed—*all* of Heather's memories.

An abusive childhood, running away with Blake to live in the woods after they suffered a miscarriage. A boy who had come from a home just as broken as hers.

Heather set her book beside her in the warm sun, watching as the man she loved chopped wood.

There hadn't been enough money for Blake to buy her an engagement ring, but he was her husband in every way that mattered. After growing up the way she had, she hoped they could still have a baby so she could prove that they were nothing like their parents while giving their child all the love in the world. As she pressed a hand to her stomach, looking at Blake now—possibly one day.

"What do you want for dinner?" Heather called. "My sister can't make it tonight, so it's just us."

He didn't answer, nor did he lift his head—he just continued to strike the wood into smaller pieces. Grunting louder with each chop.

Frowning, Heather stood and walked toward him. "Blake, did you hear me?"

Silence crawled through the air, the breeze stilling, the insects' songs halting, leaving only the echo of Blake's axe slamming into the tree stump. Harder and harder. No longer chopping wood. He finally glanced up at her with clenched teeth, his knuckles turning white as he gripped the axe.

An expression rested on his face that Heather had never seen, rage for her swirling in his gaze. Heather hesitated, taking a step back, remembering her childhood, knowing how to run and hide when necessary. But Blake was faster—he lunged forward, swinging his axe, the blade cutting clean through Heather's swan-like neck. The pain radiated only for a moment, but Sadie felt it all. And somehow, she was still there, watching as Blake dropped his axe and fished out a pocket knife from his jeans. He flipped the blade open, his eyes inhuman, lifeless, while he drew a bloody smile across his throat. Thick crimson spilled down his chest from the wound as he collapsed on the ground beside Heather, his body still.

This was the couple who'd lived here, who'd died outside the cabin… A cabin that Sadie could now see perfectly—only the garden was blossoming, the home freshly painted.

And then Sadie was ripped away from the two dead lovers, drifting back into the swirling darkness, falling and falling, until another young woman came into view. Long blonde curls, her shirt sleeveless and tucked into plaid shorts. Sadie almost caught more of her features until she dropped inside the stranger's body.

The woman's memories barreled into Sadie. Her name was Kathy and she had a perfect life growing up, the ideal family, but she'd always wanted out of the small town. After meeting her fiancé, Keith, they had a pact to one day leave, pursue her dream to act in movie pictures while he did special effects make-up. When she couldn't carry their baby to term, they decided to finally leave. They were camping out in the woods one last time before driving to California, to discover what new adventures awaited them.

Kathy placed another marshmallow on the end of her stick and held it over the fire. She'd already eaten several s'mores, but she couldn't deny fixing an endless amount. In Hollywood, one had to watch their weight, but she wasn't worried about that at the moment. She could still feel the loss of her baby inside her, yet she placed the memory in the little box at the back of her mind for now.

Glancing up at Keith, Kathy smiled as he cleaned his rifle, his chestnut hair hanging in his face. "Do you want me to make you another s'more before you go hunting?" she asked.

Keith didn't answer, only continued to rub at his gun with the cloth, his movements rough. His hand picked up speed, running up and down it harder and harder. The woods grew silent, just as they had with Heather and Blake, same as they'd been with Sadie. Sadie held her breath, knowing this was the second couple who had died in these woods and what would happen to them soon enough.

"Earth to Keith, can you hear me?" Kathy laughed, nudging his leg with her bare foot.

He looked up then, his stare blank yet heavy with intent.

Kathy's laugh cut off, a chill crawling up her spine, and she drew the stick away from the fire. "Stop staring at me like that. You're scaring me."

Keith raised his gun, and just as Kathy turned to dodge out of the way, a bullet rang through the air, piercing her skull. Her body collapsed, and she lay twitching for a few moments before becoming still.

Sadie blinked away the fading pain and watched in horror as Keith propped the rifle against the ground. He placed his mouth over the rifle, then pulled the trigger. She screamed, her sounds deafening to herself. But then she was falling once more into the sweeping world of darkness…

Again and again, Sadie collided with another body, where the young woman was murdered by the man she loved. He would then turn the weapon on himself or use another. In every occurrence, silence echoed, accompanying the tragedies, and always in the woods somewhere. With each spell into the darkened hellish pit, Sadie ventured farther back through time—decades, centuries. The women had been strangled, shot, stabbed through the chest, slit throats, so many deaths. As for the men, in every occurrence, they'd looked as though they were possessed, their eyes hollow.

This time when Sadie was dispersed into the darkness, a sparking sensation fluttered around her, *inside* her, and her gaze pinned to a woman wearing what looked to be a black dress with a collar from centuries ago, her obsidian hair braided down her back. Recognition set in—she knew that face—it was the woman who had been inside the mirror that had reflected back at Sadie.

As Sadie entered the woman's body, she gasped, struggling to find air. So much pain and darkness pierced through her like a sharp blade that Sadie screamed, not knowing if she would ever stop.

The woman's name was Harlow, and she was the youngest in her family. Her mother had suffered numerous miscarriages due to Harlow's father's beatings before eventually dying from infected lashings he'd given her. Out of her three oldest siblings who'd made it to term, Harlow's two older brothers had passed away because of her father's abuse—he'd made them continue to work the fields when ill. That left only Harlow and her older sister with their father.

Their father was a witch, and Harlow and Ada had inherited his abilities. If the town discovered it and accused them of being witches, death would soon follow. Witchcraft meant one consorted with the devil, even though that was false.

Sadie had never experienced such darkness firsthand.

Her skin crawled as the memories shot through her. But Harlow hadn't always been that way. Sadie caught glimpses of special moments—Harlow dancing at night in the woods beneath the full moon, even though she knew it was forbidden. A young man named Jasper discovered her there, a man who was a witch like her, except from a coven. He was a painter, and she was a storyteller, the perfect match. Harlow's father forbade her from seeing him and wouldn't allow marriage because he was a witch. She was to be betrothed to a nonwitch, the way her sister Ada was with Eben. She'd known the threat, but she hadn't cared.

The rage within Harlow grew, and she'd snuck into the night to see Jasper anyway, yet her father had found them. As he tied a noose around Jasper's neck, Harlow stabbed him in the throat, killing her father.

Sadie took deep breaths because that wasn't all. What came after was far worse. Jasper's coven discovered what Harlow's father had almost done to him, and even though he was dead, they chose to take it out on her.

After lashings and placing her head beneath water numerous times, they went to burn her alive when Jasper took out the entire coven by using magic. Harlow knew that soon enough her village would do the same if they ever discovered what they were. That fear for her loved ones twisted into something angry, deadly.

They resided in the space below ground where Jasper's coven would meet, and made it into their home. Together they started plucking animals from the wild, turning them into moths to protect them, using their eyes and ears to warn them. But that wasn't enough to stop Harlow's fear. The villagers of Salem came next, and so did those accused of witchery because of it. Harlow ripped their essence away, feeding off it, and created their protectors, made of animal and human bone. The portion that was unnecessary of the essence was hidden away in a room below ground, altering into something savage.

The fiends … the moths … Sadie had seen them.

Ada and Eben had begged her to stop this madness, which only made her fear twist more.

None of that was what made Sadie give pause, though...

Now, as Sadie rested inside Harlow, the young woman spun in circles out in the woods beside her favorite tree, staring up at the clouds, waiting for night to fall so she could continue the same beneath the stars and moon while coming up with a new tale to write in her journal.

The crunch of leaves sounded, and Harlow smiled, her spinning coming to a halt, but she didn't turn around. Jasper's chest pressed to her back, his hands drifting up her thighs. "Ah, there's my sweet nightmare," he purred in her ear.

"What havoc do you have in mind today?" Harlow asked, placing her palm over her growing stomach. The bump was already showing beneath her clothing, but soon her dresses wouldn't conceal it.

Jasper slowly spun Harlow around, backing her up against the nearest tree. He wrapped one of her legs around his waist, his warm body sliding against hers. This man was beautiful, otherworldly. His deep red hair hung just past his shoulders, his green eyes meeting hers. Powerful energy exuded from him in the way he moved, his assertive stare. She always found herself drawn to him, wanting to be ensnared by his hungry gaze.

Harlow's memories of Jasper were both seductive and sweet, and his heart had darkened, the way hers had—but never toward one another, or Ada and Eben, nor would her child ever have to suffer. Above them, the ivory moths swarmed in circles, their beautiful wings fluttering against the wind.

"What's bothering you?" Jasper asked, pushing a lock of hair behind her ear.

"Ada won't stop interfering."

Jasper lifted Harlow, both her legs now circling his hips, and she moaned. "You've threatened them already."

Even though remorse filled Harlow for a moment, her sister and Eben had forced her hand to use the threat.

"Perhaps. For now, show me your wickedness." Harlow ground herself against Jasper, needing him to fill her and spill his seed inside her. A lovely villainous grin spread across his face as he unfastened his pants.

Out of the corner of her eye, Harlow caught movement, her gaze settling on a blonde braid. Ada stood farther away behind a tree, holding up her bleeding hand, chanting words, strange words that echoed inside Harlow's mind.

Jasper growled, releasing Harlow to her feet as he clutched his head. Harlow stumbled as the world grew quiet. The moths above fell to the dirt like rain, their bodies still. In Harlow and Jasper's lair below ground, she could feel her fiends doing the same, the trapped spirits sinking to the earth too.

Seething, Harlow attempted to spell her sister to stop, but the sound wouldn't leave her lips. Heart beating wildly, she found Jasper no longer holding his head, only staring at her with hollow eyes she'd never seen before.

Jasper took a blade from his boot, inching toward Harlow as she stumbled back. Screams came from her sister, but before Harlow could turn back to Ada, Jasper thrust the blade into her heart, then tore the knife up her chest. Flames of pain licked through her, yet only a barely audible wheeze escaped her.

He ripped the blade out, his gaze remaining hollow. She gripped her chest as she wilted to the ground and coughed, choking on her blood as two hands lifted her. When Harlow met her sister's dark irises, she knew she should have killed her instead of protected her.

Sadie stared out through Harlow's dead eyes, watching as Ada chanted to Jasper. But she couldn't tell if she was instructing him to press the blade to his throat or if he was doing it of his own accord. The blade sliced perfectly across, blood pouring down his throat as he slumped to the dirt.

Drawing in a gasping breath, Sadie's eyes flew open, her gaze meeting glass. She was still inside the box. Her chest heaved, her body shaking as she took in the memories she'd just witnessed. Tears stung her eyes, and she banged against the glass with everything she had—she would make it shatter this time.

River rushed into the room toward her. He pulled back the lid and took her into his arms.

"Why did you show me that?" she screeched, beating at his chest.

"I tried," he whispered, holding her closer as he brought them to the floor. "Part of me tried harder than the other, but I told you there would be no going back."

Sadie curled in on herself and scooted away, her back

hitting the crystal—not glass—box. "He killed her every single time! *You* killed her every single time!"

"You're warm," he said, rubbing his fingers across his jaw.

"You called her my sweet nightmare. Like you call me," she breathed.

River's throat bobbed. "Even warmer."

"And she," Sadie stuttered. "Harlow. Called you her vicious dream. *I* called you my vicious dream. Not that day but so many others." The nicknames between them had been used in every life.

"You're so very close," he rasped.

Sadie's past lives merged into her mind, time becoming meaningless. "I wasn't only Harlow, though—I was *all* of them. I was both women who died in these woods. I know who the images are of in the mirror. I remember *everything*." Her fists tightened as she clenched her jaw. "We were … witches in our first life. Monstrous in our right. We were the *cause* of the witch trials in Salem!" The thought churned her stomach, yet that wicked part of her, that selfish branded part of her heart, had no regret.

"Hot. Right on the mark."

Harlow's, *Sadie's*, hand had touched her belly. "I-I had a child growing inside of me. *Your* child. Ada did something. Made you do it," she spat.

His jaw tightened as he nodded. "We were reckless, needed to be put in our place."

All of her lives since then would've agreed with him, but that dark part of her wanted to go back in time and shred her sister into pieces. Even after the suffering Harlow had caused, she had trusted Ada.

"What made it different this time?" Sadie whispered, her heart thundering in her chest. "Why didn't you kill me? What goes on inside your head?"

River sighed, leaning on the crystal box that belonged to him. "In the previous lives, when the silence comes, everything inside of me shuts down, and the only thing left in me is the urge to see that you're dead. It's not me wanting to do it—it's whatever lingering spell Ada cast upon us. I don't know what was different this time unless the spell is wearing off, or maybe it was because you weren't there yet, and I had time. There was this drive for me to take you to the woods when you got home, and something inside me somehow knew I would hurt you there. All I wanted was silence, so I wrote you the letter, then hung myself to protect you. I thought it would save you. But Ada's spell still clutched my essence in the ashes, which is why, when you spread them, I got trapped in these woods with everything we created together."

"The moths, the fiends…" Sadie started. "We did that together. The part of the fiends' essences that we couldn't use, we trapped down here until they became something far more deadly than the two of us had ever been." Inside her head, it was as though multiple personalities were molding together, becoming one.

"That's the thing," River said softly. "They are no longer down here. They're trapped in the woods."

17

"Dark hearts make beautiful lovers."

"You commanded the malevolent spirits to be out in the woods?" Sadie hissed, pushing up from the floor, her fingers biting into the edge of the crystal box to keep herself from trembling.

River shook his head. "No, I didn't."

Hidden within all of Sadie's memories, the spells she'd used to cast lingered, and it felt as if she were brushing off layers of dust to bring them closer to the surface. Until it was as though they'd never been locked away at all.

Sadie closed the crystal box's lid, running her palm across the symbols, silently chanting to locate the spirits. She and River would use these beds to perform chants, rituals, see things from the past, drink the rage growing inside the malevolent spirits behind their closed door. And then they would lap up their bloody tears, tasting every bitter drop of them to keep her from fear.

"My location spell isn't working." Sadie whirled to face River.

"My spells and magic don't work either. It has something to do with what Ada did to us."

Ada… Sadie clenched her fists, her nails pressing in so hard she thought she would bleed. She then fled the room, remembering every inch of this underground place, her *home*, every door, every crevice.

Her heart pounded as she unbolted the door and peered inside at nothing but a stone room filled with iron chains and symbols to bind the spirits. That was the only way to keep them here, to prevent them from massacring everyone inside the village at one time. The chains that once held them were empty, as if they'd never been there. She lifted a cuff, finding it locked and unbroken.

"I told you they aren't here," River said, kneeling beside her.

Letting the chain slip from her fingertips with a heavy clang, she turned to face River. "You said they're in the woods, but where? We have to get them back in here. We may have been monstrous, but they are even more so."

"During the day they aren't shadows like the rest of us. They are quiet inside the trees, even when darkness rolls in. But at midnight, they breathe, they whisper, yet they seem to be bound inside. As for how the trees are moving, I don't think it's them doing it."

Sadie thought about how their whispers had been getting louder, raspy low screams. As for the fiends, they hadn't come down with Sadie any of the other times because they'd been protecting her and River, keeping watch over the part of themselves that was evil.

In the past, the fiends always had minds of their own, yet they followed and listened to Jasper and Harlow as if they were their king and queen. Sadie thought about how the creatures had bowed their heads to her when she would come at night—even without her old face, they still knew who she was, who River was. But if the spirits somehow escaped their prisons, they wouldn't listen. That was why she never would've unleashed them, and if they did find a way out, she was unable to use a spell to stop them.

Yet she tried again anyway. Sadie clasped her hands together, attempting to dip into a deeper spell, pull any energy she could as she chanted the words to bring them back here.

"I don't know what to do," she whispered, her voice shaking. "Do we just hope for the best? That they remain hidden in there?" Sighing heavily, she ran her fingers over the cocoon symbols along the walls and tried to get them to light up the way the crystal box had when she'd been inside. But she hadn't used her magic to see into her past—it must've been remnants of her old spells.

"I've tried to break Ada's spell, reverse it, do anything I can think of. But I can't ignite a lick of magic," River said.

"Is this what she wanted?" Sadie snapped. "This macabre never-ending cycle of you taking my life, then your own. What would be the point of doing this? Why didn't she just leave us dead like she—like she—" She couldn't finish the rest as a choked sob came out of her. "Our baby…"

River wrapped his arms around her, pulling her close, and rested his chin atop her head. "I know you want to tear her apart, break the world into a thousand pieces to go back in time so you can do so, but you know why she did it. I know why."

"That doesn't make me any less angry. In all our lives since then, except for this one, I got pregnant, then had a miscarriage…" She trailed off as a horrified thought crossed her mind. "That's our child, isn't it? Every *time*. And it has something to do with Ada's spell, doesn't it?"

River took in a sharp breath. "I believed it was a hex put on us, and when our baby died, it would mean one would never be born. Your theory is making more sense, though." His throat bobbed, and he drew Sadie up from the stone floor, bringing her out of the room. "You've been here much longer than the last few times, and I don't know how much time you have left before you wake."

Tears pricked her eyes, thinking of her child dying over and over again. An innocent… But the lives she'd taken had been innocent too. Was this her punishment for eternity? "I want to stay here with you and never leave. I don't want to wake up." She folded her arms around him and murmured against his shoulder. "I don't care if you continue to have the urge to slit my throat."

"You've always been a brave one, my sweet nightmare."

"Not always." Sadie remembered back in Salem when she didn't stand up to her father until there was no other option. She should've tried sooner, even though she'd only been a child when he'd hurt her brothers and mother, yet maybe she could've saved them. If she'd killed her father sooner, then perhaps she wouldn't have turned into what she'd become.

River pushed a lock of hair behind her ear. "I believe

if I don't hurt you, it could possibly break the spell if you continue to live your life. I can't end my life here either—I've tried."

Sadie jerked her head up and cupped his face, that anger from Harlow building inside her. "Don't try that again. We'll figure out a way to break the hex."

"We just can't be reckless," he relented.

Sadie thought about each life after Salem—Blake and Heather, Keith and Kathy… Some of the lives were better than others. But as terrible as some of her parents were, none were as awful as her first father. He was tainted, and her mother hadn't been a witch, yet that was what he'd wanted, to have power over her. And that was why he wouldn't allow Harlow to marry Jasper because he'd wanted all his children, the two that remained, to have power over their spouses in the way he'd had. The bastard.

After killing her father and the deaths of the coven, she should've run away with Jasper, but she'd chosen a more destructive path, not knowing if a new village would be worse than hers. A pit formed in her stomach, growing larger—she'd been the root cause of the Salem Witch Trials… A history she'd learned about in school and had even vacationed with River in the very same town. She'd been infatuated with the town while there, and too many conflicting emotions were knotting together inside of her.

Before she could think any more on the matter, a piercing shriek came from somewhere above ground, rattling the walls. A horrific sound like she'd never heard in this life, but one she knew incredibly well from her first, familiar, so achingly familiar, haunting and beautiful. It was a sound that was created from the essence of their victims. Grotesque. Cruel. Perfect. She'd been a true witch, not gracious and charming, but dark and *dangerous.*

Her hand clasped her mouth. "They aren't whispering screams now. They're screeching, escaping."

"Something doesn't feel right," River said, shutting his eyes, concentrating.

If she could use her chants, she would feed off their screams and their tears as she used to, then find a way to cast a spell to attempt to go back in time to Salem. But a horrified thought crossed her mind. Something she did care very much about. "The fiends! We need to get them down here!"

She lunged for the stairs, and River clasped her by the wrist, tugging her back. "Don't be reckless, my sweet nightmare."

"Then we'll be reckless together," she said. "As always."

A wicked smile crossed his pretty mouth, and he gave in to her temptation. They ascended the stairs in a mad rush, and Sadie now recognized the wards along the walls. Protection spells to keep anyone from above out. Long ago, she'd etched them in alongside River, using their blood and various brews to bind the wards. The only way another could enter was if they spoke the secret words. Her stomach sank as realization struck her. Unlike the symbols on the crystal box, these didn't last and continued to need to be strengthened … with spells. That she could no longer wield…

As they exited from below ground, the trees remained bound together. Shrieks and pounding reverberated inside them. Jagged cracks formed up their trunks, on the brink of splitting open. The moths swarmed above as

Sadie screamed for them and the fiends to *hide.*

River grasped her hand, squeezed it while he started to chant for the trees to part, for the malevolent spirits to cease, but neither did, only the sounds of cracking and screeching.

If the spirits escaped and anyone locked gazes with their blood-filled eyes, their bodies would crack. Maybe that was what she should let happen to herself—she deserved it. But no, she needed to find a way to break this, to save the others. The spirits were complete darkness, darker—so much darker—than the blackened spot marked on her aura.

A silver form with gnarled limbs and a wispy body shot through the air. She watched with a lowered gaze, unable to do anything as the moths fell around her like snow, then ash when their bodies cracked and turned silver against the ground, their beady dark eyes now blood red.

With a bloodcurdling shriek, the spirit stormed away. Sadie lifted two dead moths, and her hands shook. Screaming tore through the woods, shaking the trees as Sadie sobbed and rested the moths back on the ground.

"We're leaving for now. Don't argue." River scooped Sadie up while she writhed, hissing at him to let her down as he fled down the steps, his grip firm on her. Screeching echoed from above, yet the wards continued to hold them back for now.

"What if they slaughter the fiends?" she whispered as he lowered her to her feet in the main room. "Maybe we shouldn't try to break the spell. Maybe you should just kill me now. Wouldn't the cycle start over?"

"That's a good question. But one I'm not willing to

risk. I'm not going to have you and our child suffer again and again."

Her shoulders sagged. That was true… If the cycle started over, if she got pregnant, she knew with everything in her that she would lose their child. A child who had done nothing wrong and needed this spell broken more than either of them. A child who deserved to live and not be punished by the deeds of their parents.

River's jaw tightened as he peered toward the stairs, then at one of the doors. "Come this way. I want to show you something."

She nodded, and he grabbed her hand, leading her to the door—their bedroom.

Inside, it looked as it had before, with the ornate wooden bed in the center of the room against the wall, a large dresser standing on four legs, and a writing desk in one corner, a rocking chair in the other. Her heart thrummed harder. The chair Jasper had made for Harlow to rock their baby in after he or she was born.

One of the doors led to their main bathing chamber and the other to the spell room. River opened the door to the spell room, and she stepped inside. In the center, an empty cauldron rested with cracked blood.

"Are you frightened of me?" River asked.

"Of you thrusting a blade into my heart?" Her gaze met his. "It's in the other room, so it would take you a while to get to it." She pressed her hand to his cheek and sighed. "That's the least of my worries at the moment. But no, I'm not. I'm prepared this time. I know the look you get in your eyes, and you don't have that hollow stare now."

He leaned into her touch as he gazed at the cauldron.

"How does it make you feel having this in our room now?"

Sadie studied River, seeing the boy she'd met in Salem, even though his face wasn't the same any longer. Jasper had been sweet, like River, yet they both always had that edge. She then remembered how the blood inside the cauldron would churn once poured in, the metallic smell wafting in the air. The blood had been the tears they'd taken from the malevolent spirits, tears they would drink when needed. The fiends had no eyes, so they would collect the tears from the spirits without being harmed. Although they could be touched by them since they'd once been a part of them, the spirits couldn't touch anyone else, only kill with their eyes locking with another. The room with the hearts had been those from the animals. They'd taken them before changing them into moths. And their hearts had continued to beat and bleed within the room to ensure they would live as long as Harlow and River did. Unless a spirit got to them. Without opening the door to that room, she knew the hearts would be shriveled, no longer dripping blood.

As she stared at the cauldron now, she thought about his question, how it made her feel.

"I don't know. I don't know if I regret the things we did or if I just wish things could've been different. Part of it feels like an old black-and-white film, whereas this life feels more real. And would I do anything of that nature now? I would like to say no. If that's regret, then maybe I do have a bit of it." She met his warm gray eyes. "But what I do regret is threatening Ada and Eben because, without the hex, our child would've been safe."

He drew her to his chest, entangling his fingers in her

hair. "The past is a part of us, a thing that never truly dies."

"It circles us the way birds search for prey."

18

"We are the wicked, we are the monsters, and together we own the night."

Sadie continued to stare at the empty cauldron in the center of the room, both haunted by what she'd done and furious not only at Ada but her father and Jasper's coven. Ada was gone, and yet her spell lived on. Sadie knew she shouldn't continue to place blame, but she remembered the lashes from her father against her back, the same from Jasper's coven with how they punished her before preparing to burn her. How her father had tightened the noose around Jasper's throat until he was blue in the face, driving so much fear in her that she couldn't breathe, could only do one single thing. Why couldn't everyone have just let them be? Why hadn't she noticed Ada in the woods before it was too late?

And really, Sadie had never gotten to mourn the loss of her child or any of the other pregnancies over the centuries in this body. Because she hadn't known. And what if she had gotten pregnant in this life? Some losses could be mistaken for heavy cycles. She couldn't think about that aspect, otherwise she would fracture and break apart. However, where was her child now? Hidden somewhere in these woods too? Or somewhere else, waiting to be born? Darkness churned within her, her nostrils flaring, and maybe it was better at the moment that she couldn't chant a spell until she calmed herself. But all she could focus on was the past…

Harlow hissed as Ada applied an herbal remedy over the lashings she'd received from her father.

"You knew Papa would say no," Ada said softly, pressing another strip to Harlow's back. "You should have kept Jasper hidden from him. I warned you to."

"I want a proper betrothal. Not to marry another and secretly meet with Jasper when my husband is away or busy with a task. I don't want to tumble another man and not know whose child it is I'm carrying," Harlow whispered. "I was planning to lie about what Jasper was, but Papa knew instantly."

"You knew as well. One witch can always spot another. Even if they don't realize it at first—they eventually will."

"Hand me my dress." Harlow pushed up, wincing at the pain. Yet it wasn't as piercing now that the remedy had been applied.

"Can't you at least wait a night?" Ada asked, handing her a simple black dress.

Harlow shook her head. "No. I should slip nightshade in his tea."

"Papa would easily know, then he would force you to drink it." Ada placed her hand gently on Harlow's arm after she pulled the

dress over her head. "I'll keep him distracted and tell him you retired for the evening. He should be asleep soon, anyway. But please be careful."

"Thank you," Harlow murmured. "You have a good heart like Mama."

"As do you. But you also have the feisty side Mama had to keep hidden from Papa." Ada smiled. Harlow remembered how when her father was out tending the crops, her mother would become livelier, take a break from chores and remove her shoes, then bring the sisters out to the back of the house where she would dance with them, spin macabre tales that made Harlow giddy and starved for more. Would take them into the woods and have them carve a word in a tree to show how they felt that day, or even help keep Harlow's stories hidden away from her father.

Harlow bid her sister goodbye and snuck out the window into the dying day. The sun was sinking into darkness, and she hurried past a few neighboring cottages and toward the woods.

As she went deeper into the foliage, she passed trees that still had the carved words from her, Ada, and their mother. Her chest tightened, but she held back the tears for her, always missing her, even years later.

Harlow slowed to a stop near the tree where she'd engraved her and Jasper's names. She sat on one of the large rocks and waited, unable to dance like she normally did when the moon came about. Jasper's boots sounded, and she stood to face him, smiling even though her back was in pain.

He lifted her and backed her into a tree, as he always did, as she usually loved, but a painful gasp escaped her lips.

"What's wrong?" he asked, taking her away from the bark and righting her on her feet.

Harlow shook her head, not looking into his worried, emerald green eyes. "Nothing."

"It's something."

"Papa lashed my back today."

"He what?*" Jasper's fists tightened, and his face grew red with anger—rage like she'd never seen on him before. Not even when her father denied them marriage had he shown it.*

"Ada used a healing ointment. I'll be fine in a few days."

He lifted her chin. "Can I see? I'll take the pain away sooner."

Cheeks pinkened, she turned to face away from him, embarrassed that he would have to see her back this way, see how she could never stand up to her father.

With delicate fingers, he unfastened the back of her dress, button by button, and pulled the fabric down to her waist.

He sucked in a sharp breath. "I'll kill him for this. I'll use the coven's darker spells."

Her father may not have belonged to a coven, but he had dark spells of his own, ones that could rival any other witch.

"It's all right."

"I'm going to have to touch the wounds." His digits pressed to the crook of her neck gently, sending a new warmer sensation coursing through her.

Squeezing her eyes shut, she nodded and held back a wince as he trailed his fingers down each gash, chanting healing words quietly.

The ache dissipated, and Harlow felt as if she could breathe again, her lungs loosening. "Thank you." She leaned back against his chest and grabbed his hands, wrapping them around her waist. "We can talk later. I want you to make me forget about today, so I only think about your touch."

"I can do that, my sweet nightmare. I can make you feel good, wondrous," he purred in her ear.

Harlow arched into him as he kissed her throat, flicked his exquisite tongue just below her ear, and his warm hands glided up her skin, leaving heated flames behind when he cupped her breasts.

She lifted the skirt of her dress, drawing it up farther for him. One of his hands skimmed back down, dipping between her thighs to cup her mound.

He groaned to find she had no undergarments beneath her dress, but they would've only gotten in the way. His fingers deliciously moved against her, circling, stroking, before two digits slipped into her heat, making her moan.

Then Jasper's hands and body were off her, a deep grunt tearing from his throat.

Harlow whirled around to find her father's tall and wide form behind Jasper, a rope around his neck.

"Stop, Papa!" she shouted.

"Put your clothing back on, whore," her father seethed.

Harlow slid her hands into the sleeves of her dress, pulling the fabric up, but left the rest undone. "Please, don't hurt him," she begged. "I promise to never see him again." If that was what it took to save his life—she would do it, would do anything. And as much as it would hurt, she would let her father betroth her to anyone else.

"No," her father spat. "He dies tonight."

Jasper's face was turning red and blue beneath the moonlight. Her father chanted words so that Jasper couldn't speak any spells.

Harlow studied the dagger at her father's hip, and she needed to risk it or her beloved would die. She darted forward, shoving them back, but not enough to topple them to the ground, yet just enough for her to grab the blade. The rope slackened, allowing Jasper to elbow her father in the ribs. A groan came from her father, and she hurled herself forward again, slamming the knife into his throat harder than she would've brought an axe down across a log of wood.

Blood poured from his throat as he gurgled, attempting to chant, but Jasper was speaking before he could, her father's mouth appearing sewn shut with string.

Her father's movements ceased, his body still, and she couldn't bring herself to cry, not in relief, not in grief, not in anger. Nothing as her gaze fell on the man who had been a monster in her home since before she was even born.

She ran to Jasper, crushing herself into him. "I'm so sorry. This is all my fault."

"No. It's mine," he rasped, his arms folded around her. "I put you in danger and should've heard him approaching."

And then another voice rang through the woods. "Harlow! Harlow!"

She and Jasper spun around to find Ada running toward them in her nightgown. "Father isn't in the house."

"He's here," Harlow said. "I killed him. He tried to murder Jasper."

Her sister's eyes widened as they fell upon their father, blood pooling from his wound. "This is good. This is bad. But more good than bad. We need to bury him, and then we'll tell the town he left us and never returned." She covered her mouth. "Let me get us shovels."

Harlow was too numb to offer to go with her, and she knew her father wouldn't come back to life, but she wanted to remain watching him, to make sure death stayed with him.

Jasper held her close, and she peered up at his welted neck. "You're hurt!"

"I'm fine," he said, his voice gruff. "I'll talk to my parents, and then they will get the coven to help you and Ada."

"I'm sorry," she whispered once more against his chest, her palm over his rapid heartbeat.

Only, his coven hadn't brought help once they found out it was her father who had wounded Jasper—they took her prisoner. Jasper then discovered a way to slaughter them with dark chants. From him, she learned the spells of his coven followed by the ones in her father's spell book that Ada had uncovered and kept.

Sadie focused on the empty cauldron, knowing that the malevolent spirits were created because of her and Jasper, but mostly her… Not only would she and River find a way to break this spell, but they would find a way to free the spirits from these woods, to reunite them with the rest of their essence that was within the fiends. Maybe then the rage would lessen, the way that Sadie's side was lessening Harlow's.

She stared up at River, who was chewing on his thumbnail. "I think I know why I love horror films and stories so much now. I've always loved a good macabre tale, just as you did with painting."

The lost expression left River's face, his lips tilting up at the edges as he gave her a sly look. "We were both always a bit secretly morbid throughout our other lives. My sculptures, my paintings—it was always buried memories. Even with your collection of moths and skulls on the walls."

"Maybe that was why we both got into moods while working. We couldn't figure out where the creativity was coming from, and sometimes trying to piece my words or your paints together only created havoc. Yet you were better at piecing yours together. My manuscripts have always needed stitching."

"Your stories have always been enticing. I miss the days in Salem when we would sit in the woods, and you would tell me one each night."

"And then you would ravish me senseless?" Sadie smiled. She glanced at the cauldron once more, wishing she could add bloody tears of her own to bring about a spell. "What do you think our child would have been like if Ada hadn't ever come?"

"Beautiful. Handsome. A bit of both?" He chuckled softly. "The one question that I wonder is if he or she would've turned out like us. But never would we have denied them being with the one they loved. Then there is the thought that maybe if the child was born, we might have changed."

"You think so? Even with me?" Sadie asked, recalling her fear, fear that Jasper would be hurt. "You don't think my fear would've grown fiercer to protect our child?"

"I would like to think that we would've overcome the fear. That maybe we could've stopped making families hurt the way we had been." He studied Sadie, his hand enfolding hers. "If I try to hurt you before you wake, run to the other room, lock the door and take the blade from the crystal box."

Sadie squeezed his hand. "I promise."

"And I promise I will try my hardest not to harm you, to find a way to help not only you, but our child."

Sadie scooted closer and rested her head on River's warm shoulder, breathing in his comforting scent. "How much longer do you think I have here until I wake up?"

"Now that you've uncovered who you are, maybe the veil gives us more time together, or maybe it's with each visit you make. But I don't know the true answer."

"It was quite a good guess." Sadie smiled, closing her eyes and listening to their breathing. It was a soothing sound. The spirits no longer roared above them, and she prayed the fiends had remained hidden well.

Sadie thought of Ada, the sister she'd loved growing up, who had helped her bury their father's body. They'd always protected one another. A spell that was a true hex—only the hex should've died with Ada, unless her soul took it with her. Something wasn't right about this... In each life after Salem, no matter the family, no matter if they were loving or awful, she'd had a sister. Her sister was always in love with someone who had been Sadie's friend first....

Her stomach sank, tying into a string of endless knots. "If we were hexed and reborn a few years later, why would Ada allow that? Why wouldn't she have checked in on us in our new lives to see if we would become wicked again? In our second life, we remained in Salem. I don't recall ever seeing her or Eben, for that matter."

River nodded in agreement, stroking his chin. "You're on the same thinking path I am. Continue."

Sadie's brow furrowed as she fidgeted with the edge of her shirt. Ada had become better at magic than Harlow and Jasper with the help of their father's spell book. Ada's fiancé, Eben, hadn't been a witch, but he'd known their secret since they were children, when he would work the crops with Harlow and Ada. But he had always protected their secret, would help with ingredients for Ada's healing remedies.

She swallowed the lump in her throat. "What if this death hex wasn't only on us but also on Ada and Eben."

"You're almost there," River urged.

"The spell continued to bring us back, and sometime during my twenty-third year of life, you would murder me. Except for this one." Sadie's heart pounded, knowing she was on to something. "And I think ... I think the spell doesn't just give us a new life. It does the same to Ada and Eben. Only the original witch can break a death hex."

"And who would Ada and Eben be in this life?"

"Charlie and Skyler," she whispered.

19

"Drink their essence, and I will bring you pleasure."

Sadie balled her hands into fists, and her jaw tightened. She had to be right about Charlie and Skyler. It seemed too strange that in every life, she had only a sister and a close friend who was a male.

"I think you're right," River said. "It's the same theory I have. Things are too similar. You always have a best friend who ends up with your sister. It could be a coincidence, but I think not. Not with how you and I always end up together." It could be a coincidence, but Skyler always wore the same genuine smile, regardless of his face. And Charlie was always the overprotective sister who would do anything for her. Even place a hex upon her…

A thought crawled through Sadie's mind, nagging at her. "Do they know? Or are they unaware like we were?

Charlie hasn't ever shown one inkling that she has an interest in spells. And I know she's never been shopping at a place like Crow Moon—unless she's hiding it really well."

"I don't know." River rubbed a hand across his jaw, his mouth set in a tight line. "But if they do know, I'm not sure why they would've gotten close to you again in each life."

"Unless they were trying to keep a close eye on me—us. But why would they do this to themselves? Why would they keep dying somehow just to come to the next life, too?"

That didn't make sense. Once Ada placed the spell, then why wouldn't she have continued living her life with Eben? Why keep cutting their lives short? Ada never would've placed a hex on Harlow, Jasper, herself, and Eben. Something else had to have happened…

"I think Ada's spell somehow twisted into something she didn't intend," Sadie murmured. "I remember her holding my body in her arms after you killed me as if something else was supposed to have occurred, or maybe she was just grieving the sister she'd once known. Either way, I highly doubt she wanted to take the chance for us to come back to possibly wreak havoc once more."

"You're her sister, after all," River said. "Maybe she had only planned for me to kill myself, not you. And if it wasn't that, then perhaps she chose to do it to protect Eben in case you ever decided to harm him. Or it could be something else. While here in these woods, I've been mulling everything over, day after day. Perhaps Ada didn't want us to die and only for us to hurt. But her spell reeked of death magic."

Sadie could still smell that sickly spicy scent drifting around her while surrounded by that absolute silence. "If the spell was only to kill you, then Ada was a fool because if I had lived, I would've taken her life and not gone easy on her," Sadie said between gritted teeth. "Even though this hex makes it so we continue to find one another, it will never be a happily ever after. If you were to continue to kill me, and I knew in the next life we would find each other, then that would still be a happy ending to me. But her spell made us lose our child, for him or her to continue to die over and over again, without taking a single breath, without taking their first steps, speaking their first words, *anything*." She flexed and unflexed her hands as tears streamed down her cheeks. Rage and melancholy entwined in her thoughts.

River squeezed his eyes shut, pinching the bridge of his nose, reeling in his anger with apparent effort. "If Ada truly is Charlie, she will have to be the one to break the spell. And if she chooses not to—"

"I will make her choose to," Sadie seethed. "If Ada wanted our lives forfeited, she could've tried something temporarily until our child was born, then performed a death spell."

"First, you need to find out if they've known this entire time. And if they have, then we can discuss what our actions will be."

Sadie imagined herself chanting a spell that would crack open Ada's rib cage so she could easily tear out her heart. But if Charlie didn't know, if her memory was like Sadie's had been, then what…? This was Charlie—the sister she loved more in this life than any other. Their bond was always strong, no matter how different they were. But what if Charlie wasn't Ada? Yet it was the only thing that made sense. Unless Ada was out there and had somehow found a way to make herself immortal, continuing to torture them. "Once I wake, I'll call Charlie and invite her over."

"I know you don't want to hear this, but put yourself in her place. What would you have done if Ada had threatened you?" River asked.

"I would've made sure she was hurt," she murmured. Sadie was much different at that time, had used hurting others to heal.

Sadie crawled forward and pressed her fingers to a skull symbol etched on the wall. She closed her eyes, chanting the words, feeling the tinge of magic in the air, the burning smell of it. But like before, the chant didn't work, even though the magic still rested inside her. It had always been there, hidden, locked away. In each life, she'd still been a witch. She just hadn't known it.

Frustrated, she sat back, wiping her clammy palms against her pants. "Could you try one more time with me?"

"As many times as you wish." He clasped a hand with hers, and they placed their other palm against symbols on the wall, bowing their heads as they chanted together.

The earthy scent became stronger, but she could feel down to her marrow that it wasn't working. With a sigh, she let her arms fall back to her sides and peered at River. "How are you always able to control your anger better than me?"

"Oh, it's there, like a leech wanting to suck and suck until it pulls all the hate and rage out of me," he said, pushing up to stand. "A part of me wants to return to

Salem so we can continue doing what we did. Then there is this other part of me fighting against it. And those parts combined lived much longer than Jasper ever did. But right now, I can't allow myself to think about those things because all I can focus on in these woods at the moment is keeping myself from harming the one person I would never choose to. I don't know where our child is right now, but they are safe for the time being. However, you're not. And I don't want to lose control. All I can see is what I've done to you in every single life, and I loathe myself for it. Is there regret and shame for everything else? Some of it, yes. My coven? Fuck no. Could things have been different after I took out the coven? Yes. But they weren't, were they? We chose the path we did." River walked away from her and sat on the bed in the other room.

Sadie shoved up from the stone floor to go into their bedroom and sank down beside him on the fur blankets. "Why did you walk away?"

"Wouldn't you? I don't know how much longer I can control these urges, and I don't want you to pretend they don't exist. I don't want to risk you, my sweet nightmare."

Sadie grabbed the front of his shirt and drew him closer. "Stop. Stop being aggravating."

He arched a brow. "Aggravating?"

"I've already told you I know the signs, so just stop with that," she said. "Unless you truly don't want to be around me. Maybe I even conjured all this up because of my grief."

"You most certainly didn't conjure it up. And I always want to be around you, always want to hear your stories, want to touch you. Touch you in ways that make your lips part in pleasure, hear those lovely gasps and moans pour from you." He licked his lower lip as he trailed a finger across her cheek, to her jaw. "Do you feel this? Do I feel real?"

Sadie slowly nodded, a warmth spreading through her as he gently skated that perfect digit down her neck.

"What about this?" he purred, bringing his finger down her chest.

"Mmm-hmm." She bit her lip, holding back from begging him for more.

As though reading her mind, a smirk played on his lips as he skimmed it down her body to the hem of her shirt. She couldn't control herself from arching into him—it had been too long—*months*—since she'd been away from his touch. And she needed it, needed the distraction, needed *him*.

Sadie helped him lift her shirt over her head. His fingers skillfully undid the clasp of her bra, and she tossed it to the floor. River then glided his digits down her shoulder, to her clavicle, to the valley between her breasts. His lips drifted to the crook of her neck, his hand cupping her breast, his thumb stroking the tender spot. "And here."

"More," Sadie whispered. His hand came between her thighs, pressed to her center over her pants. She moaned.

"More?" he asked, his eyes hooded.

"I want you to make me feel good. I want to make you feel even better."

His hand slipped beneath the fabric of her pants and panties, his fingers brushing her sensitive flesh. Her heart pounded in anticipation as he rubbed her clit, dipping his digits inside of her heat.

Her breaths came out ragged as she pressed her forehead to his. "Are you still thinking about ending my life?"

"At this moment? No," he breathed. "I only desperately want to be inside you. I want to feel you grind against me. I want your heart beating in sync with mine, my sweet nightmare." And then he captured her mouth in a fierce kiss.

"I want you to take me like you did that second time in Salem when neither of us wanted to think."

An impish smile played across his lips. "That I can do."

Sadie lifted so he could yank down her pants, allowing her easy access to peel his shirt from him. She unbuttoned his jeans, and he kicked them off until no barriers were left between them—only bare skin.

No more secrets were locked away. The good, the wicked—it was all there, alight within them.

As River's mouth claimed hers once more, she reached down to his length and gripped it. He groaned as she circled the head with her thumb, then stroked him using firm pressure.

Their kiss deepened, his tongue licking seductively across hers before he nipped her lower lip.

River's tongue then drifted down to her neck as he lay her against the feathered mattress. "I want to taste you first," he said in a gruff voice. She didn't deny his demand, allowing him to trail kisses of heated flames down her body, taking a peaked nipple into his mouth, flicking his tongue across it.

Sadie's heart pounded with desire as he settled his head between her legs. With one long, slow and delicious stroke, he carried his tongue up her center. And then his tongue played, feasted, and drank her in. When he plunged it inside of her, she tugged his hair, bringing him even closer.

"I need more," she begged.

River crawled up her until they were aligned, his mouth returning to hers. "In all my lives, I've loved you stronger than the last. Through your darkness, through your lightness, through every fucking thing." And then he buried himself inside her with a single thrust. Sadie gasped in pleasure at the same time he growled.

He slammed into her, giving her what she needed, taking the focus away from any pain. She dug her fingers into his back, then he rolled them over, sitting them both up so she was in his lap. River gripped her hips, urging her to move faster. Sadie tightened her hold on his shoulders, her nails biting into him, and she knew marks would be left behind in their wake. She pressed her mouth to his as she rode him, ground into him harder. One of her hands drifted to his hair and grasped it just as hard. They weren't tender like the last time they'd been together after the Halloween party, but more raw, needful, as if the world might collapse on them at any moment.

And then a tickling sensation stirred, taking root, *spreading*. The blissful feeling erupted, crashing through her as she continued to roll her hips, yearning for him to feel just as good. A deep and guttural sound ripped from his throat as he growled her name.

Their chests heaved, and he kissed her lips with a smile, the animalistic side of him hiding for now, while he carefully lowered her to the bed, then settled beside her.

They studied one another, their eyes, their lips, and he

pushed a lock of hair behind her ear. "I love you," he whispered. "I love that your heart isn't perfect." He placed one more soft kiss to her lips—as if he might never get to do it again.

Sadie wrapped an arm around his waist, and he draped his over hers, her thoughts leaving the bliss they'd both experienced and turning to something much darker.

She bit the inside of her cheek to bring her pain somewhere else. "After the coven, I shouldn't have asked you to follow me into the darkness due to my fear. I should've faced my fear another way."

"I wouldn't have followed unless I'd wanted to."

Sadie remembered the fear he'd had back then, too—the fear he'd tried not to show. Witch hunts had begun long ago, even before they'd been at fault for some of the accused. So the fiends would watch over them at night in the woods to warn them if anyone discovered their location, while the moths would let them know if anyone found out Ada was a witch.

"Now we just need—" Sadie's words were cut off by heinous screeching, reverberating, rattling the walls.

20

"You could shatter the darkness if you wished."

Sadie jerked forward at the terrifying sound, knowing the malevolent spirits were below ground, trying to get past the wards and through the walls. But she was no longer in a bed beside River—she was back inside the cabin, fully dressed. Awake. Staring at animal skulls and framed moths along her walls.

She knew why she'd had the urge to collect them. And she still remembered *everything.*

"No, no, no," Sadie whispered, bringing a hand to her mouth. She shoved off the futon and bolted outside into the morning light. The fiends' silhouettes swarmed toward her, but it wasn't them that halted her in place—it was the *trees.* This time, not only were they in different positions, but they were entwined with one another, creating an impenetrable barrier around the woods that cut off the outside road, only the sky high above them exposed, a mirror image of her underground home.

Sadie should've suspected something worse would happen after the trees had swapped places. She felt some measure of relief at the presence of shadows swirling around her, drifting across the cabin to protect her. They hadn't been broken apart—yet. But the moths…

Fighting tears, she studied the trees, knowing the spirits were back inside of them, trapped for now. As she moved toward them, they edged backward, making it seem as though she was in the same place and would never catch up. It had to be the hex doing it, but she wouldn't leave River here anyway—not now.

"River!" Sadie called, looking down at the shadows, not catching wind of his scent. But he didn't answer or spell out any words into the dirt for her. "River, can you hear me?" she shouted louder.

Even though she was closed in along the edges of the woods, the path inside was still open. Sadie glanced one more time at the stitched trees and took off through the foliage, booking it toward where she'd seen River last. Within the quiet, a chill crawled up her spine when she noticed not a single animal laying across the ground. This wasn't a good sign at all. Unless they were farther out, it meant they were all *gone*.

"River!" Sadie screamed, her voice echoing. When she came to the now-hidden entrance, she slapped her hands against the dirt. "River, answer me!"

Nothing. No words. No shadow. No smell. A terrifying thought crossed her mind. What if the spirits had managed to break through the wards and get to him? "No, he's safe," she whispered. "He has to be."

She wanted to believe if something had happened to him that she would feel it. But she hadn't felt him the day he'd died, the day he'd hung himself to protect her. If one person was ever meant for the other, he was meant for her. Born of dark and light, selfishness and kindness, enemy and savior.

It would be hours until midnight arrived, and Sadie couldn't waste time standing there waiting for him to answer. Her fists tightened at her sides, knowing she needed to have this spell broken, and to do that, she needed to find out if Charlie and Skyler were truly Ada and Eben. If they weren't, she wasn't certain what would come after. One step at a time, though.

Placing her hands together as if in prayer, Sadie recited a long-forgotten incantation, to see if maybe she could cast a spell now that she was awake. Magic hummed within her as she chanted, but the trees caging her in wouldn't part. Biting the pad of her thumb, she broke the skin and let a drop of blood fall to the ground, yet the woods remained untouched. She screamed in frustration, wishing the sound could make the earth quake beneath her feet.

Sadie trekked back through the woods to retrieve her phone from inside the cabin, and the shadows followed her to the porch, where they remained. A thought struck her. Something she needed to try, something that could bring this full circle. Maybe having Charlie and Skyler here with her at midnight would be the key to unlocking *everything*. She would have to tread lightly and not alarm them if she wanted to ensure they remained with her until the veil dropped, though.

She called Charlie first to see about coming over for a

late movie, but it wouldn't go through. There wasn't a signal… *This can't be happening.* She tightened her grip on the phone and sank down on the futon, staring at the screen as if she could cast a spell to make it work.

Nothing.

Throughout the day, Sadie couldn't concentrate on anything besides trying to make the phone get a signal. She paced back and forth, her feet loud against the wooden floor, then she went outside to see if she could break out through the trees, the same thing as before happened, and she couldn't reach them.

Sadie would just have to wait for Charlie and Skyler to come to her if her phone didn't start working. And by then, she hoped it wasn't too late.

Her body shook, her chest swarming with an overly tightening sensation, and to keep from breaking down, Sadie grabbed her notebook and sat in the swing outside to use words as a distraction. But she was too angry, too melancholic, too antsy, and couldn't stop looking at her phone or wondering about River. However, she now realized that the screenplay she'd been working on was one of the truest things she'd ever written, and if she did finish it, no one would know that it was except for her and River. And *possibly* Charlie and Skyler.

As the sun set, the wind crawled from its daily hibernation, blowing a cool breeze across her skin. Only there were no insect or animal sounds, and a pit formed in her stomach at that.

Gathering her things, Sadie went back inside until the veil dropped. Even though she hadn't been worried about wildlife before, she didn't know how safe it would be to keep her body outside now that there were spirits that could possibly escape the trees. She couldn't cast wards to keep them out of the cabin, so, for now, she lit sage, knowing it most likely wouldn't do anything without a spell. She just needed her damn phone to *work*.

As she burned the sage, memories clawed their way through her. Her child dying and dying. And dying. River's coven and their tortures, her father's cruelty, her own cruelty, the Salem Witch Trials. In a way, she'd become her father, only instead of being cruel to the ones she loved, she was heartless to everyone else. But perhaps she was worse because she'd threatened Eben, who'd stood by her side for years, who might be Skyler…

A thought crossed her mind—what if she'd never been a witch? Hadn't ever held magic? What would've happened when her father denied her marriage? Would she have run off with Jasper, or would she have still buried a blade in her father? Perhaps someone would've even accused her of being a witch if she'd remained in her home.

She peered one more time at her phone. No signal. With a frustrated sigh, she slammed it down again.

It was one minute until midnight, and Sadie watched like a hawk until the numbers changed to twelve o'clock. She hadn't gotten to talk to Charlie or Skyler, but relief rolled through her as the alluring music outside rolled in, the deep melody calling to her, begging her to wake River once more. The way it had been commanding her to do all along.

But this time, a new sound barreled through the song, and Sadie froze—screeches and screams wailing in the distance. The spirits were no longer locked inside the trees.

No weapon could slice through their form, only spells that she couldn't use. Wishing herself luck, she slipped out the front door and fled in the direction of the lanterns. A few of the trees inside the barrier were drooped to their sides as if they were melting. The music and wailing accompanied one another, sending chills through her. She glanced up and shielded her eyes when several silvery forms floated beneath the moonlight, so she trained her gaze on the ground.

If she looked directly into their bleeding orbs, her body would crack, and her eyes would match theirs, just as the moths' had.

Heart pounding, Sadie ran faster, wincing as twigs snapped below her feet. The spirits' screams echoed, and she wouldn't hold any fear if she could wield her spells. Chants silently left her lips anyway, but their raging screeches continued to roar. She hadn't spotted a fiend yet, and she hoped they remained hidden.

Behind Sadie, the screeches grew ravenous, thirsting to unleash their anger on someone, *anyone.* She tore through the trees, skirted around their trunks. The trees shifted, sliding across the ground, and she held back a scream. She wasn't certain if the spirits were in those trees or if it might be the hex again.

Sadie needed to get to River, confirm he was truly there. Not once had he come to her that day. If she could, she would get him the hell away from these woods, but that wasn't possible. A silvery form weaved between the branches, and a pig-skulled fiend stepped out from a trunk.

She was about to shout no, but it was too late—the spirit severed the fiend's skull from its spine, the cracking sound reverberating through the night. As the spirit gnashed at the rest of its body, another fiend crept out to distract it.

"Stop it," she pleaded, but it was too late. There wasn't a damn thing she could do, so feeling heartless, she fled toward the underground stairs, flying down the steps, praying River was there to sort this out. But when she entered the main area, he wasn't standing there.

Sadie's breaths were uneven as she threw the door to their bedroom wide, only to find it empty. She opened door after door after door. The supper room, the malevolent spirit room, the room of hearts that were now dried up as she'd suspected, and then finally, the conjuring room with the glass coffins.

Her chest heaved, her shoulders relaxing when her gaze fixed on the crystal box she'd been in the night before. River rested inside, the dagger in his hand. The lid hummed beneath her fingertips as she lifted it, the hinges quiet.

Sadie didn't know if he would wake this time, but as soon as her fingers brushed his face, River's eyes flew open, his gray irises meeting hers as he inhaled sharply.

"Why are you in here?" she asked.

"I go where the dagger is left behind, but I've been trapped in here ever since you were ripped away from me. The box had been sealed, and the magic kept me in it. Maybe you should just leave me in here."

Sadie took the dagger from him, then dropped it on the floor. "I'm reckless, remember?" She crawled into the crystal box with him, and he enfolded his arms around her. "The wards seem to be holding, but I don't know for how much longer."

"Did you talk to Charlie or Skyler?" he asked, running a hand through her hair.

"My phone's signal hasn't worked all day. A cabin out in the woods … it's expected. But I think it has something to do with the trees creating a barrier. The spirits were trapped in them during the day, but the hex or something wouldn't let me reach the barrier."

"Fuck. This isn't good. If we're both trapped here with no ability to cast a spell and can't contact them…"

"I know." Sadie sighed.

"If it's them toying with you, somehow making the spirits do this, I swear I'll—"

Sadie put her fingers to his warm lips, hushing him. "When I get a hold of them, or if they come to me, I'm going to get them to stay until midnight. To see if the veil opens up for them too. If not, we'll somehow find a way to take care of it. With or without a spell."

"As we always do," he whispered.

They stayed there for hours, embracing one another, trying to cast new spells that didn't work. If Sadie wasn't able to get a hold of Charlie or Skyler the next day, they were going to have to gather the ingredients and herbs she had around the cabin or in the woods and try a new spell that could temporarily open the woods for her. But she feared deep down it wouldn't pan out.

A boom shook the entire room, louder than the night before. Cracks formed, spiderwebbing along the walls.

Sadie and River both jerked up, and he shoved them out of the box, then set her on her feet.

"We don't have much time, but something else feels wrong," River rasped, picking up the dagger and tossing it into the box away from him. "I feel a rope tugging inside me, and soon it's going to snap in place. I don't know how many more days I can control myself around you, my sweet nightmare."

Two strong hands grabbed Sadie by the shoulders and shook her, yanking her away from River.

21

"Let them hunt us if they wish, but we are the true hunters."

Darkness surrounded Sadie, and she thrashed hysterically to escape the firm grip of whoever or *whatever* was shaking her by the shoulders.

"It's me. Sadie, it's me," a familiar voice said.

Sadie finally got her eyes to open, her body relaxing as her gaze met Skyler's golden-brown irises.

But then a wave crashed into her, reminding her of who Skyler could be. She tensed, squirming away from his touch. If he were truly Eben, then that meant they'd grown up as close friends in Salem, had been like siblings in every life since then. Not once had they become distant in any life, only the first, when he'd discovered what she and Jasper had been doing. Yet Eben hadn't been with

Ada that day in the woods, so Sadie wasn't sure how he was a part of this.

"Skyler," she whispered, gasping for air. He was dressed in his police uniform with his hair swept back.

"Oh, thank fuck," he exhaled. "I thought you weren't going to wake up." His voice came out concerned, maybe even a bit frightened. She'd rarely seen him this way, only when they'd been younger and had gotten lost in the wooded park trail near his parents' house. Ever since becoming a police officer, Skyler knew how to handle his emotions, even if that might not be how he was feeling on the inside.

"Is it morning?" Sadie asked, heading to the window, her throat dry as she spoke. She needed water. All she continued to hear was the booming of the walls, the sound of them cracking. It had been toward the end of the night, so she prayed the spirits hadn't made it inside to River, that they were trapped back in the trees.

"It is. Charlie asked me to swing by before work. I'm sorry that it's so early." He blew out a breath. "She and I tried texting you a few times yesterday, and I was going to come here, but there were several emergencies. Also, please never leave your door unlocked, especially when you're sleeping."

"I'll lock it next time," she answered, pushing back the curtain of the window to look outside. The trees barrier remained there, yet Skyler's police car was inside.

"Charlie wanted me to tell you she's stopping by to cook dinner later today since you weren't texting her back."

A pit formed in Sadie's stomach, even though this was what she was waiting for, to come face to face with

Charlie, but a part of her wanted to deny it, go back to remembering her sister as she was. If she was, in fact, Ada, Sadie would have to contain herself from bringing a blade to her sister's throat. She needed them both there at midnight to see if her plan would lead them on the same path.

"When you get off tonight, how about we all watch a movie here?" she asked.

"Just like the good ol' days."

"Exactly that." But did he know of the bad ones too? Pursing her lips, she turned to Skyler, her heart beating rapidly as she studied his face. The furrow between his brows was there as it always was in each life, that same expression when he was concentrating, just like he was doing now. It was such a simple expression, but it felt wholly Eben.

As Eben, he'd always helped steady her, had been a good friend. Even after he'd found out she was taking the essence of villagers in Salem, he'd kept her secret. But what he'd really wanted was for her to stop, so she'd threatened to take his parents' lives if he didn't let her be. She knew why he'd become determined—with villagers being accused more often, he feared for Ada. But Harlow had a hold on things and was ensuring her sister was protected. Or that was what Harlow believed.

Sadie folded her arms. "How did the trees look when you arrived? Anything out of the ordinary?"

"No," he said slowly, knowing something was different in her demeanor. "Same as when I saw them last. Has something changed?"

As she spoke, a shadow drifted inside along the floorboards, a hint of honey and sandalwood brushing her senses. River. Relief washed over her that he was there, and even though he moved in front of them, Skyler didn't seem to notice.

"Nothing's changed," Sadie finally said, lying. Yet she needed to dig. She wasn't truly angry with Eben—it was Ada. "I know your beliefs on ghosts, but what about witches?" She bit the inside of her cheek, drawing a speck of blood. "Specifically, Salem."

"Are you going to give me a history lesson now?" He arched a brow, the corners of his lips curling up.

"No, just your feelings on the witches." She remembered when Eben first discovered she could cast spells, how he hadn't held any fear, only interest. How once, when his shoulder was throbbing from working the fields, she'd healed him quicker.

"As in do I believe the accused witches of Salem were real? No, I don't believe they held magic."

"Not the accused specifically." She sighed, sinking down on the futon. "But do you believe there are witches who can cast spells for good and evil?"

"Well," he drawled, lowering himself beside her, "I think some people may have better intuition than others. But if you're asking if I believe someone can cast real spells while fiddling around with a cauldron and go for rides on broomsticks, then I think you know my answer."

"No witch rides on a broomstick." Sadie rolled her eyes. Yet it would've made things much easier to escape her father in Salem if she could have. She watched as River's shadow crept along the fur rug, halting, seeming to listen more intently as she continued, "What about reincarnation? Do you believe that people can be born again and again?"

Skyler leaned against the back of the futon. "No. I would hope not, anyway. One life, or at least one good life, is enough for me. Why are you asking about this anyway? Did you discuss more things with Kalina at the shop? I honestly think she just wants your money."

Sadie squinted, her gaze locked on his, wishing she could read his thoughts. "This has nothing to do with Kalina, but never mind."

Skyler lifted the book from the coffee table that she'd purchased from Crow Moon, and he flipped through the pages. There were so many questions she could ask, yet a part of her didn't want him to remember their past, to remember what kind of monster she'd been toward him when all he'd done was try to help her. But that fear drove Harlow into what she'd become. And she couldn't stop asking questions now, not when her unborn child needed to be saved.

Taking the book from his lap, she set it back on the table. "What are your thoughts on murderers, Skyler? Do you believe in redemption?" It wasn't an unusual thing for her to question—she'd always asked scenarios about films and true crime before.

He peered up at the ceiling, mulling it over for a moment before his eyes returned to hers. "Well, Sadie, I believe in right and wrong and a thin gray streak that slashes straight down the middle. But if you're asking me if a murderer should get another chance in this life, it would depend on the circumstance. What they did."

In this life… In this life, she hadn't hurt anyone, only collected dead insects and animal skulls—she'd never even hunted before. River glided closer, drifting along the futon beside her. "That's fair," she started. "Let's say reincarnation did exist, though. What if this person had done monstrous things in a past life, was a witch, had once been good but then used her spells to reap the essence of innocent lives. Then came a spell cast by a different witch who somehow put the other under a hex which killed her. Only, she didn't truly leave this world and was spelled to be born over and over. And in each new life, this witch never did anything too terribly wrong again. Could she be redeemed?"

"Is this something you've been seeing in the woods?" Skyler ran a hand across his jaw, watching her closely. But there wasn't a hint of recognition that sparked in his eyes at her words.

"No, just a scenario I've been thinking about." She shrugged.

"I know what we're doing here." A wide grin spread across Skyler's face. "This is part of the screenplay you're working on, right?"

"You saw right through me." Sadie forced a smile. "I'm seeing where to take the story."

As Skyler opened his mouth to say something, his phone beeped, and he glanced at it with a sigh. "I better get to work." He stood from the futon, stretching his arms. "I think maybe you shouldn't ask Charlie any of these questions, though."

"And why not?" Her gaze slid to his, wondering if he'd been hiding secrets all along.

"You know why. She'll worry like hell." He paused. "So nothing's gotten worse here?"

"Just the same unsettling silence, but I haven't seen any more animals on the ground." Only the spirits within the trees that would destroy anyone who laid eyes on theirs.

"That's interesting," Skyler said. "Maybe what you're experiencing is fading then."

No, it's only getting worse, especially when the veil drops. "We'll find out. But I'll see you tonight."

"I'll see you later then."

After walking him to the door, she remained looking out the window, watching Skyler back his car out through the trees as if there wasn't a barrier trapping her inside the woods at all. If she didn't know better, she would've thought he was a witch himself. But she honestly believed Skyler didn't know he was Eben.

She turned to find River beside her on the floor. "You don't think Skyler knows either, do you? If you do, slide out through the front door."

He didn't.

"Let me try something." Sadie lifted her phone, hoping it would work, but the signal was still down. She'd wanted to search the names of Skyler and Charlie's other possible past lives, to see when they'd died and how. Based on calculations, they would've had to die young, yet she couldn't pinpoint why they would want to do that if it was manipulation. "I suppose we'll just have to wait for Charlie to arrive."

Around four o'clock, a rapid knock came at the door, startling Sadie from the theories she'd been writing down in her notebook. River had lingered inside with her, only leaving a few times to check the woods. She'd watched his form slide across the ground, inspecting tree after tree.

Charlie stood on the porch with two plastic bags in one hand, and Sadie's jaw unintentionally tightened as she recalled Ada's magic affecting her in Salem, her child dying inside of her.

"I asked Skyler if he wanted to watch a movie tonight after he got off work, and he was okay with it," Sadie said after letting her sister inside. "You're still off tomorrow, right?"

"That's fine. What horror movie is it, though?" Charlie smiled and brushed past Sadie. She stepped on River's shadow while crossing the room to set the bags on the table. "And yes, I'm off tomorrow. We're going to the beach if you want to come."

"I'm in the mood for something witchy." It came out more bitter than Sadie intended as she studied Charlie. "I suppose I'll go, but you know how I feel about the sun." If her plan didn't work at midnight, then tomorrow, when they came to pick her up, she would see if the woods would let her and River's shadow go with them. But deep down, she knew they wouldn't be able to leave.

"I don't know why you hate the sun." Charlie shrugged.

"I'm a vampire in secret," Sadie drawled. Or a witch... She clenched her teeth so hard as she continued to watch her sister that she thought they would crack. River's shadow slid beside her feet, seeming to try and calm her.

Charlie started on the pasta in the kitchen, all while Sadie barely spoke a word. After dinner, Charlie dusted around the cabin, telling Sadie how she needed to keep up with things while an old witch movie played.

As night fell, Sadie couldn't hold her emotions in any longer, not as she thought about how her baby had started to kick inside of her, the way her hands had held her stomach, feeling each movement. Sadie never would've hurt Ada before, no matter how strained their relationship had become the last few weeks in Salem. And especially never Charlie, but if this was her toying with Sadie and River? Then she would force a blade to her throat, and if she wouldn't break the spell, she would kill her to undo it.

"She was warned not to touch a Ouija board and did so anyway, so she sort of gets what's coming to her." Charlie rolled her eyes, placing a piece of popcorn in her mouth.

"It makes perfect sense," Sadie said coolly, her gaze shifting between Charlie and River's shadow. "She's trying to save her family."

"It will only make things worse."

The blood in Sadie's veins boiled, and she ripped the bowl of popcorn from her sister. "I'm done playing games, Charlie," she snapped. "Are you Ada? Did you cast a spell on me?"

"Who's Ada?" Charlie's brows rose up her forehead, her eyes wide, looking at Sadie as if she were losing her mind. "What are you talking about? You're not making a whole lot of sense. Ever since you've moved in here, saying you've been experiencing paranormal things, having lifelike dreams about River, you've been acting different. I told you I would let you make your own choices, but this isn't going to help you, Sadie."

"I don't know. I don't *know*." Sadie took a breath, her chest heaving. Maybe she was wrong. This didn't feel like a game Ada would play—she hadn't been like Harlow. The only times Ada had ever been sneaky was when she'd helped Harlow hide things from her father and bury his body. "Sometimes I feel as if I've lived multiple lives. That maybe this hasn't been my only one."

"Are you having nightmares like before again?" Charlie leaned back and draped a blanket over Sadie as she used to when they were younger.

Sadie's gaze fell to River, who was now sitting on the edge of the coffee table, his silhouette whole, and he shook his head before sinking back to the floor in shadow form. She agreed—she needed to stop for now and wait until after midnight to see if her suspicions played out first. To see if Charlie and Skyler could follow her within the veil. "No, I had a new one. Of other possible lives."

"Even if we did, this is the life we are in now, and it is what it is," Charlie said. "But they're just dreams. You're awake now."

Throughout her lives, Sadie had always written dark tales, had let her fear control her in Salem. She wouldn't let fear do that again. "We'll find out."

"Find out what?" Charlie asked just as the sound of Skyler's car purred outside the cabin.

"It's a secret." Sadie grinned, placing her index finger over her lips.

22

"Do they know what we've done?"

"You still can't stream out here?" Skyler asked, flipping through the DVDs Sadie had set on the table.

"I usually can on my phone. If the signal is working." She shrugged, staring at River, who was now in his whole silhouette form, seated on the floor, his back against the wall, one knee to his chest with his arm propped on it.

"What are you looking at?" Charlie scrunched up her face as she studied where Sadie's gaze was trained.

"Just wondering if I should add more framed insects over there." Sadie smiled.

"Mmm, let's go with this one," Skyler said, handing the folk horror DVD to Sadie. He then sank down beside Charlie on the futon, wrapping his arm around her waist and nuzzling his face into the crook of her neck. Charlie pressed a piece of popcorn into his mouth, so easily, so in love. Her sister and Skyler were Ada and Eben—she knew it like she knew her own heart. Their body language confessed it all, just as it had in every other lifetime. The way Charlie scooted closer to him, resting her hand on his thigh, how he would constantly sneak glances beneath his thick lashes at her.

Sadie's fists tightened and magic stormed within her, aching for a key to unlock it so a spell could burst free from her lips. Clasping her hands together, she silently chanted a spell under her breath for the futon to collapse, but still, nothing rose.

River stood and came toward her, cupping her cheek. He ran his index finger across her lips, distracting her, yet she only calmed a fraction. Neither noticed him nor even looked from the corner of their eyes in his direction.

Sadie placed another bag of popcorn in the microwave and waited, her thoughts turning to her unborn child. Then came the miscarriages, her depression, her worry, her helplessness because of them. But she always had River's shoulder to lean on in the past, how he'd still brought a smile to her face, then how their lives were ruined because Ada's spell had made them both die. Once the veil brought down its dark claws, if everything went according to plan, they would remember.

River stood behind her, his nose skating up her neck. She arched into him, her arm falling back around his neck, and her gaze met Skyler, who studied her with a frown. She cleared her throat, coughing, drawing away from River. Even though she couldn't see River's expression, she knew a smirk was there.

The microwave beeped, and Sadie emptied the popcorn into a bowl, her stomach growing queasy over the buttery smell. Gritting her teeth, she shoved the bowl into Charlie's hands. "Here."

"Are you all right?" Charlie asked, staring up at her with her brows pinched together.

"Peachy keen." Sadie needed to remind herself that they didn't seem to know about any of this. If Skyler had known, she didn't think he would've let Charlie be alone with Sadie out in these woods. But what if her plan didn't work? What if they didn't experience anything at midnight? Neither one of them could see what Sadie saw in the woods. The strangeness hadn't started for Sadie until after she'd slept here the first night, though. Then came the quiet during the day, followed by how it shattered into noise at night, and finally, the music of midnight. But she'd had an initial undisturbed sleep, then a few dreams after that, so would they? Or would they all be in the same place if it worked?

As the film played, Sadie glanced over at Charlie—her sister wrinkled her nose as she watched the woman in the white gown holding up a lantern and walking through the woods. Most people would assume her sister hated the movie by the look on her face, but that expression always meant she was finding a film decent. Sadie continued to watch Charlie out of the corner of her eye, her nerves shooting off inside her like firecrackers. For a moment, Sadie wondered briefly if she was on the verge of a breakdown, that maybe she had conjured all this up, that maybe she wasn't really sitting across from her, but no, she wasn't.

"I think I might call it a night," Charlie said with a yawn, placing the empty popcorn bowl on the table.

Sadie fumbled with her phone to check the time—ten

minutes until midnight. She couldn't leave… "No! You have to stay."

"I'm tired, Sadie. But hey, we'll be together at the beach tomorrow."

"Stay!" Sadie shouted, her nostrils flaring. This was the part of herself she hadn't known existed, that had been tucked away. The dark part of her that had been marking her aura.

Skyler scowled. "What have you been seeing? I was going to ask you about it later, but I can't pretend like everything is fine and dandy. Your eyes have been drifting to the same spots near the wall throughout the movie. And don't get me started on the kitchen."

"He's right," Charlie said. "I wanted to pretend with you that everything was all right, but it isn't."

"Just stay until midnight," she pleaded, grasping Charlie's wrist. "You'll see, or you won't see when it comes. We can discuss things after."

"When what comes?" Skyler asked, his gaze focused on hers. She could see the emotion there, that he was contemplating what he should do if she were to lash out. Sadie had never been dangerous, but now she knew she had the potential where she could be.

"The music I told you about. And now the past," she said, her voice trembling. Her heart pounded harder, and she fought back the urge to shake them.

"What past?" Charlie placed her hands on Sadie's shoulders, and she yanked out from her hold.

"*Our* past," Sadie seethed. "And don't look at me like I should be locked away in an institution. You will understand. And if you don't, I'll explain it all. You will find a way to undo what *you* did to me and River."

No one uttered a word as Sadie gripped her phone, urging the numbers to move. "Give me until twelve." They both nodded, but she could see in their eyes that they were beyond worried. River came to her then, wrapped his arms around her waist and rested his chin on her shoulder, grounding her.

Perspiration beaded her brow as the seconds passed into minutes. But when the time changed to 11:59, it felt as if the world stood frozen, and she avoided the heavily concerned stares from Charlie and Skyler. "One minute."

Then the numbers changed. 12:00. River's arms left her waist, his form disappearing from the room.

"It's midnight," Charlie whispered as if she were trying to calm a wild horse. "Nothing's changed. Whatever is going on here isn't healthy."

Sadie's lips tilted up at the edges as she dropped her phone onto the futon. "You're wrong. It did work. Listen closely."

The instruments were soft at first, followed by a deep melody, gradually picking up its pace as though it were being chased. Then the answer rose, soaring somewhere within the wind outside. Screeches and wails tore through the air farther away.

For a moment, Sadie believed that it was only her hearing it, but Charlie's eyes widened, and she ran to the door. Before she got there, Sadie grabbed her by the waist, tugging her back. "Do not go outside," she bit out, her voice hushed.

"Something is out there," Charlie said softly. "It sounds demonic."

Skyler's chest rose and fell, the only sign of his uneasiness. A confused expression formed on his face as his eyebrows drew together. His gaze focused on Sadie, squinting, seeming to recall something. "I know what the sounds are coming from, and you can't go out there," he murmured to Charlie, then his throat bobbed as his eyes locked with Sadie's. "You're Harlow."

Skyler knew, and Charlie didn't… "Did you know all along?" Sadie narrowed her eyes, her heart pounding faster as she studied him. "I only recently discovered *everything*. Years and years of *not* knowing."

He shook his head. "No, I didn't know. I haven't known in this life or any of the others. Not until now." Perhaps there was a reason he remembered right away inside the veil, just as River had.

"What are you two talking about?" Charlie hissed, her eyes wild.

Sadie ignored her sister, focusing on Skyler. "Before we discuss any of this, she needs to remember now. We don't have time to wait, and I know the way she can. It's how I found out. She's coming with me into the woods, and you will not fight me on this."

"With those things out there? I'm not going to risk her getting hurt," he said. "You told me the stories of what they can do."

"It's funny," Sadie snapped, "I've already been hurt countless times. It all involves me getting killed by my beloved. The. End. It's quite the tale, isn't it?"

"You don't know, then?" Skyler ran a hand across his jaw as he cast a glance at Charlie.

Sadie blinked. "What?"

"Because of Ada's spell, I do the same to *my* beloved."

"You kill her?" Sadie took a step back, stumbling.

He nodded, and nausea bubbled in Sadie's stomach.

She knew their lives had to have ended sooner, but she hadn't thought it was because Skyler was killing Charlie each time.

"What the hell are you talking about?" Charlie whisper-shouted.

Sadie needed to comfort Charlie for now—this was the sister she loved, the one she would always fight for, more than ever before. With a heavy sigh, she rested her hands on Charlie's shoulders. "You are going to come with us through the woods. We can't stay here because this cabin isn't protected and they can come in. I know how this is going to sound, but it will help you remember. Outside there will be silver spirits that may come after us. Keep your gaze trained on the ground, and do not look into their eyes. Not one time. If you do, you will die. Do you understand?"

Skyler scowled, mulling over what she'd said. "She's right. You wouldn't be protected here. Trust her words on this. Trust me."

Charlie's lip wobbled and her face paled.

"This is your warning. Do you understand? If you want, I can even blindfold you," Sadie said.

"I don't need a blindfold," Charlie answered, her voice shaky. "But I swear if you two are screwing with me and this is all a practical joke, I'm never talking to either of you again."

"I wish I could say it was." Skyler grasped Charlie's hand, gently squeezing it.

"I'll lead the way, and we need to move fast." Sadie peered out the window, finding no sign of silver silhouettes floating through the air, only their wails in the distance.

Slowly, Sadie drew open the door, looking side to side before waving them on. They rushed toward the lantern-lit trees, keeping their feet as light as they could.

The trees were still stitched together, holding their barrier shape, while some of the others were leaned to the sides again as if they were a wax candle and a flame had melted them.

Skyler kept silent, but her sister let out a low gasp and Sadie motioned at Charlie to keep quiet. She could tell her sister was fighting a scream as she covered her mouth. Charlie was going to remember the spell she cast even if Sadie had to tie her to a chair and force her to recover the memory. But a sinking feeling coursed through her as she wondered how her sister had been killed in each life…

Up ahead, the goat-skulled fiend crawled out from behind a tree and Charlie gasped. Sadie mouthed at her not to worry. There wasn't a sign of the others and she hoped they were hidden, but as they passed bones along the ground, she knew they weren't all safe. She remembered the pig-skulled fiend being ripped apart.

The lanterns continued leading the way and Charlie stared at them, but she didn't question it, even as her body trembled. A silver form then slithered out from a tree above them.

"To the hole where you dug before," Sadie rushed out, nudging Skyler forward.

They sprinted past several trees when something strong yanked Sadie back by her hair and screeched beside her face, making her ears ring. Squeezing her eyes closed, she ripped herself free and bolted after Skyler. Not once did she glance over her shoulder as she cracked open her eyelids. "Keep going and don't look back," she shouted to Skyler, who was pulling Charlie beside him. The spirits could touch *them* now, something they could never do before. But in this state, it was Sadie's essence that was here, not her true body. Her form at the moment was the same as theirs. She dodged a few fallen logs, then pushed away the vines, finding Skyler and her sister halting inside the circular tree formation. Still, no moths lingered.

Shrill screams shot through the air and Skyler held onto Charlie, not budging.

"We need to go *now*. The wards were still holding last night but may not for much longer. Trust me in this life, Skyler. I promise this will help her to remember and isn't a trick. You must both speak these words to enter." She whispered the spell to them both, words she'd never told anyone.

Skyler tightened his jaw, relenting as the screams grew closer, and he and Charlie murmured the words. Sadie then led the way down the two flights of stairs, relieved the words had allowed them to follow. Cracks lined the walls, but the wards held. For now.

Same as the night before, she found River inside the crystal box where the dagger had remained, only the lid wasn't closed this time since they'd left it open.

"He's here?" Skyler rasped, stepping closer to the box.

"River is in there," Charlie gasped, her arms folded in front of her, her body vibrating harder.

"Yes, each night I come down here, he has to be touched to wake. He goes where the dagger is."

As she reached out to wake River, Skyler grabbed Sadie by the wrist. "You're not doing that yet."

Sadie ripped her arm away from him. "You will not

tell me what to do."

"Not until Charlie remembers first. I don't want her vulnerable somewhere."

"He won't hurt her. *I'm* the one he wants to hurt."

Skyler narrowed his eyes.

"Fine." Sadie let out a breath, knowing what their top priority was. Making Charlie remember. "But I will wake him once she's finished." She lifted the lid on the second crystal box, gesturing for Charlie to lie down inside. "I know what this looks like to you, but it's the fastest way. We don't have time to wait to see if you will recall things."

"Listen, I followed you through something more real than any haunted house I've ever been to with you. River's body is somehow here and hasn't rotted, even though I know he was ash before. There are skeletal, furred monsters and screeching things flying in the air outside," Charlie spat. "I'm not going inside what looks to be a clear coffin either. Tell me what's going on, Sadie."

"Please, just get inside," Sadie begged.

Charlie shook her head and backed away from them as if she was about to be slaughtered. If she didn't get inside the box, Sadie just might have to rip the blade from River's fingertips and make her get inside.

"We don't have time for this, Skyler," Sadie said between clenched teeth.

Just as Charlie turned to run, Skyler hauled her to his chest. "You'll understand after," he said gently. "Please believe me, know that I won't force you to get inside. Just please do this. Sadie's life, your life, depends on it. I love you." He might not force her inside, but Sadie would if she didn't go in.

Skyler slackened his hold on Charlie and released her.

She slowly faced him, tears filling her eyes, her body trembling. Sadie thought that her sister would try and bolt again, but then she slowly nodded, moving toward the box.

Charlie's body continued to tremble as she lay against the silk fabric, her eyes widening in fear when the lid closed over her. And though it hurt Sadie to see her sister this way, satisfaction stirred within her while she watched the one responsible for her own agony experience some small measure of terror.

The symbols on top of the lid illuminated a light blue, and Charlie's arms fell limply at her sides, her eyes falling shut.

Taking a shallow breath, Sadie inched back beside Skyler as the sounds of the spirits rang through the walls. Then they waited. And waited. For her sister to regain consciousness, to remember everything Sadie had done, to remember what *she* had done. For her to see the hate burning in Sadie's eyes when Ada gazed back at her.

23

"Nothing will break us."

Harlow stood in front of the cauldron, watching as the spirits' bloody tears churned inside. Her fear never wavered, to the point where she rarely left her home, only to meet with her sister. Ada believed she'd moved to a new town with Jasper. But she'd remained here all along, plucking the essence of people from Salem. She knew she was putting her sister at risk, but she would make certain nothing ever happened to her.

Rustling came from the bed in the other room—Jasper waking. His bare feet against the stone floor sounded, and she glanced back to find him sauntering to her, his body still bare of any fabric.

"Mmm, it looks as though you're tempting me to crawl back into bed with you." She smiled.

"Or you may be tempting me to take you right here," he purred.

Harlow's smile slipped from her face, and she couldn't hold it in any longer. She dropped to her knees, sobbing into her hands.

Jasper knelt beside her, tilting her chin up so her gaze met his bright green irises. "We don't have to do anything, Harlow. You can tell me one of your stories in here, or we can dance in another room."

"It's not that," she sobbed again.

"What is it?"

"I'm with child," Harlow hissed. She'd never wanted children, not after having a father like hers, not after having seen her brothers die because of him or the other siblings she'd never gotten to meet.

Jasper grinned wide, his emerald eyes beaming. "Our child?"

"Yes! Who else's child would it be? You did this to me."

"I quite think it takes two lovers to make a child, my sweet nightmare. You and me."

She glared. "You're right. It's all my fault. I didn't remember to take the potion as I should've. You were always too—"

"Tempting?"

"Enough, but yes." Harlow rolled her eyes. "What are we to do now? With you and me both being witches, he or she would certainly be destined to be one."

"Do you want to have the child, then? There's still time…"

This child was barely a month old, but with as many wretched things as she'd done, to drink the potion now … to have the tiny heart stop beating. She couldn't. And she wouldn't want anyone else to have their child either. "I want to keep it."

"Do you want to relocate?" he asked.

The thought hadn't crossed her mind… They had time to figure out what step they should take next. "Perhaps when the child is born. I want to stay here to continue watching over my sister and Eben to make sure they remain safe. But for now, take me to the bed, my vicious dream."

Sadie brushed away the memory, now believing she should've gone with Jasper, started over, taught their child about spells but also how to hide them. To not let fear control oneself—the way she had.

Skyler stood beside her, and she could feel a slight tension there. Not only that, though—the comfortable bond they'd always shared also lingered.

"Did you know what Ada was planning to do?" Sadie asked. Ada discovered that they hadn't truly left Salem when she'd become suspicious and used a location spell to find her.

Skyler sighed, gripping the back of his neck. "I helped her with the spell. I'm not a witch, but I gathered and mixed the ingredients she needed. Ada had told me not to come, yet I couldn't listen, not when I had this gut instinct that something was going to go wrong—it was a spell she'd never cast before. When I arrived in the woods, Ada was holding your body, screaming and crying uncontrollably. Instead of wanting to go to her and help, all I could feel was a taste of something demanding, urging me to kill Ada, the spicy smell of the magic begging me to. *Not* because I yearned to, but because her spell had gone awry."

"So you knew she was plotting to kill us?" Sadie narrowed her eyes, pinning him with icy daggers.

"Even after all you'd done, she wasn't plotting to kill you, Sadie," Skyler said slowly. "She was always there to protect you, and she was only trying to strip you both of your magic. You threatened us—to murder my family."

"Because she shouldn't have used the location spell to find me. You kept hounding me to stop what I was doing." Sadie's voice rose. "And it wasn't only for me or Jasper, I was protecting *her*!"

"You knew she wouldn't want to be protected that

way." Skyler blew out a breath. "I understand now why you were asking about redemption. You're feeling remorse, aren't you?"

"I want to rip out her throat, Skyler," Sadie whispered, taking slow and even breaths to calm herself. "Because of that spell, my baby died. She's the reason I've had miscarriages in every life, and not with a different child, but the *same* one."

He frowned. "Baby? What are you talking about? You had a baby in Salem?"

"I was *pregnant* with a child in Salem. They had yet to be born, and I was almost five months along."

Skyler's face paled. "I swear on my life, she wasn't ever planning to kill you. Not once did she speak those words."

"People do a lot of things they don't mean to in life, but does it make them any less guilty?" Sadie spat. "I know I deserved what was coming to me. Do you think I'm that foolish? But an innocent child does not deserve to die over and over again. *My* child." She peered up at him, tears raining down her cheeks. "I never should've threatened you or my sister. I couldn't admit it back then, and it's no excuse, but I let fear rule me, shape me into what I was. However, I will never be sorry about trying to protect the ones I loved. And that included you. The world back then could've rotted for all I cared as long as I kept those I loved safe."

"But that's the thing—you were driving fear into others. The one thing you didn't want to have," he said softly.

Sadie took in his words, her chest tightening, the room feeling as if it was spinning around her. Even though he was right, she hated hearing it. "I know now I should've run away and started fresh with Jasper, but I didn't."

"After what the coven did to you, that was why Charlie was relieved that you weren't in Salem when the trials were going on. But then she found out you'd been there this whole time, the cause of it. And you know what? You saw how we only tried to get you to stop. That was all."

"I know," Sadie said softly.

"Anyway, do you recall when we were children and I found out you were a witch? You told me you would let me remember as long as I didn't tell anyone, but then you threatened to spell me into a rabbit if I did."

"It wouldn't have been for eternity, though." Her lips tilted up at the edges for a moment, then dropped. "If Charlie does remember, do you think she can break the spell? Even when she has died, the spell has continued, not broken."

Skyler peered down at Charlie. "Over the years, not once have I seen her use magic. Not since Salem. I don't even know if it's been stripped from her too."

Her sister had never feared magic in Salem—she'd always embraced it. But in the other lives, she shied away from the mention of supernatural things… Was it, deep down, because of what she'd done?

Sadie shifted closer to Skyler as she studied River's sleeping form. "Do you feel the urge to hurt Charlie yet? River feels it with me. Somehow, he had felt it before, and that's why he hung himself. To protect me."

Skyler shook his head. "It doesn't come until after he takes your life, I think. It's like lightning striking my heart, flipping a switch, and no matter where I am, I go to your sister."

A loud bang to the crystal lid sounded, snapping Sadie's attention to Charlie. Her sister's fists pounded harder, her gaze focused, determined. No longer did fear reside in Charlie's eyes.

"She remembers," Skyler whispered.

A mixture of emotions washed over Sadie—this wasn't just Charlie. The Ada piece of her was now there, just as Harlow's was with Sadie. Skyler drew back the lid and Charlie sat up, shakily slipping out from the box.

"I remember everything," Charlie said in a low voice, gripping the side of her skull as if she could remove the memories.

"You did this," Sadie spat. "You toyed with an unknown spell and trapped us in this cycle."

"Because I didn't know what you had become. You lied to me about leaving Salem, and then you were reaping the essence from innocent people and creating havoc in your wake. With your recklessness, you were going to expose yourself! You can't blame Papa and Jasper's coven for everything!" Charlie shouted.

"Papa should've left me alone, let me marry Jasper. His coven would've accepted me. It was Papa's fault!" But she knew, even though she refused to admit it, that she'd done this. "And if we're discussing innocent lives here, what about my child? I was pregnant when you cast your spell. Did you know that?" Sadie's words didn't come out as harsh as she'd wanted. Instead, she knew her sister heard the sound of heartbreak within them.

Charlie stumbled backward, colliding with Skyler's chest. "I did, but not until I unleashed the spell, then I felt it, felt the baby's heartbeat, *his* heartbeat, and that's why the spell misfired. It had only been meant for you two, but when I tried to reverse it, I got caught in the hex, as did Skyler. I never would've tried to end your life."

Her baby had been a boy… Her sister hadn't meant to harm her, which she should've known, but she'd still believed that Ada could've changed… "Why wouldn't you want me to die, though?" Sadie asked. "You discovered what I had become, had witnessed my threats."

Charlie heaved a sigh. "Because there was still good in you. Your heart wasn't wholly dark, no matter how much you believed it was. There was always a part of you to save."

"And River?"

"The same. But that doesn't make what you did right. That doesn't mean there shouldn't have been repercussions."

Tears pricked her eyes. "Do you still have your magic? Every miscarriage I've had has been the same child, am I right? He dies in each life."

"It is. I'm sorry."

Sadie held back a sob and nodded, knowing all along it had been.

Charlie closed her eyes briefly, her brow furrowed. "I do have magic still, but if you're asking if I can break the hex, I'm not sure I know how."

"Can you take the bind off my magic? I can help you."

Charlie hesitated while glancing back at Skyler. "Possibly, but I'm not sure that's a good idea."

Irritation coursed through Sadie, even though she understood the reasoning behind her sister's answer. But if she couldn't help, then she didn't know what would occur next, what would happen to River and their child. "I can't leave the woods anymore. And if you're afraid I'm going to hurt you, I could easily do it with an axe or a knife if I wished," she growled.

Charlie bit her lip. "It's not me I'm worried about."

"I'm not going to hurt Skyler either."

"It's not him." Her gaze held Sadie's, worry flickering there. "I'm pregnant."

24

"I love the taste of your lies."

Sadie frowned at Charlie's words just as Skyler cursed under his breath. Pregnant? *Pregnant?* It wasn't possible… Of course, it was possible, but…

"You just got back with Skyler recently," Sadie pointed out. "I don't think you can find out if you're pregnant after a handful of days unless you've performed a spell. Have you?" Or had her sister slept with someone else in between their breakup? She watched her sister for a lie, wondering if she had known what she was after all.

Charlie sighed. "I'm not a few days along. I'm three months pregnant."

"What?" Sadie blinked. "So you've been with Skyler all this time?" Under different circumstances she would've been thrilled, but what did this mean?

Charlie shook her head. "No. We recently got back

together, but after what happened with you and River, I didn't know what to do. I went to Skyler's and spent the night with him." She bit her lip and peered up at Skyler. "I should've told you sooner. I know I should've. I was planning to tell you tomorrow at the beach. It's not just that though…"

A baby… Sadie couldn't help but think of her own child and she knew precisely why her sister had trailed off, why she was looking at her now with fright. "That's my child. You're carrying the child that River and I created," she murmured. Instead of envy, Sadie felt only the urge to protect her sister. To protect the child, *her son*, who had died so many times.

"Yes, it's the same energy. I feel it now. Before, my magic was locked away until I remembered. I've never conceived in any life. Not until now."

"River altered something when he killed himself instead of murdering me." Sadie shakily put a hand to her mouth. "I think it's time for the four of us to get reacquainted *now*." She pressed her fingertips to River's cool cheek, feeling him warm beneath her touch as he gasped, jerking forward.

River's attention snapped to Skyler and Charlie, the dagger falling from his hand and clattering to the floor. "Our theory was right?" he asked Sadie, his breaths ragged.

She nodded, then told him everything that had happened since he'd vanished from the cabin, ending with what was recently revealed. "She's carrying our baby. He's alive inside her."

"I didn't mean to harm anyone," Charlie said, her hand protecting her stomach as if River might rip their child right out of her.

"Keep him safe." His gaze softened before hardening. "You need to break this hex. Remove the binds on our magic."

"Charlie, please do it," Sadie begged. "I promise I won't hurt you or the child. But we need to rid ourselves of this hex."

"Do it," Skyler said.

Charlie nodded and closed her eyes, chanting a spell to remove the invisible binds. A hand seemed to reach deep within Sadie, peeling back layer after layer to release the binds on her magic. But then Charlie inhaled sharply, beads of perspiration gathering along her brow, her eyelids fluttering. "I can't. The hex needs to be broken."

"Then *try*," Sadie pleaded.

"I did, but—"

Screeches tore through the air as cracks spread farther along the walls and dust rained from the ceiling. So close, *too* close.

"Strengthen the wards!" Sadie shouted to her sister.

Charlie recited the ancient spell as her body swayed. "It's too late. The wards here are fracturing, and because of your past spells, I'm unable to place new ones. If we can make it back to the cabin, I can put some up there."

Sadie cursed herself and her fear for protecting themselves so much so that they couldn't even protect themselves now.

"The veil needs to lift." River's jaw tightened as small debris fell with the dust. Soon the entire ceiling would crash down on them.

Charlie's lips moved, her words silent before she shook her head. "It isn't lifting. We were all together past midnight here, and we all now remember. The spirits are feeding off that, becoming stronger. Our only chance now is to get to the cabin so I can put wards in place. Then we can figure out the rest."

Fingers, silvery and crooked, pried their way through a crack in the wall. They were running out of time, especially since the spirits could touch them, force them to open their eyes and stare into their bloody orbs.

"Go!" River shouted, grabbing Sadie's hand just as she collected the dagger from the floor. He pulled her with him toward the stairs while more silver twisted hands shoved through the walls around them. Charlie and Skyler were close behind as they rushed up the staircase. The screams echoed, following them, and she didn't know how much time they had before the spirits would break free. That was if some weren't already waiting for them at the top of the stairs.

As she and River hit the night air, there wasn't a single silver form drifting above. The wind's song howled, raging faster, a nervous tinge entwined with it. The trees surrounded them, bound together like they had been on other nights.

"They won't let us climb them. I've tried. Can you open them with a spell, Charlie?" Sadie whispered, knowing if she couldn't, there wasn't a chance of escape. Not when a spirit could easily yank them back below ground.

Charlie closed her eyes, holding up a hand. "The trees are empty, but they are under the hex's control, so I may not be able to. Let me see your dagger, and I'll try." She took Sadie's blade and sliced it across her palm. Blood oozed from the wound, and she pressed her hand to a tree, then another, as she whispered a chant, asking them to part, if only for a few moments. Sadie didn't think they would listen, but then the two trees leaned back, making an opening that left just enough room for them to scramble across.

Sadie and River slipped through after Charlie. She gasped just as Skyler stepped beside her. Bones lay scattered across the ground in every direction. Her gaze fell to a goat skull, and her chest tightened. The fiends.

"We needed to let go of them anyway," River said. "It's better for them to be released now."

He was right—she knew he was, but it didn't lessen the clenching of her heart. Unable to mourn their loss for now, she darted through the woods.

They picked up their speed, skirting around trunks to avoid the screeching that wasn't far behind. Sadie leapt over a log, and a hand grabbed her by the hair, only unlike before, she was lifted off the ground, being pulled higher into the air. She writhed, shouting obscenities while piercing throbs radiated across her scalp. River didn't miss a beat and scaled a tree, grasping her by the ankle just as she was about to be drawn even higher. He caught her when she fell, but they both tumbled forward, colliding in a heap along the ground. Pain shot up her spine, her scalp on fire. She grunted, pushing up from the dirt as the spirit shrieked.

They avoided looking at the spirit and sprinted, running faster, catching up to Skyler and Charlie. Around them, deep groans filled the woods as the trees twisted and turned, their branches unfurling, their roots lifting. Charlie held up her hand, pressing onto her wound for more blood while she chanted, not stopping but slowing the trees from latching onto them.

The cabin slipped into view, and they were so close when a spirit swooped down and plucked Charlie up by the neck as if she was a piece of fruit that it wanted to suck dry.

Sadie dove for Charlie, but Skyler shoved her to the side as another spirit shot out from behind a tree. He tore Charlie from the silvery form, pushing her toward River, who easily caught her.

When Skyler turned, the spirit was faster, curving in front of him. Skyler squeezed his eyes shut, and Sadie barreled forward, yet not quick enough as the spirit forced his lids open with its gnarled digits. Sadie latched onto the back of the spirit, not focused on if it were to whirl around and connect its gaze with hers—she only wanted it away from Skyler. The spirit was cold as ice, her own warmth stolen as she held on, numbing pain spreading from her fingertips up her arms. Charlie thrust the blade into its side, but the spirit didn't so much as flinch.

"Get off of him!" Sadie screamed and pulled harder. River grasped the spirit by the waist, yanking with her while Charlie chanted, tears streaming down her face. In an almost robotic manner, the first spirit drifted back into the woods, yet the other screeched and pierced Skyler with its stare. Charlie's words grew louder, desperate. Then after only mere moments, the spirit finally released Skyler and stared toward the trees. Charlie's spell cast it back into the woods, blood spilling from her hand. But it was too late. Skyler's face was frozen, his eyes turning to orbs of crimson, cracks spreading along his flesh.

"No!" Charlie shouted, her hand falling as she rushed toward him, his body collapsing to the ground in her arms. "No, no, no."

Sadie grasped her sister by the wrist, trying to rip her away from Skyler. "We have to go now."

"No!" Charlie shouted.

Sadie turned to River since her sister refused to run, to save herself, to save her baby. She was going to get them all killed. "Do it, River!" she pleaded.

River didn't hesitate and lifted Charlie over his shoulder. He didn't loosen his grip as she pounded on his back, running her into the cabin. Sadie slammed the door shut while River set Charlie on her feet.

"Ward the cabin!" Sadie breathed as she hurried and collected a bundle of sage from the kitchen.

"I can't," Charlie cried, her hands shaking. "I need to get back to him. He's going to become one of them."

Sadie lit the sage, then grabbed Charlie by the wrist, preventing her from leaving. "Skyler would want you to, all right? For the baby, for you, ward the damn cabin." It didn't have to be for her or River, but for this innocent life growing inside Charlie that had never gotten a true chance.

Charlie relented, using the dagger she still had to open the wound further. She handed the blade back to Sadie and took the sage, whispering, the words sounding like a thousand echoes, the acrid smell of burning stirring. White triangular symbols illuminated the walls as her sister warded the cabin. Sadie knew that spell, knew it wouldn't hold forever, but it would for the night. They didn't have all the herbs they needed to make something stronger.

Once Charlie stepped away, it hit Sadie, sinking in that Skyler was gone… "I'm so sorry," Sadie murmured.

"This wasn't how things were supposed to happen. I shouldn't have ever cast that spell. I thought I was helping," Charlie sobbed, then ran toward the bathroom, slamming the door behind her. Tortured wails echoed through the walls, not coming from the spirits, but Charlie, crying louder than any of the screeching vibrating outside. Sadie's heart cracked, just as Skyler's skin had, but she knew to leave her sister alone for the night.

As Sadie turned to River, her knees buckled, and she collapsed to the floor, even though her own cries remained trapped inside her. River scooped her into his lap, her breaths coming out ragged in the crook of his neck. "This isn't her fault," she croaked. "It's mine. I should never have given into the darkness."

He ran a hand through her hair, holding her close. "Perhaps it's mine—once I got a taste for the darkness, I liked it. I still do, just as I know you do. It's like someone trying to quit their addiction. It's possible, but it will always linger. We just have to decide what path to continue on and stop looking back."

"Those spirits are evil and tore the good parts of themselves into pieces, killing them, and now Skyler…" Sadie clutched onto River, knowing precisely how her sister was feeling. It was how Sadie had felt when she'd lost River. And now, she wasn't sure what to do since Charlie couldn't unbind their magic. The wards were up for now, but unless the hex was broken, they wouldn't wake up.

River lifted Sadie and carried her to the fur rug, then laid beside her in front of the dead fireplace, his chest pressed to her back. The spirits swarmed around the cabin, their wails clashing with the wind's music, their fists banging against the wood, the glass, but the wards continued to hold. And she wondered if one of them was now Skyler.

"Do you want to take my life right now?" Sadie asked as River's chest rose against her.

"No," he murmured, his warm hand trailing across her stomach beneath her shirt.

Sadie rolled over to wrap her arms around him and whispered in his ear, "Liar. But I wouldn't fault you if you did." In fact, in that moment, she wished he would.

25

"Allow me to make them suffer."

Sadie hadn't even attempted to sleep—she just lay there, holding River. Charlie's sobs in the bathroom accompanied the sounds outside during the night, but Sadie's own eyes remained dry, her heart hollow with grief.

Just as the spirits' screeching silenced, so did Charlie's crying. Morning light seeped in through the window behind the curtains, and she thought for a moment that she'd woken up since there was no musical wind, only the quiet outdoors. But River was beneath her touch, and that proved they were still enveloped by the veil.

Sadie drew back, meeting River's gray irises. "I have to talk to Charlie. She needs to make the wards along the cabin stronger, and we may not have the brews, but I know a few things that can help. It looks as though the spirits have left, so I can probably get her to do a spell. Can you grab the bag of salt from the cabinet for me?"

He tucked a lock of hair behind her ear. "Of course. Go talk to her and I'll see what else I can find."

"Thank you." She pushed up from the floor, avoiding looking at her laptop, where Skyler had just been the night before, watching a movie on it while sitting on the futon.

Taking a deep breath, she knocked on the bathroom door. Her sister didn't answer, so she knocked again. "Charlie?"

What if the wards hadn't held in there? Heart pounding, Sadie threw open the door, frantic as she searched for Charlie. She shoved the shower curtain aside, finding her sister resting in the tub, shoes and all, her gaze fixed on the ceiling.

"I'm not going to kill myself," Charlie said, keeping her eyes trained on the ceiling as if it was a starry sky where she could wish upon all the tiny lights to give her something she couldn't have back. "Although, I did think about it. But that's all they are … dark thoughts that we all have. Only some of us show them more easily than others. After I remembered everything, remembered the spell I cast, remembered how Skyler would take my life in the same way River must have been doing with you over the years, I thought that I would have time to figure out how to break this cursed hex. Once I did, I believed that I could finish the life I was supposed to have with Skyler." Her hands fell to her stomach, where a child, *Sadie's* child, was growing. "Not only that, though—I believed that maybe I could find a way for River to come too, for you to be with him. In this life, the way it used to be, when no one tried to tear you two apart, only this hex that was because of me." She choked on a sob, then finally turned to Sadie, her eyes red and puffy. "We're not that different after all. If the things happened to me that had happened to you in Salem, I would've held fear too. You took from Salem, I took from you, and now the spirits are taking from the both of us. It's a vicious little circle, isn't it?"

"You're wrong," Sadie whispered, crouching at her side. "You wouldn't have held fear. You're much stronger than I am. Everything in life is a gray area. Right. Wrong. The reasons for those rights and wrongs. Jasper and I had discussed relocating while I was pregnant, but I wanted to stay and watch over you. I would like to believe that I would've changed paths once my son was here, once I saw his innocent face. Maybe I would've wanted to be better for him. Maybe. As for Skyler, I've loved him like a brother in every single life. He's been a shoulder I could lean on, just as you've been." She took a shaky breath, clenching her fists to keep from trembling. "You and I have always believed in an afterlife. Once Skyler is free from this spell, he will be there waiting for you, and for the time left that you have on Earth, you'll take care of the child growing inside you. I believe wholeheartedly that you can break this hex. You were always a better witch than me—I just used my magic more often, more viciously. Yet it was to protect not only us but you and Eben. As for River and me… I fear the place we'll be sent to when we die won't be as beautiful as where you will go."

Charlie shook her head and stepped out of the tub, wrapping her arms around Sadie. "I believe in redemption. I believe in it fully. Now, let me see your hand."

Sadie placed her hand in Charlie's, and her sister guided it to her stomach. Charlie closed her eyes, softly chanting. A heartbeat sounded in the room as if the walls themselves were beating. Charlie's heart. But then another thumped, softer, faster. Sadie blinked back the tears she'd been holding in, remembering how, in several lives, she'd gotten to hear the child's heart, but not like this. And it was strong, fierce.

"I think this was what he needed after Salem." Sadie paused. "You."

"And you." Charlie sighed. "I heard you discussing the wards with River. I'll perform a stronger spell now that the spirits are gone, but even then, it won't last forever. Just collect the bones we saw in the woods. Surround the cabin with them, then we'll sprinkle salt to strengthen the wards with our blood. The wards here are already fading, and if the spirits return, they won't hold. Before that, though, I need to see Skyler…" Charlie's voice trailed off, but she didn't curl back into herself.

"I'll walk with you." Even though his body wouldn't be there, Sadie needed to go too, needed to say goodbye, needed to thank him for all he'd done for her. "Come on then." She led her sister into the living room, where River sat on the edge of the futon, the large bag of salt resting on the coffee table in front of him.

"We're going to do a quick stop, and then you and I will collect the fiends' bones for Charlie to perform a protection spell on the cabin," Sadie said.

"Whatever you need." He nodded to Charlie. "The both of you."

Outside, the sun was bright, the barrier still folded around them. Even if they could leave, there wouldn't be a purpose, not until the spell was broken.

Sadie froze as her gaze fell on a form near one of the pine trees. Skyler shouldn't have been there… But as they inched closer, he most certainly still was. His skin was a silvery hue, lines marred his flesh as if he were a cracked doll, and then there were his eyes that were now the shade of blood, not a speck of any other color in their depths. He stared blankly toward the sky, his essence remaining here...

Charlie cupped her mouth as she knelt beside him and rested her head against his still chest. "How is he still here?"

The moths couldn't come back as malevolent spirits because they hadn't ever been human—only someone like Skyler could've become one. But what if… "Charlie," Sadie whispered. "I think we may have been wrong about him being dead."

Charlie lifted her head and furrowed her brow. "Look at him… He's not alive, Sadie. His heart is dead."

"I know what it looks like. Yet his essence is still here." Sadie itched to use a spell, to chant what she wanted to do as magic pulsed within her. "Hide him for now."

Hope shone in Charlie's eyes as she rested her palm directly over Skyler's heart. With her other hand, she lifted a small amount of dirt and sprinkled it over his chest. She repeated a spell for the ground to hide his body while moving her hand in circular motions. Cracking snapped throughout Skyler as his body broke further. The lines across his flesh deepened, his mouth widening. His flesh turned into silver flakes, collapsing to the earth in what looked to be a pile of ash. The ground swallowed it up, piece by piece, protecting him from harm.

"I'll leave you with your thoughts while River and I gather the bones," Sadie said as Charlie pressed her hand to the dirt once he was gone, knowing her sister needed to be alone.

Charlie nodded. "I'll try to figure out a spell to break the current one."

Sadie got River from the cabin, and she told him what happened as they went deeper into the woods to where the broken bones had been.

"I think you're right about Skyler." River pushed back a tree branch for her to duck under.

"Unless he wouldn't turn into a spirit until the following midnight, but that wouldn't make sense." Sadie's chest tightened when they stumbled upon the skeletal remains. Bones scattered across the woods as if the spirits had taken them apart and thrown their pieces everywhere.

She lifted the goat skull and chewed the inside of her cheek to hold back her mixed emotions—it had been the first fiend she'd ever created, the one who'd protected them the most. With a sigh, she held the skull close while gathering as many as she could carry.

They went back and forth to the cabin, resting the bones around the perimeter until there was enough. River then sprinkled the salt over the bones while Sadie grabbed a bundle of sage. She lit it and handed it to Charlie. Her sister performed the spell using her blood, and deep symbols etched into the wood, a pale blue light flickering.

Charlie sat on the porch steps, continuing to write spells in a notebook to try. She had attempted some earlier while Sadie and River were collecting bones, but the woods still held them prisoner, and no one had woken.

As night pulled down its blanket, Charlie had fallen asleep in the chair, passed out over her notes. Sadie studied her sister, the urge to protect her still there.

"What are you going to do if the hex is broken and our baby survives?" River asked.

"He's ours, isn't he?"

"He's part us, part them, and part his own. You'll have to decide what you want to do."

"We, River. *We*." He wasn't going to leave them.

"Let's get her inside for now." River gently lifted Charlie, and she let out a small sigh, but her eyes remained shut.

As River lay Charlie on the futon and went into the bedroom, Sadie sat on the coffee table across from her sister. Biting her lip, she scanned over the hundreds of failed spells while trying to think of another way to unlock their magic, just as she'd done for most of the day. She'd gone in and out of the cabin, brewing concoctions with leaves and other things from the woods, but her spells hadn't come to fruition.

There had to be another way to break it free, to snap the thread into place. There was always a way to undo something, and she wouldn't consider slaughtering her sister to achieve it. She only needed to find the right key for the lock inside her. The magic thrummed within her heart, but a new fear arose—if she could wield it, would she give into the darkness again? Her fears? A new one had come about—the fear that her child wouldn't be born, and then, what if something happened to him after?

Soft music poured out from the bedroom, and Sadie

noticed River hadn't come back. She found him on the floor, his back propped against the bed as he studied his hands, listening to a record. Sadie sank down beside him and laced her hand with his, then rested her head on his shoulder while closing her eyes, thinking of their times together in the past.

"My father won't allow us to be together," Harlow said.

"We could run away," Jasper murmured, his warm lips trailing up her throat, temporarily tamping down her fear.

"Let's wait. I don't want to leave my sister," Harlow whispered, fear coursing through her.

"He'll give in eventually. I do have quite the charm." His hot tongue skated up her jaw. "Witch or not."

"That you do, my vicious dream." She arched into his touch just as he buried himself inside of her.

Two hands cutting off Sadie's air supply ripped her from her thoughts. She opened her eyes to meet River's gaze, empty and cold, as she gasped for air, his hands squeezing her neck harder. The whites of his eyes were spotted with red, his expression hollow. Her body bucked and jerked, small squeaks escaping her mouth as she fought to scream. The magic within her begged to come out through a spell, to make him stop.

River! Sadie screamed inside her skull. Her lungs felt as if they would burst, and her essence was fading, her eyelids collapsing.

Feet pounded against the wooden floor before River was yanked away from her. Charlie held the dagger to River's throat, her nostrils flaring. "That was your one chance. Come near her like that again, and I'll slit your throat. I know you're battling these things because of me, but that doesn't mean I will allow you to bring her death."

River's eyes were no longer swirling with emptiness. As his chest heaved, a haunted stare was now there, and he didn't even try to push Charlie away. "Maybe you should," he rasped. "This time, I can't control it."

"You will not harm him!" Sadie shouted, still battling to drink in oxygen. "Please."

"Then, for now, he will need to be tied up," Charlie said.

26

"I will always protect you."

Sadie searched the shed for rope, but it was split and frayed—even a small child could easily tear through it. She would just have to make do with fabric from her room. As she shut the door to the shed, haunting music swept through the night. Midnight had arrived.

When a screech ripped through the air, she flicked off her flashlight, then hurried inside the cabin, shutting the door behind her. The sound trickled closer with the breeze, and she watched behind the curtain of the backdoor window as a dark outline of a spirit crept closer. It banged against the glass, releasing a heinous scream.

She should've never kept the spirits in her home back in Salem—it was the reason they were here now. Skyler was hurt, dead or not, because of her. Yet these spirits had chosen on their own, with no force from her hand to harm him. Skyler, who would've wanted to save them.

"I hope you suffer more," she whispered, gritting her teeth.

"Sadie!" Charlie shouted. "Did you find any rope?"

"It was deteriorated." Sadie slowly stepped away from the door, then hurried to the bedroom. "I'll grab a few scarves, though," she said, stopping in her tracks as a low groan fell from River's lips. He lay on the bed, perspiration dotting his brow, and as soon as his gaze fixed on Sadie, he growled, jolting forward. Charlie shoved him down by the chest, speaking words that prevented him from rising while he writhed, *hissed*, as if he were possessed by a demon.

Sadie yanked open the drawer to fish out the silk scarves she'd saved from Halloween several years ago. She didn't hesitate as she grasped one of River's arms, even while he swiped at her, and tied two around one wrist to make the bind stronger, then she mirrored her movements with the other. Charlie helped with his legs, each of them tying one ankle to the footboard.

Bed shaking, River growled louder, madness shining in his gaze, aggression that he wanted to unleash on her. Sadie's chest heaved as he watched her with bared teeth, beads of red flickering in the whites of his eyes. Her heart clenched at seeing him this way, with violence directed toward her. She loathed having to tie him up, but for now, it was their only option.

"Come here," Charlie said, motioning Sadie out into the living room. "He'll be better off in there. I know he's your other half, the other side of your coin, your soulmate if they exist. I get that, I do, but you need to leave him alone for the time being. He's getting too aggressive when you're near, and you need to wait for him to calm down, if he does at all. I know how you two can never stay away from each other, but do it for him. Let him rest tonight."

If he does at all. What if he didn't return to himself… "I can leave him alone," Sadie whispered, peering down at her hands.

Charlie eyed her as if she didn't believe her. "What else is it? I feel the anger brewing inside you, as it did toward Papa."

"The spirits. I want to punish them for Skyler." She held up a hand as Charlie opened her mouth to speak. "I know I can't, but it's what I feel. I feel the way I did with Papa, the way I did when River murdered his entire coven. If I could've done it, I would've too. I still wonder what Mama would think about what I did to Papa. Would she have hated me?"

Charlie blew out a breath and gathered Sadie in a hug. "Mama would've been relieved about Papa. He hurt her, her children, and you did what she couldn't bring herself to do. I never once believed what you did was wrong, and I wouldn't change a thing about it." Sadie now understood why Charlie had always seemed like more of a mother, and it was because of Salem, when their mother had passed early, their two brothers following a few years later, and their father never being a true father at all.

"I still hate him," Sadie said under her breath.

"I know." Charlie took her arms from around Sadie and stepped back. "You helped me a lot today, and I didn't think I would need it to figure out how to break this hex, yet I do. Nothing is working. But I'm going to continue to try. Could you get me a few candles?"

"Of course. I'll do anything you need tonight." Sadie

collected two candles from the kitchen cabinet. She lit the wicks and brought them to the coffee table before taking a seat on the fur rug beside Charlie. As her sister closed her eyes and concentrated, Sadie tried to dip into her spells, begging the magic to come forth as she silently chanted to banish the spirits back into their chains below ground. She remembered the sound of her son's heartbeat that Charlie had allowed her to listen to, and it only made her try harder until she could no longer keep her eyes open.

"Wake up," Charlie said, gently shaking Sadie's shoulders.

Sadie opened her eyes, lifting her head and arms from the table where she must've fallen asleep. The candles were burned down to the wicks, and she didn't know how long she'd been asleep like this, but light spilled into the room from the windows. She stood, popping her back, her gaze meeting two steaming mugs of hot chocolate on the kitchen counter.

"Which do you want?" Charlie asked. "Light or dark? The other will be for River, am I right?"

Light or dark… It was the same as the brews she and River would exchange in Salem. Another habit that had carried on through their lives. "Yes." She shrugged, reaching for the dark one.

"I should've known sooner. Even before remembering all this." The corners of Charlie's lips tilted upward as she handed the mug to Sadie. "An idea came to me this morning. You spread River's ashes in the woods—can you show me where you released them?"

"His ashes are what brought the hex and everything else here. But they would be long gone by now…" she trailed off, remembering what Charlie had done with Skyler's remains. "Or wait, they would be part of the ground."

"Precisely that. I want to see if I can feel more of the hex through his ashes." She nudged the other mug toward her. "You can take this to him before we leave. He's calmed down for now. But if he starts up again, try not to linger."

"Thank you." Sadie took the steaming hot chocolate and found River wide awake, peering up at the ceiling.

"You shouldn't be in here," he said, his voice gruff. "However, I can't deny how much I want you near. Whether it's holding you close or me between your legs. But last night went too far."

She arched a brow. "I think I could easily take you at this point. Now sit up a little—I brought you something to drink."

"Mmm, and I can't deny that either," River purred, adjusting himself and parting his lips as she brought the drink to his mouth. He slowly sipped from the mug while she tipped it back for him. Sadie ran her free hand through his damp hair, tempted to unbind his ankles. It would be rather hard for him to free his wrists with his toes.

"I wouldn't touch those if I were you." River's face lifted to hers, his gaze swirling with a different kind of thirst. "Although, I don't mind you taking advantage of me while tied up."

"Even in this predicament, you somehow make me want you even more." Sadie cocked her head, giving him a small smile. "I'm taking Charlie to your ashes. Will you be all right?"

"Don't worry about me. Focus on your sister and our child. If you need me that bad, though, you can always bring me on a leash." River smirked.

Sadie rolled her eyes. "Stop being ridiculous." She pressed her mouth to his in a soft kiss, and she couldn't stop herself from deepening it, letting her tongue dance with his before meeting Charlie outside.

Her sister was surveying the area, the trees still folded and entwined around one another. Only now, long fissures crawled up the trees.

"The spirits will soon be out throughout the days, too," Charlie whispered, brushing her finger along a thin crack.

Sadie stepped toward the outer barrier, and the trees inched backward as they had before, reminding her that they would never allow her to catch up.

"Come on," Sadie said, leading Charlie through the eerie quiet of the woods. She studied the trees, observing their cracks until they reached the oak. "I spread his ashes here, right in front of its trunk."

Charlie focused on the engraved names as she knelt before the tree, lifting a handful of dirt into her palm. Closing her eyes, she moved her lips, speaking soft words that Sadie couldn't hear. For a brief moment, speckles of silver flickered within the dirt before burning out—River's *ashes.*

Charlie blinked, moistening her lips. "Let me try again. Something is here—I *feel* it. Hold my hand."

Sadie knelt beside Charlie, then grasped her sister's hand. As soon as their skin brushed, a tickling sensation spread through her, not her own magic, but Charlie's. Her sister repeated her earlier chant, and the sweep of Charlie's magic pierced through Sadie's blood, seeping down to her bones, not pulling or mixing with her own, but trying to *read* something inside her.

Charlie gasped, squeezing Sadie's hand. "It makes sense now."

"What does?" She couldn't see anything—she had only felt Charlie's power weaving through her.

"As I thought, the spell twisted in Salem because of you being with child. It forced River to take your life, then his, and because it stripped away your magic and your child, it prevented you from having your son make it to term in each life. River disrupted the hex this time by ending his life first, so the spell is trying to correct this turn of events by having his essence kill yours, which would, in turn, kill your sleeping body."

"I sort of knew that already, though."

Charlie shook her head. "That's not all. Skyler's essence would then have to kill me. That's why he was still here. He isn't dead. He will rise again once River ends your life."

Sadie ran a hand down her face in exasperation. "That doesn't solve anything, though. How do we break this hex?"

"There is a way. *One* way." Charlie chewed on her lip, her eyes shining with sympathy. "Things will have to be in reverse. *You* will have to kill River's essence. If you do this, the spell will end, and it will reunite the malevolent spirits with the other part of their essence of themselves, taking them out of this world as it should've long ago."

Sadie's eyes widened in horror. Kill him… Kill *him*? "I don't give a damn about the spirits," Sadie spat. "Find a way so River doesn't have to die. Find a way so he and our child can both live. There has to be a way."

"There isn't, Sadie," Charlie said softly. "River tried to save you by taking his own life, making a change, and in turn, the spirits were awoken after all these years. Not only that…"

Sadie's nostrils flared, knowing precisely what her sister was about to say, wishing she could refuse to hear it. "If he kills me by his own hand, we won't find each other in the next life—our child wouldn't be there either. There would be no next life, no meeting beneath the veil because he's becoming one of them now, isn't he?" She thought about the red spots that had been in the whites of his eyes, ones that would grow to become orbs of blood.

Charlie slowly nodded. "He is, but that isn't all. If he becomes one of those wretched spirits and ends your life, the woods will open and release them all. Chaos will ensue. To save River, you will have to sacrifice him."

27

"You can fly, even without wings."

To save River, you will have to sacrifice him… Charlie's words pounded inside Sadie's head so hard she believed her skull would crack. River was becoming one of them, and she hadn't suspected it, not even when blood had dotted his eyes. River killing himself hadn't put a dent in the hex—it had morphed it into something darker.

"You honestly don't think there's an incantation to reverse it?" Sadie asked. "You're so good with spells and conjuring up new ones." But she knew better than anyone that most true hexes couldn't be reversed, not without repercussions. Even such spells as bringing a loved one back from the dead were generally how it was in the movies—they were altered.

Charlie shook her head. "No, and if there was a spell to reverse time to take us to Salem, I would try it. But turning back time doesn't exist, no matter how much I wish it did. I can attempt to do something for the rest of the day, but when midnight comes, you'll have to make a choice. He doesn't have much time left."

Even after the lives she'd stolen in Salem, the only person she'd ever murdered with a weapon that wasn't with a spell had been her father. She couldn't imagine thrusting a blade into River's chest, his throat, or anywhere else for that matter. "I can't," she whispered, her hands shaking. "I know he's killed me countless times, but he was under a spell. This wouldn't be me under an influence."

"I would influence you if I could," Charlie said. "But I don't know if that would make the hex worse than it already is. River took his life of his own will this time, and I believe you will have to do the same. This is a way to save him, yourself, the world."

"I don't care about the world," Sadie spat. "I care about him, you." She peered down at Charlie's hand, where one rested on her stomach, protecting the child growing inside her belly, the one that had belonged to Sadie and River in all their past lives. If River were to kill her and the spirits were set free from the woods, they would massacre people. That meant Skyler would reawaken to end Charlie's life, end their baby's once more. River's parents were out there—so were Kalina and her daughter…

"I can't do it for you, Sadie." Charlie sighed. "I'm leaving this choice, this decision, up to you this time."

"If it comes down to it, I'll do it," Sadie whispered. "But I don't even know what will happen to him after—it would mean he'd be gone forever." Her body grew rigid, and everything within her wilted.

Charlie wrapped her arm around Sadie's shoulders, drawing her closer. "If it were Skyler, I would do it. No one would want to become one of those things. It would be better to be gone from this world. I promise I'll continue trying to find a way, though. I only wish we had more time."

"Me too." Sadie wanted to hold her sister back, but she felt numb, too numb to even bring up her arms.

"Let's reposition the bones around the house, and I'll strengthen the wards one last time," Charlie said.

Sadie walked back to the cabin and checked on a sleeping River before helping Charlie rearrange the bones, then she added the remainder of the salt. Charlie flipped through the book that Sadie had gotten from Crow Moon, finding nothing useful. Neither one could get the barrier to open to go back to the metaphysical shop, and Charlie's phone hadn't worked since the veil had dropped, so she couldn't search for anything.

Charlie sat on the porch steps, and from her frustrated expression, she needed space, to be left alone to concentrate. Sadie's hopes were withering.

She headed inside the cabin, finding River still asleep, his head tilted to the side. Skimming her hands over the records, she put one on and turned the volume down a shade as she lowered herself to the floor to watch over him.

After a while, Charlie came into the cabin and started tossing leaves and berries into a pot. Sadie went back and forth, helping her boil more pointless brews that tasted of dirt and didn't lift any layers of the hex, until Charlie demanded she spend time with River. So that was what she did—except while he slept she dwelled on things in Salem, those she'd hurt, until midnight wasn't far off. She couldn't hold back anymore, couldn't let him continue to sleep if she might not have time with him after this. It didn't matter if she was being selfish—she pushed off the floor, tucked the dagger into her boot, then rested on the edge of the bed, placing a hand against River's warm cheek.

His eyes cracked open, and they weren't swirling with a hint of red—they were clear.

"Hi." He smiled, then winced as he seemed to realize where they were, that he was still tied to the bed, with a desire to end her life in some way, any way.

"Don't call me reckless. I have the dagger to defend myself, but you're coming with me for a bit. I promise I'll tuck you right back into this hellish bed." She started to untie the rope at his left ankle.

"What is it?" he asked, a line settling between his brows. "I can tell you're keeping a dark, dirty little secret."

"You can always read me." She smiled, moving to his right ankle. "I'll talk to you about it after. For now, tell me your favorite moment between us when we were in Salem."

"Oh, there are plenty of those," he cooed. "But it had to be the first time we met when I found you beneath the stars in the woods with animal bones sewn to your dress and black feathered wings attached to your back."

"You asked what I was doing." She grinned, wishing those wings were here now and that they could somehow fly them away. But it was hard to dream at that moment, to wish.

"You told me to mind my own business and to shoo.

But then, as I pried, you admitted that you were trying to figure out a way to fly for the night."

"Then you told me you knew what I was, and I told you the same." Sadie's heart swelled at the memory. "You sat beside me, casting a spell, even though it didn't work."

"Then we continued to meet, *dance*, beneath the moonlight."

Just as they had danced in these woods below ground as Sadie and River. "When we go outside, pretend we're back there now," she murmured, releasing his wrist. "Beneath those stars, in those woods. You and I and our dreams."

"Anything you wish, my sweet nightmare," he purred. But in his eyes, she could see his fear, fear that he would hurt her. But her fear was stronger, the fear that she knew she would hurt him.

Sadie opened the window so they could crawl out, just as she used to do in Salem when she would meet him during the night. Charlie was still in the kitchen, but she didn't stop to rush into the room to call her back, to tell her to quit being reckless. Sadie could defend herself, and if she needed Charlie, she would scream for her because she wasn't taking River far.

"So, this is where you planned to lure me?" he drawled. "Just outside the window?"

"Yes." She grinned, glancing at the trees, their cracks, knowing they soon wouldn't be able to hold. "Apparently, they will be listening to us."

"Good," he said. "I like an audience." With quick motions, he lifted Sadie and pressed her back against the cabin.

A heat spread through her, and they both cast their

gazes up at the stars. "Make a wish," she said.

He followed her stare, peering at the clusters of white flecks. "Done." He brought his head down, capturing her mouth with his.

"You didn't give me time to do mine." Sadie laughed against his mouth. But then she made her wish, wished that at some point she would reunite with River again, not be apart from him for all eternity. But maybe that was what they deserved… "Done." She kissed him back, and in that single kiss, she knew there would never be another like him. No matter the life. No matter the time. No matter their wickedness or their goodness.

They didn't bother to remove their clothing as he unbuttoned his pants and freed himself. River hiked up her skirt, sliding her panties to the side. He then glided along her center before burying himself inside her, making them both moan.

As he thrust, as she gripped his hair, as they kissed hard and deep, a whirlwind of emotions bloomed inside her, melancholic and beautiful. It was as if the silk curtains were being drawn closed to a story, a film. *Their* story.

"I love you," he ground out as his pace picked up, the friction growing stronger, his hands digging into her just as much as hers were into him.

And then bliss tore through her, ripping a groan from her at the same time a growl escaped him. Their chests heaved together, and he remained buried inside her, kissing her forehead with his.

"I love you," she said as he slowly slipped out of her and lowered her to the ground. "But I need to tell you something, River."

"You don't have to tell me." He shrugged. "I see it in

your eyes. I already know I'm becoming one of them. I *feel* it. That hollowness, the darkness marked on my aura spreading."

Sadie threw her arms around him, murmuring into his chest, speaking to his heart. "Charlie uncovered how to break the spell. There's a side of me that wants to be reckless, steal you away." She could take him right now, keep on running through these woods, lock him in the shed, even when he changed into a malevolent spirit. A world without him wouldn't be a world at all. But she couldn't. Charlie's wards wouldn't hold him in, and he wouldn't want this for himself or the child Charlie was carrying. "I don't care if you were one of those vile spirits—I would love you just the same."

He lifted her chin with steady fingers, not a twitch or tremble of nervousness there. "What do you have to do?"

Yet her entire body did tremble. "I have to kill you."

28

"When we die, will we shine as bright as the stars, or will we burn?"

"Do it," River demanded. There was no hesitation in his words. He slid his hands to her face, cupping her cheeks, the pad of his thumb brushing away her tears. "Do it. If I could do it myself again, I would. I wish it would have saved you before."

Sadie slowly nodded. She had tucked the dagger into her boot, but she refused to let the spirits have whatever remained when she took his life. "Not here. Let's go back inside."

"Wherever you wish."

She inhaled the crisp air and climbed through the window with River behind her. Just as he closed the glass, Charlie appeared in the doorway, the notebook of spells in her hand. "You could've left through the front door." She rolled her eyes.

Sadie took the notebook from her sister's hands, her gaze poring over it. "Did you find anything?"

Charlie pursed her lips, and that was the only answer she needed. "I'm sorry, River."

"I always did like you, Charlie." The last word came out a groan, and he hunched over, his skin turning a light shade of silver.

Sadie jolted forward, grabbing him by the shoulder to bring him to the bed. He whirled around, knocking her to the floor. Charlie chanted, and River froze, his body jerking to a stop before he broke free from her spell, lunging for Sadie.

Charlie yanked him back by the shirt, and Sadie took hold of his left arm, forcing him to the mattress as he writhed.

"I suggest not untying him again and making a decision because he has no time left," Charlie hissed through her teeth while tying his wrist.

"I know it was reckless, but I had to give him one final goodbye. For you, for him, for the child, I'm going to protect you all." Sadie worked on his other wrist as River let out a string of curses in a deep monstrous voice that sounded nothing like him.

They left his feet unbound, and Charlie glanced at the clock. "Midnight's approaching. Let me set up the candles, and once it's done, I'll bless his essence."

Sadie didn't say a word as she slowly removed the blade from her boot, the one that River was given to murder her with.

Charlie placed a candle on both bedside tables, then

lit them. The flames swayed as Charlie shifted closer to Sadie. "I should've been braver earlier on, killed Papa myself. Then things would've been different for us, for you."

"Your heart's too good, and it's better you didn't." She faced her sister, the sound of River's growls echoing off the walls, sending a shiver up her spine. "I don't mind holding the darkness for us both."

"We can't change the past," Charlie said softly.

"No, but we can alter the future." Sadie glanced down at her sister's stomach, wondering if breaking the hex would truly give the child she was meant to have, which was now Charlie's and Skyler's, a chance. She thought about how he would've felt in her arms once he'd been born if she hadn't died in Salem. "Titus," Sadie said softly.

Charlie tilted her head, her brow furrowing. "What?"

"That was what we were going to name our child if it had been a boy. Maybe you can use it." Her voice shook as she said the words.

"I like it." Her sister smiled as her eyes became glassy.

"Now, give me a moment." Sadie stepped away from her sister and turned to River, edging closer to him as if she could prolong the inevitable. His eyes were narrowed on her, his lips twisted in a snarl while continuing to growl at her. He had never chosen to hurt her, but she was choosing to kill him. And though it was what he wanted, what was necessary to save everyone, Sadie's heart broke at the thought that River would be truly and completely gone. Even if he was a monster, it would still mean he would be out there, and now, he wouldn't be.

Tears pricked Sadie's eyes as she lifted the blade, holding it above his chest. "I don't know if I can do it," she sobbed. She'd done horrific things in her past, yet she couldn't stand the thought of ending River's life. No matter if it turned her from a villain into a hero. In Salem, she would've chosen to find a way to become a malevolent spirit alongside him, but now, their child was involved. And she wanted them both.

Sadie took a breath, remembered River in each life—his smiles, his laughs, his touches, their fights, their forgiveness, how she would never want anyone else but him. Dark or light.

It was one minute until midnight, and she knew the spirits were inside their trees, waiting for the time to come when they could crawl outside the cabin and lure River away from her to become one of them.

River stopped bucking, the red spots of his eyes spreading, but his expression was pleading, not filled with malice. "Do it, Sadie," he ground out. "And maybe, just maybe, we'll find each other wherever our souls may go."

The crimson of his eyes was swallowing the remainder of the whites, and this time, she knew he wouldn't return to himself ever again. His silver skin was fading, becoming more ethereal, and once midnight arrived, if she continued to stare into his eyes, she would die. And that was what the hex wanted.

Death wasn't something she feared, but she did fear not being able to save River, and this was the only way she could. Hands shaking, she clenched the blade as tight as she could, then drove it down, breaking through his rib cage and piercing straight into his beautiful heart.

River gasped, his back arching, his fingers bending as if wishing they could dig into something. Blood spilled down the blade, blooming from the wound in his chest when Sadie ripped the dagger from his heart. She tossed the blade to the floor with a loud clatter and covered the hole in his chest even though he wouldn't be healed. Her beloved's body was still, his breaths locked away, and his pulse no longer thrummed.

Behind her, Charlie chanted low words, blessing his essence while Sadie wept. She climbed into bed beside River, not releasing her palm from his chest. A moment later, he started to fade, his entire being growing lighter, her hand and head slipping through him, falling against the mattress until his body was gone.

He was gone.

Charlie continued to bless River's soul while Sadie curled her knees into her chest, sobbing into her hands. River's calming scent lingered, but it was fading, just as his body had, as if he'd never been there at all. In this life, she'd lost him for a second time. And she didn't know if this was truly the end of *them*.

Sadie's chest tightened, and she couldn't get air to her lungs fast enough—she wished they would stop working, that her heart would cease beating. The urge to thrust the blade into her own flesh screamed in her thoughts. Arms wrapped around her, but not the ones she wished for. She noticed something then, as Charlie whispered words of a spell, an invisible hand tugging at Sadie, and when she blinked, she gasped for air, her heart slamming against her sternum while she took in deep breaths. Charlie was beside her, mirroring her movements. They were both awake, standing in the living room where they'd been before the veil had dropped. The dead moths and animal skulls seemed to stare at them from the walls, reminding her of everything that had happened…

"I'm sorry, Sadie," Charlie murmured, tears beading her lashes. "River was brave, never once fighting his sacrifice, even before he knew everything. I believe in second chances, and I believe he will get one." Sadie would pray every night, wishing that he would.

Her eyes widened as she looked around the room, realizing something was missing. *Someone* was missing. Even if he wasn't alive, a body should've been there. "Where's Skyler?" He'd been with them before, and his body couldn't have turned to ash the way his essence had.

"Skyler!" Charlie shouted as she searched the rooms throughout the cabin.

Sadie threw open the front door, and light surrounded her, the world now alive while she felt dead. Everything was as it had been before she'd spread River's ashes in the woods. The barrier was gone, the wind blew, rustling the trees, insects buzzed, and birds chirped. She now knew the animals she'd seen sleeping, and then dead, hadn't truly been the ones here—they'd been the essences of the ones she'd taken long ago, who were now also free.

Skyler's police car was still there, but there was no sign of him. Was there a chance that when Charlie fed his body to the ground it did something to him here? Horrified at the thought, she ran into the woods, screaming his name. "Skyler!"

Farther away, a shout echoed, her name being called, followed by the snap of twigs. She raced toward the call, leaping over logs when a tall form in a police uniform broke through the trees.

"Skyler! You're alive. Don't ever try to save me like that again." Tears streamed down her cheeks as she rushed toward him, throwing her arms around his neck. "The hex is broken, but River is gone. Truly gone."

"I'm so sorry, Sadie." Skyler crushed her to his chest when another voice rang through the woods. Her sister.

Sadie moved backward, and Charlie barreled into Skyler, squeezing him. "What are you doing out here?" Charlie asked.

"I was trying to find a way back to you, regardless that I couldn't cast a damn spell."

A thought struck Sadie, hard and fast—maybe, just maybe, River would walk out from behind the trees too.

She bolted toward the old oak where she'd spread his ashes, carved their names into its trunk, but when she stood before it, he wasn't there. So she went further, darting toward their underground home, where she'd found him night after night beneath the veil. But of course it wasn't there, and neither was he.

Sadie dropped to her knees, pleading. "River, show me a sign you're all right." She waited and waited. However, he didn't answer—no shadowy silhouettes appeared. All that was there was a hollowness inside her, a feeling that would eventually break her.

She closed her eyes, silently chanting, and the barrier that had prevented her magic from working before broke, no longer trapping her spells. A spark, cracking like a whip, slipped out of deep hibernation, then rose. As she opened her lids, the sky darkened, the trees rustled, and she stopped, knowing she would do something horrific that she couldn't take back.

Heavy footsteps sounded from behind her, and Sadie glanced over her shoulder to find Charlie rushing toward her, her chestnut hair bouncing, her hazel eyes wild with worry.

"I didn't do anything," Sadie whispered, lifting a handful of dirt and letting it slide through her fingers back to the ground. "I stopped myself."

For now, I shattered the darkness.

EPILOGUE

"When you believe our story is over, it is only the beginning."

Sadie finished reading over her screenplay for the last time. It was complete and true to her heart. To her and River, to Skyler and Charlie. To Harlow and Jasper, to Ada and Eben. To Titus. To the victims of Salem.

She left the screenplay on the coffee table, along with a sealed envelope to Charlie.

Sadie took a breath and walked outside into the dark night, trekking through the woods until she came to the familiar oak tree. She ran her fingertips across the engraved letters of her and River's names, thinking about how she'd never lived a full life, but with all her lives combined, it was as though she had.

With the spells humming in Sadie's veins, aching to

break free, she'd cast a few in the woods, placed protection on any living thing that needed it while here. But that urge was still there, to use a dark spell, to find a way to draw River's soul back down here. Even though she wouldn't harm anyone at that moment, who was to say she wouldn't tomorrow? She didn't truly trust herself, and she owed this world that much, owed the victims in Salem where she should've been punished for her crimes.

The noose she'd hung earlier was already waiting for her, dangling from the branch with a chair beneath it. Sadie stepped onto the chair and placed the noose around her neck. She believed in redemption, and this was her final step in achieving that.

Titus had been born, and she'd gotten to hold him once, to see that he'd survived. He was the most perfect baby as she knew he would be. Chubby cheeks and a button of a nose. A part of her wanted to take him from Charlie, run away with him, and she knew that would never change. So to protect her sister's beautiful new family, she needed to do this.

Sadie stepped from the chair, the noose digging into her throat, her breaths being cut off. As her body struggled for air, Sadie's mind was at peace. Her eyes fell shut, her essence lifting from its shell.

It wasn't the darkness reaching for her, but a silhouette inside a bright light. Sandalwood and honey caressed her nose as it drew closer. *River.* When his hand clasped hers, she thought about the last line she'd written in her screenplay, one that was no longer haunting to her but the beginning of a new chapter, whether beautiful or wicked.

And then there was silence.

Did you enjoy And Then There Was Silence?

Authors always appreciate reviews, whether long or short.

Want another deliciously dark story? Try out Dearest Clementine: Dark and Romantic Monstrous Tales

"Beautiful. Unique. And utterly romantic."

Clementine has been taken by a creature of darkness. Dorin is a fiend in love who must find Clementine before losing her forever. While on his desperate search, Dorin pens eight dark and romantic monstrous tales, written only for Clementine. Each story serves a purpose, and that is, do monsters have the ability to love, too?

SADIE'S HORROR MOVIE WATCHLIST

May (2002)
Ginger Snaps (2000)
The Bride of Frankenstein (1935)
The Others (2001)
Crimson Peak (2015)
A Nightmare on Elm Street (1984)
The Invisible Man (1933)
Midsommar (2019)
The Company of Wolves (1984)
We Are What We Are (2013)
The Witch (2015)

SADIE'S MUSIC PLAYLIST

"I Think We're Alone Now" – Tommy James & the Shondells
"Can't Help Falling In Love" – Elvis
"Come Together" – The Beatles
"Paint It, Black" – The Rolling Stones
"Light My Fire" – The Doors
"The Sound of Silence" – Simon & Garfunkel
"Behind Blue Eyes" – The Who
"Have You Ever Seen The Rain" – Creedence Clearwater Revival
"All I Have To Do Is Dream" – The Everly Brothers
"Stairway To Heaven" – Led Zeppelin

MORE FROM CANDACE ROBINSON

Wicked Souls Duology
Vault of Glass
Bride of Glass

Marked by Magic
The Bone Valley
Merciless Stars

Cruel Curses Trilogy
Clouded By Envy
Veiled By Desire
Shadowed By Despair

Cursed Hearts Duology
Lyrics & Curses
Music & Mirrors

Immortal Letters Duology
Dearest Clementine: Dark and Romantic Monstrous Tales
Dearest Dorin: A Romantic Ghostly Tale

Campfire Fantasy Tales Series
Lullaby of Flames
A Layer Hidden
The Celebration Game
Mirror, Mirror

These Vicious Thorns: Tales of the Lovely Grim
Between the Quiet
Hearts Are Like Balloons
Bacon Pie
Avocado Bliss

Faeries of Oz Series
Lion (Short Story Prequel)
Tin
Crow
Ozma
Tik-Tok

Vampires in Wonderland Series
Rav (Short Story Prequel)
Maddie
Chess
Knave

Once Upon a Wicked Villian Series
Spindle of Sin

Demons of Frosteria
Slaying the Frost King
Frost Mate
Frost Claim

Acknowledgments

I'm always terrible at writing these things, but I thank you so much for reading this story. This one was an emotional ride, and I absolutely love this book so much. It was a tale I've been holding inside me for a long while and I'm glad I was finally able to pen it. And I hope you enjoyed Sadie's story!

To my husband and daughter who know how much I love horror movies and therefore can relate to Sadie completely on that level! You both have supported me so much and it keeps me sane.

Jackie, you helped me so much through the edits, and to SiriGuruDev for breaking apart scenes for me that helped make them better. You guys are lifesavers!

Amber H., you saved this story from any pesky things and I'm always so grateful for that! Jerica, I appreciate the funky parts you gave me that needed to be fixed. And to Hayley, Amber D., Ann, and Victoria, seriously thank you for everything.

With each book I write, the characters take a spot in my heart, and I have a secret to tell, Sadie and River hold a very big spot in there.

About the Author

Candace Robinson spends her days consumed by words and hoping to one day find her own DeLorean time machine. Her life consists of avoiding migraines, admiring Bonsai trees, watching classic movies, and living with her husband and daughter in Texas—where it can be forty degrees one day and eighty the next.

Made in United States
Troutdale, OR
01/25/2024